THE AUTHOR

Nick Cann was born in London in 1959.
Since 1981 he has worked as a freelance
journalist and graphic designer.
In 1989 he moved to Northern Ireland
where he runs his own editorial design
consultancy.
The Tour is his fourth published novel.

KHARA PRINGLE

01. 08 . 20 19

THE TOUR

NICK CANN

indiego.co.uk

FIRST PUBLISHED IN THE UK IN 2018 BY

indiego

HOLYWOOD, COUNTY DOWN

© indiego 2018

ISBN 978-0-9549066-3-4

WRITTEN BY NICK CANN

FRONT COVER ILLUSTRATION BY NICK CANN SENIOR

EDITED BY VICTORIA WOODSIDE

PRINTED BY GRANGE PRINTING

BOUND BY ROBINSON & MORNIN

FOR DENNIS HACKETT

WITH THANKS TO:
The Boys on Tour who are, or have been:

James Kealy,
Chris Hill, Terence McCracken,
Gareth O'Connor, Sean Clifford,
Ian McArthur, Kevin Doherty,
Sean T Murphy, Kevin O'Connor
George Harley, Brian McDermott
Paddy Gillen, Anthony Thompson, Kevin McGrath,
Gerry McLaughlin, John McElhinney
Colin Macadden, Mike Dick, Billy Andrews, Keith Chase
and Gareth 'Magoo' Magowan

ALSO:
Dawn, Sophie, Chloe, Jack, Poppy
Wendy and Judy and Derek and Valerie Geddis

AND FOR THEIR TECHNICAL ASSISTANCE:
Captain Scott Beadle, Jo Rice, Al Cassels, Paul Hewitt,
John Wallace, Eirinn Clifford and Lidón Prades Ortiz

ACKNOWLEDGEMENTS:
Wing Commander Brendan (Paddy) Finucane DSO DFC

1

One month earlier
Puerto Santa Cruz, east of Caracas, Venezuela

The fumes billowing from the flatbed chugging along the quay suggested that it was burning more engine oil than diesel. A classic Ford, the truck's paintwork was riddled with rust spots, its chrome pitted and matt. The curve of its bodywork, however, created an allure that was almost female. Though old and battered it was from a graceful age of automotive design. The faded gold italics swirling across the cab door were those of a fruit and vegetable wholesalers, a third-generation family business located somewhere near the commercial centre of Caracas.

As it drew alongside the sixty-foot ketch moored at the end of the marina, the truck clanked to a halt and coughed up a last belch of exhaust. Half a dozen local men jumped down from the rear of the lorry and strolled towards the yacht. The crew of the *Contessa Rose*, four Europeans, were already ambling over to greet them, offering nervous smiles and a handshake. The locals nodded without changing expression and kept their hands firmly clamped by their sides.

"Mr Valentine? Are you Mr Valentine?" A besuited Venezuelan asked in a heavy accent.

"Yes. Do you have our supplies?" the yacht's skipper replied, employing a genial tone.

The local nodded again then turned to walk back to the truck, beckoning his cohorts to follow. They reassembled at the tailgate and started to offload a pile of hessian sacks. The sacks, about forty of them, were each the size and weight of a bag of coal. They were all unmarked.

"¡No, no, Rudie! ¡Ponlos en fila! ¡En fila!" the besuited Venezuelan, Rafael Mendoza, barked at his foreman. "¡En fila, dije!" he repeated, slapping his forehead and shrugging before retreating into the cab, not wanting to attract attention.

As ordered, the workers spread out to form a human chain stretching from the flatbed down towards the ship's prow. Meanwhile the crew gathered at the water's edge to help stow the goods.

Though concerned, Mendoza thought it best to keep out of the way. Back in the driver's seat he straightened his tie, smoothed down his suit jacket, adjusted his shirt cuffs and then lit up a Marlboro to calm his nerves, finding the wafts of nicotine preferable to the stench of the port in thirty-degree heat. Every now and then he peeked over his shoulder to check on the progress of his men.

Satisfied that all was going to plan, Mendoza decided to stay put until the offloading was complete, not wanting to infect his men with the same nervousness that he was struggling to suppress. He could hear them chattering and laughing and this pleased him. At any other time he might have yelled at them to get on with their work, but knew that the chatter – a sign of normality – would help them blend into the hustle and bustle of the port. That there was an absence of anyone in authority in their vicinity encouraged Mendoza to assume that the right envelopes had been passed into the right hands. He exhaled a small plume of smoke, closed his eyes and waited.

Once they'd got into a rhythm, the men passed the sacks down to the ketch quickly and smoothly, maintaining an unbroken and steady flow, wanting to skedaddle home to the security of Caracas as soon as possible, their cash reward bulging in their pockets. They had insisted they were to be paid in American dollars.

As soon as the last sack had been passed along the line Mendoza stepped onto the quay, stubbed out his cigarette and commanded his men to climb back on board the flatbed. He gave the yachtsmen a brief thumbs up and clambered into the cab, started the engine, turned the lorry and trundled it off towards the harbour exit, the truck puffing more exhaust into the air behind them. The ship's crew, meanwhile, finished stowing the last of the sacks and took up their stations for manoeuvring the ketch across the harbour and out to sea.

To the casual observer the scene playing out on the quay was nothing new or strange. The day-to-day comings and goings of a busy port made the marina the ideal departure point for the export of their valuable cargo out of South America and across the Atlantic without fuss. The crew hoped for a fast crossing and a successful rendezvous at the designated island off the west coast of Ireland.

Rafael Mendoza blew out his cheeks, relieved that the exchange had gone to plan. And he felt no guilt. To him this was business. The selling of a commodity which had provided his wife and children with a standard of living denied to most in his community. His children were now benefitting from a good education and had far better prospects than he'd had at their age.

Financial security for his family had been his sole motivation at first, but not now. There was no stopping now. Even if he wanted to, others wouldn't allow it. He'd become indispensable to his suppliers in Columbia – violent men – by creating a vast income in foreign currency. He reassured himself, however, that cocaine was a recreational drug and, if enjoyed sensibly and in moderation, was no more harmful than alcohol. Also, their target market comprised older, wealthier Europeans and Americans. It was their choice. A lifestyle choice. He'd convinced himself that kids wouldn't be in receipt of their product. It was a cleaner business than that, altogether. To Mendoza his work was a public service. It almost seemed respectable. Well, almost.

2

Saturday, 8am
Greenwich, south-east London, 15 March 2014.

The alarm clock failed to go off. Didn't ring. Not a peep. Cue panic and pandemonium.

What kind of fuckwit still has a battery alarm clock in the twenty-first century? Colin Draper cursed.

He hurled back the covers then froze.

Shit! It's Saturday! he realised, remembering that for once he'd given himself the day off work.

And what a stupid idea that was, he thought, knowing there wasn't the slightest chance the break would make him feel any better – spare time being the depressive's number-one enemy. That and booze. And bad luck. And wheat.

A bottle of vodka was the first thing that caught his attention following a glance at the clock. Of course the bottle loitering on the bedside table was empty save for a cloudy inch at the bottom, a cocktail of drink and drool. A survivor from the previous night's binge. Nearly a litre of the stuff downed; sorrows enhanced rather than drowned; regrets now etched in alcohol onto the consciousness to swamp anything positive in his less-than-happy existence.

But then there was the wedding to think of. *Oh, Christ! The wedding!* His daughter's.

How ironic that whilst yesterday he was overwhelmed with the finality of the trip to court to sign off on his divorce from Saffie's mother, he now needed to concentrate on the final preparations for Saffie's wedding. It was just over a week away.

A gut-wrenching traverse from the ridiculous to the sublime. It would be hilarious if it wasn't so fucking tragic.

Yes, he'd make a joke of it – massage the details into an anecdote, a routine to entertain friends and colleagues, and retold for years – but he'd practise it first till he had the story word-perfect to debut in his father-of-the-bride speech.

And the wedding? Sitting at the top table with his ex-wife would be the highlight of the comedy routine. There they'd be soft targets for the warped entertainment of those friends and relatives who had been murmuring of their demise for years. Sitting ducks for their sniggering gossip. And he'd play up to the theatre. He would shrug, wink and mime the throat-cutting gesture for anyone who caught his eye. He'd make them laugh and play the fool; anything to mask his true feelings.

At last he smiled. Then he giggled. Now he couldn't stop laughing at his dilemma. As his shoulders started to shudder he could do no more than lie flat on his back till the hysterics subsided. And, as the first pinpricks of a hangover began to jab into his brow, he rolled over to try to get some sleep before the serious throbbing began.

When he awoke a couple of hours later, Colin Draper felt no better. He decided that today would be a write-off. A day for pyjamas and the telly. No one would mind. No one would care. And definitely not at work. He'd already told them he was taking the day off and they'd be sure to welcome that. For one day at least *Mr High and Mighty* wouldn't be fussing about the site to distract them from whatever task was at hand.

He flipped the pillow in search of a cool patch and resolved to do nothing that involved movement in a vertical plane until the worst of his hangover was past; guesstimating that it would take till late afternoon at the earliest before his head felt any lighter than a medicine ball.

A visit to the loo might help first though. He'd see if he could make himself sick and evacuate his bowels, but that would be the only activity he'd be capable of in the morning. And if he could find it, he'd retrieve the eye mask saved from his last transatlantic flight and dumped somewhere amidst the jumble in the bathroom cabinet.

As he stepped into the bedroom from the en suite he felt something squelch underfoot. Stopped. Looked down.

Ah, a pizza box.

Yep, he appeared to be standing in a takeaway pizza box with a giant wedge of margherita oozing up between his toes like a tomatoey cowpat.

Then the phone was ringing.

He shook the pizza box off and hobbled over to the receiver trying not to trample tomato sauce into the carpet.

"Hello, can I help you?"

"Why are you whispering, Colin?"

"Hi, Mum. I'm not whispering. I'm just a bit hoarse."

"You need to take better care of yourself, Colin."

"Yes, Mother."

"Anyway, did you call? My phone says you called me, Colin."

"Yes, Mum, last night. We talked briefly. You've probably forgotten."

"Have I? Oh, sorry, dear. Yes, well ... What did you want?"

"Only to say hello."

"Oh, sorry, Colin. Sorry to bother you now then."

"Don't you worry, Mum. It's no bother at all. It's always lovely to hear from you. You call me any time you like."

"Yes. Sorry, dear."

"Please. It's no problem, Mum. Look, I'll call you this evening as usual."

"Lovely."

"OK then?"

"Oh, how's Mary?"

"Fine, Mum, she's fine."

"Good ... good. Well, bye-bye then."

She rang off.

Short-term memory loss. An early symptom of dementia. Colin Draper sometimes wished he could summon up short-term memory loss at will without having to rely on binge drinking to perform the deed.

Before he had time to retreat to the bathroom the phone rang again.

"Hello?"

"The venue called, Dad."

"Oh?"

"They want to go through the seating plan, you know, finalise the menu, discuss table decorations, blah blah blah. And ASAP."

"Fine. When are you seeing them, Saffie?"

"Tomorrow."

"On a Sunday?"

"Yeah."

"Will your mother be there?"

"No. She's on a shoot in Mallorca. Not home till Monday."

"What about Phil?"

"Yep, he'll be with me. We're both going to stay at Granny's till the wedding. Except Phil's staying with his best man at The Bull's Head the night before, of course."

"Good, I'm glad Phil's around. Now, have you ticked off all the two-weeks-to-go things on your wedding planner?"

"God, you sound like Mum."

"Saffie!"

"Oh, go on then, Dad, shout them out."

"Marriage licence?"

"Yep."

"Practised your wedding make-up?"

"Done."

"Tried on your wedding dress?"

"Done."

"With shoes, underwear and accessories?"

"Done."

"Full wedding rehearsal?"

"Done."

"Arranged for your honeymoon cases to be taken to the reception venue?"

"Done."

"Made final checks on cake, flowers and photographer."

"Done."

"Final briefing for ushers and bridesmaids, etc."

"Done."

"Good. You're all covered then."

"One day you'll make someone a wonderful wife, Dad."

"Look, just because I'm in touch with my feminine side—"

"Dad, are you OK? You sound terrible."

"It's only a cold, Saffie. A throat thing. It's nothing."

"Well, take it easy. We'll be needing you in good voice on the big day."

"Of course, of course. Don't worry!"

"OK. Take care."

"I guess your mum will want to say a few words too, Saffie?"

"What do *you* think?"

"Mmm, no comment. Look, I'll call you soon, sausage. Let me know if you need anything else."

"Will do. You're a pet, Dad. Speak soon. *Mwah*!" Saffron Draper enthused, air-kissing into the receiver before ringing off.

Draper smiled. Was relieved she had something pleasant to do to distract her from her parents' divorce. But *Saffron*. What a name. Her mother's choice, not his. He preferred Penny.

Another trip to the loo then back to sleep. He dared to sneak a peek at himself in the bathroom mirror first.

Eyes? Bloodshot. A look that reminded him of Ben Johnson crossing the line in the hundred-metres final at the Seoul

Olympics: eyes so red that his head appeared to be on the point of exploding.

Tongue? Also red, but that a healthier sign.

Colin Draper leaned in for a closer inspection, hoping that his deep tan was due to working out of doors rather than liver damage.

Satisfied, he retired to the bedroom. He was tempted to leave the phone off the hook but expected there'd be too many others in need of his wit and wisdom to permit such an indulgence.

Lunchtime came and went celebrated with a couple of paracetamol, a piece of toast and a cuppa. Then a snooze till teatime.

When he awoke around four, his head felt clearer.

Thank God the threat of nausea seemed to have passed and the challenge of sitting up and following the headlines on the news channel achievable. But then pangs of guilt started to nag. Why wasn't he on-site? Something was bound to go wrong.

Luckily he'd found that his current building project sparked his imagination enough to distract him from the ups and downs of his personal life. The alienation from Mary, the separation and divorce became less of a torture when he had a property renovation on the go; it was good to be busy.

The latest was a four-storey Edwardian town house in Pimlico. He'd picked it up in an auction three months earlier. Property development was a new line of business he'd fallen into when his graphic design agency had started to go belly-up. And it seemed to be working. His timing had been acute. London property prices were booming again. There was good profit to be had in refurbishment – enough to cover his lavish lifestyle anyway and, potentially, enough to finance the divorce.

The town house was nearly done. A good job thanks to his team, a loveable crew of hard-working tradesmen from Eastern Europe who were highly skilled and, usually, very dependable. They liked Colin Draper and were grateful for his building projects but resented his insistence on micromanaging every aspect of their work.

"You worry about the pounds and pence, Mr Colin, we'll worry about the health and safety," Tomasz, his Polish plasterer and foreman, would urge with a grin.

Then the landline was ringing again.

"Hello, Colin Draper," he mumbled, yawning.

"Is that you, Colin, you big girl's blouse?"

"Oh, God! Hugo, what the hell do you want?" Draper groaned.

"We're taking you down to the bierkeller. The Moose and I will pick you up around six."

"Look, after last night what the hell makes you think I'd want to go anywhere with you two *ever* again? Especially to a pub. In fact *anywhere* that sells alcohol."

"Because you love us, you silly bollocks."

"You and Moose might be OK as blokes go, Hugo, but you're not really my type I'm afraid."

"That's not what Mary says."

"Oh, fuck off, Hugo."

"Good. That's settled then. We'll see you at six, sharp."

Colin Draper put the phone down. Didn't smile, didn't frown. Deadpan was the etiquette when dealing with the Reverend Hugo Saunders and The Moose.

The reverend was a reverend in name only since his early retirement due to poor health. His had been a debilitating condition but one from which he had seemingly recovered; a mini miracle some had suggested rather cynically.

Draper levered himself off the couch and headed for the shower, marvelling at his own ability to conjure up a second coming.

On entering the cubicle Draper donned the shower cap he'd nicked from Mary when he'd left home six months ago. He didn't care that it made him look like a milkmaid as long as it kept the water away from his dark and curly thatch; hair that could spring into an Afro the instant it was exposed to the slightest drop, drip or drizzle of water.

Dressed, Draper poured a coffee.

Slouched on a bar stool he surveyed his small studio flat.

He couldn't have purchased the property in Greenwich at a better time. Certainly couldn't have afforded it now. Gazing over from the open-plan kitchen-diner, across the sitting room and out through the rear window, it always pleased him that the view was filled by the branches of a sycamore living on the other side of the park wall. The tree provided the privacy of curtains without the claustrophobia.

The property had been intended to be another plank in his raft of buy-to-lets, but the separation from Mary had put paid to that. Fortunately, he could cover the mortgage.

And what about Mary? Was it a coincidence that their troubles had coincided with his design business going under? Did his pecuniary shortcomings have to be marriage threatening? Not to him. But then Mary, who was a conspicuous consumer, found the thought of living in poverty highly offensive.

Draper had a gulp of coffee then reached for his iPhone. He tapped in a message: *Mary. Hope yr OK. Call me if u need anything CX*, had another sip and waited for a text to come back, his attention caught by a squirrel skittering about in the branches outside. He sat staring into the boughs of the tree long after the squirrel had gone, transfixed by the light flickering through the leaves and the sycamore's seedpods bobbling on the breeze like Clackers.

Then he dared himself to remember his time with Mary and their life in Yarmouth on the Isle of Wight, their home town. He glanced down to his iPhone. She hadn't replied. He would try again sometime, would keep on trying even though the combination of the effort, the expectation and the reality built a pressure that made his head feel like it was splitting in two. Relief came in a self-pitying spasm of tears that brought him to his senses. He stopped, took a deep breath and sighed. *Bloody binge drinking.*

The buzzer on the intercom broke his train of thought.

Draper grabbed the phone from its stand on the wall above the kitchen worktop.

"Yep?"

"It's Hugo. It's beer o'clock. Time we were in the pub, dear boy."

"Oh, God! Do I have to?"

"Yes."

"Really?"

"Yes."

"Fuck it! I'll be down in five."

"Make it one."

Draper jogged down the stairs and out the door where he was immediately bathed in warm evening sun. Greenwich Park appeared postcard pretty in the golden light, but was packed with courting couples and tourists.

Hugo Saunders and The Moose were peering at him from the opposite pavement. They were slouched against a wall whilst tanning their teeth in the tar sucked from a soggy roll-up.

"God, you're a miserable-looking pair."

"Thank you, Colin."

"So, where're we off to?"

"Where do you think?" Hugo countered through a khaki smile. Hugo and The Moose turned to one another, nodded and then headed off.

It was about a mile to their favourite local, but worth the trek to witness the eccentricities of the landlord, Ken, also for the fine ale and the view down the river once you got there.

Draper dawdled behind the other two. The Moose was a man-mountain who strode in large mechanical steps, his feet clomping in a shuffle that reminded Draper of Frankenstein's monster – hardly balletic. The Reverend Hugo was scampering alongside and struggling to keep up like a small boy walking with his father. Hugo's attire was charity-shop tatty. He generally opted for a fawn, tweedy look befitting his former station in life. The Moose was nearly always resplendent in black T-shirt and jeans; a combination that complemented his dark features and mop of raven hair. The Moose's greatcoat trailed behind in the wind like a cloak.

"Are you OK, Colin?"

"Do I seem OK to you, Hugo? Would you be OK? No. I'm not fucking OK," Colin Draper fumed, gazing out over the Thames towards Woolwich whilst sipping his first pint of bitter. He thought better of gulping it down. Didn't want to drink too fast, didn't want to drown his sorrows for a second evening in a row. A three-pint night would do the job.

"But you're here ... with us ... in the Smuggler's ... drinking beer. It's Saturday night and you're single. What's not to like?"

"Whatever you do, Hugo, don't take up counselling. What do you think, Moose?"

But, as usual, The Moose wasn't for making small talk.

"Seriously though, are you going to be OK, Colin? We're setting off on our golf trip tomorrow and you're going to be stuck here in Greenwich all on your own."

"I've got friends. Real friends, Hugo."

"Somehow I doubt that, Colin."

"Listen, I'll be fine. In any case, I'm very busy at work and I've got Saffie's wedding to consider."

"When's that again?"

"Next Sunday."

"A church wedding on a Sunday? That's unusual."

"Saffie's idea. It's her birthday."

"Oh, OK."

"So, you see, I've got a hell of a lot on, Hugo."

"You poor sod."

"Maybe I'll pop down to the coast tomorrow and go sailing for a bit."

"I thought Mary'd sold your boat."

"Ah, thank you very much, Father Hugo. Thank you so much for reminding me. Anyway, mine's not the only boat on the Solent, you *eejit*," Colin Draper replied, raising his glass and winking.

"*De nada*, Colin."

The Smuggler's Arms had the character of a pub from a bygone age that, like a steam railway, attracted nostalgia buffs and anoraks in droves. There was an open fire stoked whatever the season and a wood-panelled interior that would make the perfect setting for a costume drama. It was smokey, regardless of the smoking ban, and its furnishings feathery and threadbare but comfortable. The beer was a hundred per cent real ale, and the staff characterful; that is to say unaccustomed to the demands of modern-day customer service. Tourists, of which there were always plenty in Greenwich, were treated with suspicion. In ways it was a private drinking club; the preserve of the locals and their dogs.

Ken, the landlord, took a sadistic pleasure in barring anyone he didn't like the look of, or who irritated him, or who broke the house rules: no mobiles, no iPads, no books, no politics, no bad manners, no hats, no children, no feet on chairs and no singing. Table service marked the Smuggler's out as a pub with a difference.

"Who's going on this trip then, Hugo?" Colin Draper asked tentatively after a long pause.

"You know, me, The Moose, Irish Gavin and Fran. The usual crew."

"Frightening."

"It was Gavin's idea. He's desperate to get us all away together. And he's mad about Ireland. But then he's first generation, of course. He's of the Irish diaspora."

"Of course."

"And he's keen for you to go too."

"Me? Really, Hugo?"

"Absolutely. I don't know why, Colin, but he's *very* keen that you go. Very keen."

"Oh."

"Well, you can't say you weren't asked."

"But you know I hate golf."

"It's not about golf, Colin."

"Wait a minute, don't tell me: it's not about golf, it's about male bonding."

"Correct! It is. That and having fun. And I'm sure it will be. And you *were* asked."

"Still, I hate golf, and I don't fancy bonding with anyone right now. What about you, Moose?"

The Moose wasn't going to respond to that one either – his attention focused on a coal barge chugging its way upriver.

3

Saturday, noon
Port de Pollença, Mallorca, Spain

A breeze rippled across the surface of the swimming pool; an unexpected but refreshing interlude for the pale-skinned couple lying on adjacent sunbeds roasting their backs in the fierce midday sun. White was the predominant colour around the pool: white walls, white furniture, white towels and white skin – all glaring in the intense heat. The sky, in contrast, was a dark, dark blue; an unbroken swathe, cloudless and daunting.

The outdoor pool area was deserted bar the dozing pair and a pool attendant lifting leaves from the surface of the water with a large net. The resort was not yet in high season.

The pool attendant stopped for a moment to stare at the couple spreadeagled before him. Couldn't decide whether they were mother and son or girlfriend and boyfriend. The man looked early-to-mid-twenties – toned and lithe and with a full mop of blonde hair – whilst the woman looked older, maybe ten years older. Maybe more. In pretty good shape, but definitely a fair bit older.

A high-pitched electronic *pling* suddenly broke the peace and interrupted the attendant's train of thought. He returned to his sweep of the pool.

"What was that? Was that your phone, Mary?" The young man asked his female companion, raising his head an inch or two.

"Yes. It's a text."

"Who?"

"Colin, if you must ask."

"*Again*? Does he never give up?"

"No, Harvey, he doesn't."

"What does he want?"

"Nothing that would bother you."

The ambient temperature in Port de Pollença was in the twenties – hot for March and too hot for the two Anglo-Saxons lounging by the pool of the five-star hotel.

"I thought we were here to play tennis, Harvey?"

"We are."

"When then?"

"God, Mary, I couldn't play in this heat."

"I know, me neither. But when do you reckon?"

"Don't worry. Rest and relaxation are an integral part of conditioning the body in preparation for any extreme physical activity."

"So, when are we going to see some physical activity, Harvey? I mean out of doors and on a tennis court, that is."

"Who's the tennis coach here, Mary, you or me?"

"Your extravagant fee would suggest it's you, Harvey."

"Good. We're both agreed then – it's me."

"How about some bloody coaching then?"

"Look, there's plenty of time for tennis."

"Considering we're only here till Monday morning and I've barely been out of this bloody bikini, I'm starting to wonder."

"Anyway, what about your daughter?"

"Saffie?"

"Yeah. What about Saffie?"

"What do you mean, *What about Saffie*?"

"Shouldn't you be ... you know ... at home ... helping her?"

"Eh?"

"Shouldn't you be at home helping her prepare for the wedding?"

"She's a smart girl, Harvey. She'll be fine."

"Does she even know where you are?"

"Kind of."

"*Kind of*?"

"Well, she knows I'm in Mallorca."

"What the hell does she think you're doing here, then?"

"I told her I was going on a fashion shoot."

"Oh, right. So I presume she doesn't know I'm here too?"

"Of course not. No, she doesn't. And you can take it from me that she doesn't need to know and won't either."

"Why? What would she say?"

"You mean, what would she say if she knew I was here fucking our twenty-four-year-old tennis coach?"

"No. I didn't mean that. Just what would she say if she knew I was here with you?"

"She'd presume you're here to give me some serious tennis coaching, you know, to improve my serve, perfect my forehand, tweak my backhand slice."

"And am I?"

"Are you what, Harvey?"

"Just here to coach you tennis?"

"Maybe not *just* for the tennis, Harvey, no. I mean, what do you think we were doing last night? That certainly wasn't tennis we were playing till two or three in the morning."

"Actually, I don't tend to think very much about anything, to be honest, Mary."

"Good."

"*Good*?"

"Yes. Good. Because if that's the case, then we're going to get along just fine."

"Oh."

"Hell, Harvey, enjoy yourself. Everybody's entitled to a bit of fun once in a while. And after a lifetime of living with Colin, I think I'm more than entitled to my share."

"What about the divorce?"

"It's done. All settled."

"God, that was quick. So, are you going to keep his name?"

"Of course I bloody am."

"Why?"

"Oh, for Christ's sake, Harvey, what does it matter?"

"Makes no odds to me. Seems a little strange, that's all."

"Look, if you must know, it doesn't make any difference."

"What?"

"If I keep his bloody name or not!"

"Why?"

"Because it's my name too."

"What?"

"Draper."

"*Draper*?"

"Yes. It's my married name *and* my maiden name."

"Bit of a coincidence?"

"No, not really, Harvey. Colin and I were ... are ... cousins."

"Jesus!"

"Exactly."

"First cousins?"

"Yes."

"How?"

"We were always very sweet on each other as kids. No one in our family appeared to notice or mind very much. I think it must have seemed rather cute at first. But then Colin was always a little precocious, a little bit too curious, shall we say. So no one appeared to notice how things were progressing between us either. Well, until it was too late of course."

"Oh."

"Can you imagine the outrage when my periods stopped?"

"And this was Saffie, I suppose?"

"No. This was long before Saffie. We were only teenagers at the time. No age."

"Ah."

"They had us married pronto, though. A bit of a scandal at the time. Then ..."

"What?"

"Things didn't turn out quite the way everyone was expecting, if you know what I mean."

"Oh, I'm sorry."

"Yes. It was devastating at the time. And very confusing."

"Of course."

"We were very young. But still, we were married. We had each other, so we decided to make a go of it and just enjoyed being together for a while. Made the most of it. We waited for five or six years then tried again and, lo and behold, we had Saffie."

"And after that?"

"How long have you got?'

"Sad though."

"What?"

"You and Colin. That you're divorced."

"People change, Harvey. Grow apart. It happens. In any case, we'll always be connected. We're family," Mary said, leaning forward, standing, stretching, then wandering over to the side of the pool and plopping in feet first. A graceful plunge that barely made a ripple and the pool attendant's cue to retreat indoors for lunch.

4

Sunday, 8am
Greenwich, south-east London

It unnerved Colin Draper when the alarm failed to go off for a second day in a row. That he'd forgotten to change the batteries worried him too. That he didn't immediately realise it was Sunday worried him more. Maybe short-term memory loss ran deep in the family genes.

From what he'd read online about how to spot Alzheimer's, *What day is it today?* was usually the first question asked in the simple diagnostic tests. But then at least he knew the year, or was pretty sure of it, could name the president of the United States and answer all the other simple questions on the list.

He shook his head to see how bad his hangover was this time. Not too bad, in fact almost undetectable and no blurred vision. The three pints may have become four but still, single figures. Luckily, for once, the Reverend Hugo Saunders and The Moose insisted on taking it easy since they had a road trip ahead of them. Their abstinence surprised Draper. Perhaps they *were* capable of adult behaviour after all.

The phone rang.

"Did you call me last night, dear?"

"No, Mum. I'm sorry. I was out with the boys."

"Did you have a good time?"

"It was alright. How about you? Do anything nice?"

"Oh, you know, not really."

"What about today? I believe Saffie and Phil are coming to stay with you. She's dying to tell you about her wedding plans."

"Is she? Coming to stay? With me? The Isle of Wight's a long way, Colin. How is she getting here?"

"She'll drive."

"Does she know the way?"

"Mum. She's up and down most weekends. She'll be fine. Don't worry."

"I'm not worried, dear."

"I'm sure it's in your diary, Mum. You'll find all the details in there."

"Good."

"I'm sorry but I really have to go now, Mum"

"Yes, sorry to be a nuisance, Colin."

"You're not, Mum. You're never a nuisance. You're lovely."

"So are you, Colin. Oh, and give my love to Mary."

"Mmm, yep. Will do. Bye, Mum. Love you."

Coffee. Shower cap. Shower.

Mid-shower the telephone rang again. Colin Draper ignored it at first, but the caller was persistent and Draper's curiosity got the better of him. He darted through to the lounge, naked, soaking wet and leaving sodden footprints across the Axminster.

"Hello?"

"You're coming, Colin."

"Jesus, Hugo! It's a bit bloody early to be calling. I've only just got into the shower."

"Never mind that. You're coming."

"Are you mad?"

"No. But you're coming."

"Where to, for fuck's sake?"

"The Emerald Isle."

"Listen, Hugo, once and for all, I am not going anywhere with you, and definitely not on a golf trip, and definitely not to bloody Ireland."

Colin Draper slammed the phone down then trudged back to the shower relieved he hadn't received an electric shock when dripping water over the telephone's base unit. He might have been grumpy at the interruption of his morning constitutional but then it's never easy conducting a casual conversation when wearing a woman's shower cap.

Dressed, he called Tomasz to check on progress at the Pimlico house.

"It's all good, Mr Colin. No worries. And it's Sunday ... You not doing something nice today?"

"Sunday! Of course it is, of course it is! Sorry, Tomasz. I shouldn't have bothered you on a Sunday. And no, no, I'm not, but thank you for asking."

The blast from a car horn caught Draper's attention. He wandered over to the window.

"Got to go, Tomasz. I'll catch up with you tomorrow. Have a good weekend yourself. Well, what's left of it."

The intercom buzzed.

Draper put one handset down then lifted the other.

"What?"

"I'm coming up."

"Do you have to?"

"Yep."

Draper buzzed Hugo Saunders in and waited for the staircase to start shaking.

"Colin Draper!"

"Hello, Hugo. It's Sunday. Shouldn't you be in church?"

"Very funny, Colin."

"What's the matter? Is The Moose not with you?"

"In the car."

"What do you want?"

"We want you to—"

"Golf? Can't. Won't."

"But Fran's dropped out and Irish Gavin's really keen for you to come."

"Tough. What's with Fran?"

"Tilly's gone into labour. She's three weeks premature."

"Not my problem. Fran shouldn't have been going in the first place. I mean, nine months pregnant! Who the fuck goes on a golf tour when their wife's nine months pregnant?"

"Not Fran, obviously. Not now, anyway."

"Too bad."

"But it'd do you good, Colin."

"No, it wouldn't. I hate golf, and Saffie's wedding's no more than a week away. How the fuck could I? She needs me. And there's work."

"Listen, A, you're pissed off and need a laugh. B, Saffie needs your credit card, she doesn't need you. C, you're a bloody good golfer – the best of us, and D, they don't need you at work, you only get in the way. I know, I've seen you on-site and the way your guys roll their eyes behind your back when they think you're not looking."

"Oh, thanks very much for the sermon, Father Hugo."

"It's only four or five days, for goodness sake. That's no time. Transport's laid on. The accommodation's practically free. There'll be you, me, The Moose and Irish Gavin. That's a great four-ball."

"No."

"Please!"

"No."

"We need you."

"Tough."

"Please, Colin."

"No."

"PLEASE!"

"*Fucking hell, Hugo!*"

"Please."

A pause. Colin Draper closed his eyes.

"When are you leaving?"

"Now."

"No. Can't do it."

"We'll go and have a swift half in the Smuggler's then call back for you in an hour."

"How are you getting there?"

"Gavin's Passat Estate, of course."

"Is that big enough for you and all your clubs and clobber?"

"Easily enough."

"You sure?"

"Why? Are you coming?"

"No."

"Please."

"No."

"I won't come to the wedding."

"Who says you're invited, Hugo?"

"My invite, that's who."

"Must be a mistake."

"Oh, please come!"

"Oh, for Christ's sake. I don't even know where my bloody clubs and shoes are."

"Great. We'll call back for you in an hour. Be ready!"

"But ... but ..."

"No buts, Colin Draper, you're coming."

And with that Hugo Saunders dashed out of the apartment and down the stairs as if escaping from the fires of hell.

Colin Draper tutted and shook his head. But slowly, very slowly, he felt a smile spread across his face, blossoming like a bud unfurling in spring or the last languid roll of a wave across a beach. Maybe he needed a little time off. Maybe he deserved to escape for a while. And it was flattering to be in demand. Not that he'd let the Reverend Hugo Saunders or The Moose know.

He gazed over at the vodka bottle now lurking by the sink, held his breath, counted to ten, checked his watch and then walked over to the kitchen drawer to look for his passport.

Of course Hugo's hour was more like an hour and a half, which left Colin Draper not only ready – clubs and shoes found, phone charged and bag packed – but ready and growing impatient.

The car hooted. The intercom buzzed.

"You're late, Hugo."

"Oh. Sorry. You're not going to drop out, are you?"

"No, I'm not dropping out. I'll see you downstairs," Draper grumbled.

Unfortunately it was pissing down – rain lashing out of the heavens. The cloudburst threatened a drenching in the sprint to the car and thus eliminated all conversation. This was fortunate for Hugo, The Moose and Gavin Doyle since as soon as Colin Draper opened his front door he found himself cast in the giant shadow of a caravan hitched to the tow bar of Gavin's silver Passat Estate.

Draper paused and pointed at the mobile home, gesticulating in staccato jabs to cue a response from Hugo who shrugged, raised his hands and gave a half-smile. Hugo ran round to the tailgate to help Draper load his clubs and bag into the boot, whilst pretending to be unaware of Draper's annoyance, and ignoring the obvious object of his exasperation.

Belongings dumped, both men quickly squeezed into the car to avoid getting totally drenched in the downpour. Hugo clambered into the passenger seat beside Gavin, who was at the wheel, whilst Draper sat in the rear with The Moose.

"The caravan? What the fuck's that all about?"

"Ask Gavin, Colin."

"Gavin?"

"It's Old Mr Cowie's, Drapes."

"Who the fuck is *Old Mr Cowie*?"

"Karen's dad. My father-in-law."

"And the reason we are towing Old Mr Cowie's caravan to Ireland *is*?"

"Because he lives in it, Colin. The caravan's his home."

"*What!* You're not telling me he's sitting in there, are you?"

"Of course he is," Gavin Doyle replied, deadpan. "I mean, there's no room for him in here, is there?"

Draper turned to look at The Moose who turned to look at Hugo.

"Listen, Colin," Hugo said, attempting to adopt a priestly tone, "since Karen passed away, Old Mr Cowie has had no one else to care for him except for Gavin here. Gavin is, basically, his next of kin. He lives in Gavin's drive."

"In that caravan?"

"Yes. Old Mr Cowie loves his caravan. And Gavin couldn't leave him to fend for himself. And, as Gavin says, there's no way we could fit him in the car."

"No, there bloody isn't. I thought you said it was going to be big enough for the four of us and all of our gear, Hugo. 'Easily', you said."

"We're all in. What's the problem, dear boy?"

"Is it safe to travel with this much luggage? I mean, can you see anything out of the rear window, Gavin? And is it legal to have someone travelling in a caravan whilst it's being towed?"

"Relax, Colin. You know, you worry too much. It'll be OK. Once this rains stops and we hit the open road, you'll be as happy as Larry. We all will."

"I'll give it five miles."

"It's an adventure, Colin. We'll be fine once we get to Ireland."

"Oh, really. And what part of Ireland are we headed for, Hugo?"

"County Donegal—"

"God's own country," Gavin Doyle said, butting in.

"And where are we staying and where are we playing?"

"Ah, here's the good news," Gavin continued. "We're staying in the B & B above my cousin's seafood restaurant in Ballyhanlon on the west coast and we're playing the old links course at Ballyhanlon tomorrow."

"If we get there."

"Then a round at Portsalon, a round at Ballyliffin and then home on Friday."

"And what's Old Mr Cowie going to do when we get to Ballywhatever-it-is, Gavin?"

"Simple, Colin. We'll drop him off at the caravan park with enough food and drink to keep him going and then during the day I'll hire a golf buggy so he can ride round the courses with me. He loves golf. He's a golf nut."

"He'd need to be."

"Then we'll take him to the pub in the evenings and tuck him up last thing at night. He'll love it. He loves Ireland. Loves Donegal. He's more or less Irish, for God's sake! First generation, like me."

Colin Draper twisted round to peer out the rear window. He could just about see into the twenty-foot caravan through the screen of golf bags and clubs piled into the boot of the estate. Old Mr Cowie was nowhere to be seen.

The caravan was in its original trim of off-white vinyl with orange detailing. It appeared to have travelled far judging by the wear and tear to its chrome fittings and weathered shell. According to the lettering, cracked and peeling on its front, the caravan was a Lightning IV, a brand name that rather exaggerated the vehicle's ability to travel at speed, Draper felt.

Once Gavin Doyle had steered them through the suburbs of London and out into the green belt – an arduous hour and a bit of traffic crawl, inertia and road rage – they hit the M25. As they travelled further away from the city and the traffic grew less congested they reached a cruising speed of around sixty miles per hour. This, however, put a severe strain on the caravan that now bobbled and bounced on its single axle like a bingo ball in a cage. Colin Draper worried for Old Mr Cowie's well-being and kept looking round for signs of him flying about in the back but saw nothing.

Soon the rain eased and the sky brightened.

"Ah, a rainbow. I think it's going to clear up now," the Reverend Hugo Saunders beamed.

"Yeah, but I bet it's raining in Donegal," Colin Draper grumbled. "And I hope we're going to take a break. We are, aren't we, Gavin? I mean, before we get to Holyhead? I presume we're heading for Holyhead?"

"Correct!" Gavin Doyle snapped.

"That's *correct* as in we're headed for Holyhead, or *correct* as in we're stopping before we get to Holyhead? I hope it's the former as I, for one, am dying for a pee."

"Both. And, in the meantime, how about some Girls Aloud?" Gavin suggested matter-of-factly.

The others stared at one another in disbelief as Gavin Doyle swung the Passat Estate into the maelstrom of traffic driving north on the M1.

5

Sunday, 11am
Port de Pollença, Mallorca, Spain

A clay tennis court. The surface, a rich terracotta. The tramlines gleaming white in the bright sun. A ball flashes past at a speed that makes it almost invisible to the eye.

"Thirty love!"

Another ball thunders past.

"Forty love!"

And another

"That's game, set and match!" Harvey Alexander screamed as he served out to seal the set with the elation of someone winning the men's singles final at Wimbledon.

"Jesus, Harvey. I thought coaching was supposed to help build some self-confidence in the student, not totally destroy it. What am I? Cannon fodder? I don't want to go home with fucking PTSD."

"I take it we've had enough for one day, then?"

"Is the Pope a catholic?"

"Being serious, though, I think your game has improved immeasurably in the last couple of months."

"Oh, has it, Harvey," Mary mumbled – more a statement than a question.

"Definitely."

"I hadn't noticed, to be honest. I'm still to take a game off you, let alone win a bloody set."

"Let's not get ahead of ourselves, shall we?"

"Cocky bastard."

"Sorry?"

"Actually, I'm starting to wonder if it was worth travelling all the way to the Balearics for just the one set of tennis, Harvey."

"It's hot, Mary. No one could play tennis for long in this."

"Rafael Nadal could."

"Really? And why's that?"

"Because he's fucking Mallorcan, you idiot!"

"But—"

"Harvey, is that your phone?"

The faint sound of a dog barking interrupted their squabbling.

"What?"

"Your phone. That's your phone. That stupid dog bark. It's your phone. It's ringing."

Harvey Alexander rummaged through his shoulder bag and yanked out his iPhone, the dog barking suddenly increasing to a savage pitch.

"Hello? Oh, Saffie! Hi!"

He turned to Mary Draper, lifting his shoulders and raising his free hand in a what-the-hell-do-I-do-now kind of gesture.

"Tennis lesson? Joint one for you and Phil? Sure. No problem at all. When do you fancy? Wednesday? Yep. No problem. Yep, two o'clock's fine. Yep. See you then, then."

Phil pressed the red button and slid his mobile back into his bag. He could sense Mary's mood had changed.

"Awkward or what?" he said blushing.

"Why the hell does Saffie want a tennis lesson in the week before her wedding, Harvey?"

"I don't know. To unwind? To see me?"

"Shit. Now mine's fucking ringing," Mary moaned, as the phone in her hand started to throb.

"Oh, fuck, it's Saffie!" she whispered, as though her daughter might have been calling from the tennis court beside them. "Darling!"

"Hi, Mum. How's Mallorca?"

"Hot."

"Jesus, everybody appears to be abroad except me. I called Harvey Alexander a minute ago. He didn't say, but he's obviously out of the country too judging by the ringtone."

"I'm sorry, Saffie, but whatever it is you'll have to be quick. I'm wanted on set any second."

"It's about the flowers, Mum."

"Yes. I saw them. They look lovely in the photos."

"Payment?"

"That's your dad's department, dear."

"Right, right. Of course. And you're home tomorrow?"

"Yes, yes. Tomorrow. I'll ring you the moment I'm through the door. You're at Granny's, aren't you? I'll catch up with you there. Have you been speaking to your father?"

"Yes. He's seems fine."

"Good, good ... Oh ... Saffie ... Hold on ... Got to go!"

Mary cut Saffie off, glanced at Harvey and shrugged. "Jesus, Harvey!"

They sat on the bench to one side of the court, glugged some water and packed away their kit."

"Mary?" Harvey asked, employing a sheepish tone.

"What, Harvey?"

"I've been thinking."

"What, Harvey?"

"You and Colin and Saffie."

"What about us, Harvey?"

"If you and Colin are cousins, then you're all cousins, aren't you? I mean, Saffie's not only your daughter, is she? She's also your second cousin. That's correct, isn't it?"

"Brilliant, Harvey. If you had half a brain you'd be dangerous. Now please stop thinking. It really isn't your forte."

"Sorry."

"I think it's time for a lie down, Harvey. Coming?"

"Massage, Mary?"

"Oh, go on then. Why not?"

6

Sunday, 12.20pm
The M1 motorway, Watford Gap Services

Colin Draper was wandering back from the service station toilets when he stopped to check his iPhone; he'd forgotten he'd switched it off overnight to save power. Firing it up he was startled as three or four text messages immediately arrived one after the other. They were all from Saffie.

Time to cover his tracks. He called her straight back.

"Hi, poppet!"

"Where the hell have you been, Dad? I've been trying to get you all morning."

"Sorry, I'm out shopping. I didn't have my phone on."

"It sounds very echoey, Dad. Where are you?"

"I'm in a kind of mall," he said, ambling over to WHSmith and grabbing a copy of *The Observer* and a bottle of water to embroider the statement with a scintilla of truth. "Was there something urgent, Saffie?"

"I was just wondering where you were, that's all."

"That's sweet. What about you? Are you in Yarmouth yet? Are you at Granny's?"

"Yes. Phil and I are with her now."

"How is she?"

"Seems fine. Bloody good for eighty-eight. We're about to take her to The Bull for lunch."

"Did she remember you were coming?"

"Yeah. I think so. I mean, she wasn't overly surprised to see us or anything."

"Good, good."

"Dad?"

"What?"

"Is she still driving?"

"No. Absolutely not. She's definitely not supposed to be. We returned her licence last year. Why do you ask?"

"I noticed her car keys sitting on the hall table."

"Bloody hell, Saffie, do us all a favour and hide them somewhere she can't find them, then let me know where, would you?"

"Will do. So, how's she getting about then, Dad?"

"She's got an account with a local taxi firm. She can call for a cab whenever she wants."

"Oh, OK."

"And, Saffie, please try and persuade her to come to the wedding. She'll come if you ask her and she'll enjoy it once she gets there. Make sure it's written in her diary."

"Yep, no problem."

"You OK then, sausage?"

"Oh, Dad, what about the flowers and order of service."

"Well, the order of service is at the printers. They're due back tomorrow. They're delivering them to your best man's address. What's his name? Alan, Angus?"

"Archie."

"Ah, yes. How could I forget? Archie Archibald. Really? I mean, who would do that to a child?"

"Dad! Stop it!"

"Sorry."

"Dad, I'm worried about the flowers."

"Oh, please tell me you've got them ordered, Saffie?"

"Of course. But the florist wants payment up front."

"No problem. Text me their number and I'll take care of it."

"OK. Thanks, Dad."

"Right, give my regards to Phil, and please tell Granny I'll call her this evening as usual."

Colin Draper slid his phone into a pocket and headed for the Roadchef, the cafe at the heart of the service station. Hugo and Gavin were sitting at one of the many Formica tables overlooking the coach park. The Moose was at the tills paying for a round of coffee.

"Where's Old Mr Cowie?" Draper asked as he approached.

"He's in his caravan. He doesn't like to leave it much. Moose's getting him a cuppa," Hugo said, bracing himself for a fresh catalogue of complaints.

"Don't worry, he's as happy as a pig in shit."

"Clover, Gavin, clover. How old is he anyway?"

"Hard to say, Drapes."

"He's your father-in-law, for fuck's sake, Gavin. You must have some idea."

"Early eighties? Mid-eighties? Something like that."

"Oh, that's very precise. But, seriously, is he OK?"

"He's fine, Drapes. Likes to keep himself to himself. Likes a bit of peace and quiet."

"Then I bet he really loves being towed behind your bloody Passat at sixty miles an hour from one side of the country to the other."

"Actually, it wouldn't surprise me if he did. He loves the open road, hence the caravan," Gavin said with a defiant smile.

The Moose came back with the coffees and a tea for Old Mr Cowie.

"Would you mind bringing him his cuppa please, Drapes?" Gavin asked with an air of authority Colin Draper hadn't noticed before, and sliding the tea towards him across the table like he was making a chess move.

"What? Why?"

"He'd like to meet you, that's all."

"Really?"

"Really. And he was quite insistent."

"Really?"

"Yes. He likes yachty types."

"Oh, OK, no problem," Draper muttered, prising himself out of his chair and looking bemused. "And you're sure he meant me?"

"Absolutely."

Colin Draper picked up Old Mr Cowie's boiling tea and sauntered off towards the car park, the cup at arm's length.

Draper tapped on the caravan door then waited. No response. He tapped another two times and when there was still no answer stepped forward, put the tea on the ground, twisted the door handle and pulled – pulled hard. The door had to be heaved free of its frame with both hands, screeching as metal scraped on metal. Once open, Draper leant in. He was struck by the overwhelming stench of stale cigarettes and beer. It reminded him of his youth – the smell of his parents' living room after one of their drinks parties on Christmas Day morning. They always had a hooley after the eleven o'clock church service and before lunch, which left its mark in sprinkled ash, wine stains and half-eaten vol-au-vents; the stench loitering long after the Queen's Speech at three. Strangely enough Draper found the aroma comforting.

"Colin? Colin Draper?" A faint voice called from the shadows.

"Hello, Mr Cowie."

"Come on in, son."

"Are you OK in here, Mr Cowie? Are you comfortable enough?"

"Of course, Colin. This is my home."

"We're not bumping you around too much, are we?"

"No. Compared to some of the journeys I've been on at sea this is like a stay at The Ritz."

"Really?"

"Of course! I've got my portable TV, I've got a kettle, teabags and a tin full of Jaffa Cakes. What more does a man need? And you know what? I can't wait till we're in Donegal. Love the views, the countryside, the people. Can't wait!"

Colin Draper moved across the room to sit with the old man, sliding along the red vinyl banquette on the opposite side of the kitchenette table. He gazed around the living area. It appeared exactly how he imagined a classic caravan should be: a combined kitchen-diner and sitting room, sofa-cum-bed, lozenge-shaped windows shrouded with grey nylon nets and wood-effect doors. The floor was covered in a burgundy lino with yellow and white flecks that looked like it had been salvaged from a 1960's barbershop.

Old Mr Cowie's personal effects were dotted about the place and resembled more the bric-a-brac in a car boot sale than the priceless momentos of a long life. The collection of cracked plates, cheap china dogs and black-and-white photos of men in sailing gear reminded Draper of the tiny snug bar deep in the bowels of the Smuggler's Arms – the walls displaying an ancient history portrayed in fading photographs of once-familiar faces with now long-forgotten names.

"Interesting collection of stuff, eh?"

"I'm amazed it's all intact after the journey we've been on."

"I'm an old sailor. I know how to stow stuff away and batten down the hatches."

"Right."

"Gavin tells me you're a sailor too, Colin. I'm sure you understand."

"Indeed. Oh, by the way, here's a tea for you, Mr Cowie."

"Thank you, Colin. That's very good of you."

"So, how long have you had this caravan, Mr Cowie?" Draper asked, peering up into the old man's face, trying to gauge his age.

Old Mr Cowie's eyes twinkled a steely blue, the whites yellowing but still pervading a warmth and charm. That he had a generous shock of white hair lent him a youthful appearance even though his skin was rugged and worn. The combination reminded Draper of the Irish playwright, Samuel Beckett – the hint of a Dublin accent completing the effect.

"I've had this one from new. It'd be nearly fifty years old by now, Colin. I've got many happy memories of caravan holidays in this touring the West Country with my wife, Betty, and daughter, Karen, when she was a kid. Did you know Karen?"

"No, not really, I'm afraid."

"Since they've both passed on, it's become a bit of a life raft, I suppose. In here I can still imagine it's 1969 and we're in Weymouth, or it's 1973 and we're in Poole, or even 1977 and we're on the French Riviera somewhere near Saint-Tropez. That was a good year, Colin."

"I kind of know where you're coming from, Mr Cowie. It used to be a little like that aboard my boat."

"Used to be?"

"Yes. Sadly the boat was a victim of my divorce."

"Divorce?"

"Yes. I'm afraid I'm divorced now."

"Recent?"

"Very."

"Oh, I'm sorry."

"I guess divorce is an abomination your generation mostly managed to avoid, Mr Cowie."

"We had conflicts of our own to contend with, Colin," Old Mr Cowie said, nodding towards a black-and-white photo of men in naval uniform."

"Of course. I'm sorry."

"I hear you were a keen sailor," Old Mr Cowie continued after an awkward pause.

"Still am, Mr Cowie. I've yet to do a round-the-world but there's time enough."

Ten minutes of chat and Colin Draper left Old Mr Cowie's caravan to rejoin the others in the cafe.

Looking round the large table as he approached, Draper imagined they must appear an odd bunch to anybody bothering to cast an eye in their direction – a diverse mix of size and style.

"Are we on holiday, Gavin?"

"Why?"

"I was just wondering why the hell you're wearing a two-piece suit with waistcoat, shirt and tie on a golf tour?"

"It's smart business attire, Colin."

"Yeah, but you look like a Ken doll. Don't you ever wear jeans when you're not at work, Gavin?"

"I sometimes wear a V-neck over an open-neck shirt."

"Christ, how very decadent!"

"I like looking smart, that's all. Just because you're stuck in a seventies time warp in your Fred Perrys and Doc Martens."

"It's adaptable daywear, suitable for any occasion."

"Bollocks, mate. You're stuck in a rut. Anyway, Hugo's the most stylish guy in town. Hey, Hugo, who's your tailor? Where do you buy your tweeds?"

"Oxfam."

"Must be the King's Road branch, eh?"

"Ah, that's my secret."

Though a little threadbare, Hugo's quality tailoring created an impression of sartorial elegance. He would appear very much the dapper country vicar if he cared to wear his dog collar but rarely did.

The Moose arrived back balancing a fresh round of coffees.

"Wait a minute, here comes our ageing goth, or is he a Catholic priest? It's hard to tell under all that black."

Having catered for the three at the Formica table, The Moose dawdled off with another cup of tea for Old Mr Cowie struggling not to slop the boiling liquid over his hand.

"Gavin, what does Moose do?" Draper whispered, leaning forward as though The Moose might be gifted with supernatural hearing.

"Don't you know?"

"Haven't a clue."

"Geriatric nurse."

"What!"

"Yes. He's a geriatric nurse."

"You mean he cares for old people?"

"Yep. That's the one."

"Doesn't he scare them doolally?"

"No. Apparently they love him."

"Really?"

"You know ... The Big Friendly Giant and all that."

"And, Gavin, please tell me, why is he called The Moose? I've often wondered but never dared ask."

"Don't know. Haven't a clue," Gavin Doyle said, raising his hands and turning to Hugo for inspiration.

"I thought it was pretty obvious," Hugo replied with a hint of disdain.

"Why? Because he's huge like a moose?"

"Are you daft, Colin?"

"Well?"

"Do you remember Angel Delight?"

"Angel what?"

"You know, Angel Delight mousse."

"What, as in the powdered dessert you mean, Hugo?"

"Yes. He couldn't stand the stuff when we were kids. Absolutely loathed it, especially the chocolate flavour. Wouldn't touch it. It always made him throw up."

"Really?"

"Yeah, not a pretty sight. For years he'd refuse to go to birthday parties in case someone's mum tried to make him eat it. Hence the nickname, *Mousse*."

"Oh, right, I get it now."

"God, Colin, you're so slow sometimes."

"But he's still The Moose to me, Hugo. Big and hairy."

"Too obvious, Colin. Nicknames need to be ironic. You know, like bald guys being called Curly," Gavin interjected.

"In that case why aren't you called *Brains*, Gavin?"

"Ha, fucking, ha, Colin," Gavin Doyle replied straight-faced.

"And talking of genius, Gavin, how *is* your latest get-rich-quick scheme coming along?" Colin Draper enquired after a protracted pause.

"It's going OK," Gavin mumbled.

"Not so good then, I take it?"

"No. Not so good, since you ask, Colin."

"I guess *Dogs Are Just For Christmas* was always going to be a hard concept to sell, Gavin." Hugo said winking at Colin Draper.

"Actually, it was just starting to take off, Colin."

"Really?"

"Yeah, really, but that was the problem."

"So, what the hell was it all about, Gavin?"

"Will you tell him or will I, Hugo?" Gavin replied sheepishly.

"Oh, I'll leave this one to you, dear boy."

"*Dogs Are Just For Christmas* was a mad idea I came up with in the pub. A bit of a joke."

"You said it, Gavin."

"Shut up, Hugo! As I was saying, it was a mad idea to buy up old, mangy dogs fit to drop. You know, on their last legs, guaranteed not to see the month out – and then sell them on to people to give as Christmas presents. You know, to friends and family. So they would then literally be dogs just for Christmas, hence: *Dogs Are Just For Christmas*."

"Are you kidding?"

"Exactly. That's the point. Originally *Dogs Are Just For Christmas* started out as that – a bit of a joke. It wasn't meant to actually happen, but I put together a calendar featuring old dogs, printed one off and gave it to Hugo for fun. He thought the whole thing so fucking hilarious he got his nephew to buy the domain name and design me a web page without telling me. You know, to keep the joke going. But then I got an order."

"Fuck! What did you do?"

"Obviously, I was tempted to come clean and tell them the truth, but then I decided, why not? So I went down to Battersea Dogs Home, picked out the perfect dog: a twelve-year-old Labrador with a terminal kidney problem and arthritis. You know, clapped-out. Then I sold it on to the customer. The only problem then was – what with client referrals and word of mouth – other orders started to roll in. A trickle at first. So back to the dog's home. It was going great guns until the trickle became a flood. That's when it all went tits up."

"How come?"

"Someone at the dog's home smelt a rat, had a snoop about online, came across my web page and cottoned on to what I was doing. Obviously that knackered the supply chain. *And* they threatened to go to the press, so I closed it all down PDQ."

"What was the final result?"

"I never got into profit. Plus I got stuck with a load of mangy dogs. Well, a few. Naturally I looked after them like gold dust and then, unavoidably, grew attached to the poor beggars. But, of course, before long they all kicked the bucket – and pretty quickly. One after the other. That was the tough bit."

"The grieving?"

"Yes. Mind you that was also the joy of the business model. Plenty of obsolescence in the product."

"Are you completely mad?" Colin Draper asked, wide-eyed in amazement.

"Ambitious, Drapes."

"*Ambitious?*"

"Yes."

"Oh, hold on a minute!"

"What, Hugo?"

"I'm just starting to remember some of your other eccentric business ventures, Gav."

"Really? I don't know what you're talking about."

"What was the other one that nearly got you into trouble?

Ah, yes, I remember – funeral photography. Yep, that's the one. Brilliant, and very tasteful. *Photo-my-funeral.com*. Yep, that was it, wasn't it?"

"Well ..."

"Then there was customising mobility scooters for the youth market: *mod-ility-scooters.com*. How's that one going?"

"Now that was a fine idea—"

"And then there was your naked board game. What was it? *Libido* something? The nude version of Twister. Wasn't exactly a big hit, was it? A total flop, I think you said. How appropriate! And finally, *Breasteese*, the dairy products manufactured from breast—"

"Enough! Enough! Can we change the subject *please*?"

A pause followed as The Moose arrived back at the table.

"Right, let's get out of this dump. I don't feel comfortable anywhere you can't buy a decent drink," Gavin Doyle moaned, seizing the moment and standing up to leave.

"Hendrix and The Stones," The Moose mumbled.

"Come again, Moose."

"Hendrix and The Stones."

"What about them, Moose?"

"They loved it here."

"What the hell's he on about, Hugo?"

"Oh, are you talking about the Blue Boar?" Gavin asked. The Moose nodded.

"Watford Services, Colin. It used to be called the Blue Boar," Gavin continued, warming to his theme. "It was built at the same time as the M1. The Stones, The Beatles, The Who, they all used to hang out here when they were gigging up and down the country in the sixties. When Hendrix joined the circuit and heard their stories, he presumed the Blue Boar was a nightclub."

"And how do you know all this, Gavin?" Colin asked with a benign smile.

"Old Mr Cowie."

"Don't tell me, don't tell me. Let me guess ... Old Mr Cowie used to be a roadie," Draper sighed.

"Yes, for Gerry and the Pacemakers, Colin!" Gavin added.

Colin Draper frowned.

"Ah, but blessed are the Pacemakers, Colin."

"Very funny, Hugo. Hilarious."

"No, but Mr Cowie knows his stuff, Colin. He's been around the block a bit."

"In that bloody caravan I suppose, Gavin?"

"I guess at his age he's old enough to recall almost anything that happened in the twentieth century," Gavin Doyle added before turning to head off to the car park. The others took his lead, stood up and followed.

"Do you want to drive?" Gavin Doyle asked, tossing the keys to Colin Draper as they approached the car.

"No. I'd rather leave that pleasure to you, thanks, Gavin," Draper replied, tossing them back again. "So, what's the plan from here?"

"Plan? We need a plan? Are we not free spirits? Are we not revelling in life on the open road? Who needs a plan, Colin?"

"What about the ferry, Gavin?"

"What about it?"

"When is it, you plank?"

"A quarter past five. It's the Holyhead to Dublin crossing."

"Well, we're going to miss that one, aren't we?"

"No, we won't."

"We're going to bloody miss it, Gavin!"

"Don't worry, I'll put my foot down. There's no more than a couple of hundred miles to go."

"What!"

"It'll only take about three and a half hours on the motorway."

"Three and a half hours in a tin can squashed together like fucking sardines. Oh, hold me back, I can't wait."

"Don't worry, Drapes. Have faith. We'll make it."

"And if we don't?"

"Easy. We'll catch the next one."

"Which would be when?"

"Oh, I don't know. Something like two or three in the morning."

"Oh, great! Brilliant! I can't get enough of this, Gavin."

"Relax. Don't worry, we'll make it. When we get going we'll put on some party music and have a sing-song. Look, we're here to enjoy ourselves, Drapes. Come on, relax. Try and get into the holiday spirit. We're the boys on tour after all."

The three passengers huddled round the car waiting for Gavin Doyle to release the central locking. He opened the driver's door, paused, then stood on the doorsill and swept a bony arm in an extravagant arc.

"One for all, and all for Donegal!" he boomed, clenching his fist and raising his voice in a grandiose manner.

"Yey!" Hugo Saunders responded in a half-hearted stab at enthusiasm.

"For Harry, England and St George!" Gavin added with a flourish.

The others rolled their eyes.

"I thought you were Irish. First generation, you said. You're called Irish Gavin, for fuck's sake, or is that another example of nickname irony too?" Colin Draper muttered.

"Depends on my mood and where I happen to be, Drapes. But it's St Patrick's Day tomorrow and we'll be in Donegal, so we'll see."

7

Sunday, 4.30pm
Port de Pollença, Mallorca, Spain

After lunch Mary Draper and her young tennis coach returned to the sun loungers beside the hotel pool. Late afternoon and shadows were lengthening – goose pimples due.

"Mary?"

"What?"

"Oh, nothing. Nothing."

"What, Harvey?"

"No, no, it's nothing."

"*Bloody hell, Harvey!*"

The outdoor pool was deserted, as ever, save for the English couple and the pool attendant who was resplendent in white flannels and anonymous behind mirrored sunglasses. He was sheltering in the shade of the surrounding wall, chin resting on the handle of his long pool net.

The couple were nearing the end of their last day in Port de Pollença. The sedentary nature of the afternoon's activity had left Harvey Alexander a little restless.

"If you and Colin are cousins, first cousins that is, how come your physical characteristics are so different?"

"Oh, for God's sake, Harvey!"

"But you don't look very alike, do you?"

"That's because *I* – as you may have noticed – am a woman, and *he* – dear Harvey – is a man."

"No, but you know what I mean. No one would think you were related, would they? There's no family resemblance."

"*What?*"

"You don't even look like you come from the same country."

"*Harvey!* What's with this sudden interest in Colin and me? It's fucking tiresome!"

"Sorry, sorry. You're right. I know it's none of my business."

Mary Draper closed her eyes in an attempt to curtail the conversation, but after a brief pause she sighed and opened them again.

"Harvey, it's none of your business but, if you must know, our grandfather was twice married. His first wife, Isabel Draper – Colin's father's mother – was originally from Catalonia. His second wife, Marjorie Draper – my father's mother – was from Chelmsford. Does that help explain whatever it is you've noticed?"

"So, you mean you're not cousins, then?"

"No, Harvey. We *are* cousins."

"I'm sorry, I don't understand then, to be honest."

"Harvey, I am sure you *don't* understand but, let's face it, it doesn't really matter, does it? And it doesn't merit any further explanation."

"No, no. Of course not, but I was—"

"*Just being curious.* I know. People often are, but then they don't always have the cheek to ask stupid questions too."

"Sorry."

"It's OK, Harvey. It's not important to me, and it's not important to Colin, and it certainly doesn't matter a damn to Saffie ... Or to anybody else for that matter."

"Yes, yes, of course. I'm sorry."

"That's OK, Harvey."

"Mary?"

"What!"

"Do you fancy an aperitif?"

"Oh, fuck it, why not?"

The pool attendant watched the English pair roll up their towels, don their towelling robes and flip-flops and trudge off towards the nearest bar. Once they were gone, he glanced down at the net in his hands, tutted and sloped over to the pool to give it a final sweep of the day.

8

Sunday, 1.35pm
The M1 motorway, north of Watford Gap Services

Since the drive to Watford Gap Services had passed with all the exuberance of a funeral, Gavin Doyle was determined that the journey to Holyhead would embrace a different mood. His initial effort to break the ice with a game of I spy, however, was met with total indifference. After one last attempt to raise some enthusiasm by introducing a 'Z' to the hackneyed phrase: "I spy with my little eye something beginning with ..." and since they were nowhere near a safari park or a pedestrian crossing, an awkward silence ensued.

Recognising the need to spare Gavin Doyle's blushes, the Reverend Hugo Saunders leaned forward to explore the glove compartment, hoping to find some CDs or any other form of in-car entertainment.

"I say! Hello, my lovelies."

"Sure, help yourself, Hugo. There's more in that holdall at your feet. Please pass them round," Gavin Doyle urged as Hugo Saunders stumbled across his secret horde of Guinness.

With the first cans open, Gavin Doyle loosened his tie, hurled it over his head and opened a couple of shirt buttons which encouraged a large sprig of orange chest hair to spring forward. Those who noticed winced.

Another mile or two down the road, Gavin produced a two-CD compilation from the pocket in the driver's door and waved it in the air in triumph.

"Oh, God, Gavin. What the hell's that?"

"*Now That's What I Call Music!*"

"OK, but what the hell is it?"

"*Now That's What I Call Music!* That's what it's called, you plonker. It's volume ten."

"Fuck me, Gavin."

"I'd rather not."

The sullen atmosphere was then dispatched with a raucous singalong of pop classics. The mixture of alcohol and the catchy chorus of Madness' "Baggy Trousers" encouraged mass participation.

When both CDs were through, Colin Draper launched into his party piece: "Pressure Drop" by Toots and the Maytals. One of the simplest and therefore easiest lyrics to remember – and what he couldn't remember he whistled. It was a short song.

"God, that was awful, Colin."

"What, my singing?"

"No, your fucking whistling. Shrill's not the word. You could shatter glass with that whistle, mate."

"Thanks, Gavin. I get that from my dad. He was a great whistler."

"Are you sure?"

"Actually, no. He was terrible. Just liked to whistle a lot. I remember once we drove to Craven Cottage to watch Fulham play QPR. We got there early. Dad was always early for everything. So we parked up and tuned into Classic FM, you know, waiting for the kick-off to get a bit closer. Then he starts his fucking whistling. Whistling along to 'Fingal's Cave' or whatever it was. Ear-splitting! On and on it went. Then I had this sudden thought: one day, there'll come a time when he's not here any more and you'll miss his whistling. So I shut up, sat there and listened. You know, smiled and listened. And, as it turns out ..."

"What?"

"I do."

"What?"

"Miss his whistling. I *really* miss his whistling. God, I'd pay anything to hear my dad's terrible whistling again. Strange the things you miss, Gavin."

"Yeah, right."

"So, do you think one day you'll miss my whistling?"

"No."

"Really?"

"Yes. Absolutely, undoubtedly and definitely not."

With Colin Draper's impromptu performance over, Hugo led them in a mash-up of hit songs from *The Sound of Music*. It was a somewhat self-conscious carload of middle-aged men, therefore, who could be heard belting out a chorus of "I Am Sixteen Going On Seventeen" as they passed the turn-off for Stoke-on-Trent on the M6.

A few miles past Colwyn Bay, Colin Draper's rendition of "Mule Train" was cut short as the Passat Estate began to veer violently from side to side accompanied by a loud flapping of rubber. A blow out, sudden and unexpected. Gavin Doyle had to fight to keep control of the car and steer it over and onto the grass verge. Luckily the flat tyre was on the Passat rather than the caravan, which could easily have been thrown off the road with the force of the puncture.

Old Mr Cowie peeped through his nets as, undeterred, the four-man team had the boot emptied, the estate jacked up, the wheel off, the spare wheel on and the car reloaded and underway in less than ten minutes. Colin Draper, however, who'd had a mental image of an hourglass never far from mind, now visualised the last millimetres of its imaginary sand draining fast through the imaginary hole in the bulb's imaginary middle into its imaginary bottom.

They progressed in silence, but careering down the home straight to Anglesey on the north-west tip of Wales like a toboggan on the Cresta Run; a good ten miles an hour over the speed limit and with the caravan swerving wildly. Palms were sweaty.

The Reverend Hugo Saunders attempted to conjure a state of calm through a cherubic smile, whilst The Moose looked blank and Colin Draper kept schtum save for a little intermittent tutting to keep a modicum of pressure on the driver. Meanwhile an attempt by Gavin to reignite the party spirit by sneaking on another compilation CD was thwarted in the nick of time when the disc was snatched from the jaws of the machine and tossed to the floor.

"For fuck's sake, Gavin. I told you we weren't going to make it, you plank!"

"Hang on, Drapes, calm down. We've got twenty miles to go and bags of time. Don't worry."

"That's all very well, Gavin, but at the service station you promised it wouldn't take more than three and a half hours to get to Holyhead. And where the fuck are we now? The ferry leaves in half an hour."

"Be fair, Drapes. Firstly, I didn't make any promises, and secondly, how the hell did I know we were going to have a bloody puncture!"

"God, it's like travelling on Apollo bloody 13. We're only going to fucking Donegal not the dark side of the moon!"

"Look, by my estimation we'll be at the ferry terminal in a little over twenty minutes. I know the way there—"

"Like the back of your hand."

"Exactly. I know the way and it's a quiet Sunday afternoon in March. There won't be any traffic. And, I know we're supposed to be at the terminal half an hour before departure, but the ferry company just say that for their own convenience. Don't worry, they'll let us on. It'll be fine. I know, I've done it before."

"Right!" Colin Draper snarled through gritted teeth.

Finally, and with about ten minutes to spare, Gavin Doyle was steering the Passat through the streets of Holyhead and taking great care not to miss the final directions to the ferry terminal.

"Thank Christ, Gavin!"

"It was never going to be a problem, Drapes, you know."

"Yes, but we're still not on board yet."

"Piece of cake. The boat's there and we've everything we need to embark. We have a reservation. We have our tickets. All you have to do, Drapes, is answer to the name of Francis Devlin when we're going through security. Simple!"

"What? Francis bloody Devlin? Why?"

"Obviously I didn't have a chance to change the booking. Your e-ticket's in the name of Francis Devlin."

"Does it really matter what I'm called?"

"No, it might not, but then again, it may. However, the good news is that I've got Fran's passport for you. He let me borrow it."

"What?"

"Let's face it – now the baby's coming he's not going to be leaving home for a month or two, is he? Give them a flash of that and you'll be fine."

"But I don't look anything like Fran."

"Well, yes and no."

"He's tiny!"

"Yes, but there's no way you can tell he's only five foot tall in a passport photo, is there? And *you're* hardly a giant yourself. I'd say that you're only about four or five inches taller."

"Nine! Nine inches! I'm five foot bloody nine!"

"OK, only about nine inches taller than he is, then."

"Brilliant! Just brilliant!"

"And you've both got similar hair and you're both, you know, a little more ..."

"What?"

"Oh, you know ..."

"Ethnic?"

"I couldn't possibly say that, Colin."

"Hold on a minute. Are you saying we all need passports, Gavin?" Hugo interjected, waking up and yawning.

"No, not for travel in Ireland, but I believe you need identification to get on and off the ferry, Hugo. And you know that. I told you on the phone last week."

"No, you didn't actually."

"Listen, whether I did or didn't is neither here nor there, but please tell me you've got some kind of ID, Hugo!"

"I've got this. Will this do?"

"Your driving licence? Ah, good man! Yep, photo ID's fine. That's you covered then. What about you, Moose?"

There was a long pause until, slowly and silently, The Moose pulled a passport from the inside chest pocket of his overcoat in the manner of a hitman drawing a handgun.

"Good, Moose. That's us all sorted then," Gavin said with a satisfied smile.

"Oh, and I presume you've got ID for Mr Cowie then, Gavin?" Colin Draper asked calmly.

Gavin Doyle looked blank.

"Shit!"

"Oh, for fuck's sake, Gavin!" Draper snapped. "Please tell me he's got some ID. A bus pass, driving licence, birth certificate. A fucking Tesco Clubcard would probably do. But please tell me he's got *something*."

"I put all that kind of stuff in a drawer in my house for him, you know, for safekeeping."

"And you didn't think to bring any with you?"

"I ... I ..."

"You fucking forgot? Brilliant! And I bet he isn't named on your ticket details either."

Gavin continued to look blank and was now reddening in the face. "Jesus, Hugo. Why didn't you remind me?"

"Dear Gavin, what am I? Your nanny? It's not my fault

you're a complete imbecile. You didn't even mention that Old Mr Cowie would be coming with us until the very last minute."

"It's not my bloody fault. It was *all* so last minute."

"OK, Gavin, but what are you going to do?"

"What do you want me to do, Drapes? Hand him over to the authorities? Put him on a train home to London? Park his caravan in bloody Holyhead for four or five days till we get back from Donegal?"

"We haven't got time for this, Gavin. Please tell me, what the fuck are you going to do?"

Gavin Doyle sat with his mouth agape; his face frozen in a blank expression.

A long silence ensued.

"Hide him."

Everyone turned to look at The Moose. Softly and in a slow menacing whisper, the man-mountain had spoken.

"Hide him. Hide him in the caravan," The Moose continued, talking with a detached nonchalance whilst staring out of the window to avoid making eye contact with any of the others.

There was a short pause.

"He's right!" Colin Draper interjected. "I might be as law-abiding as anybody—"

"You can say that again."

"But he's right. We'll have to hide Old Mr Cowie in the caravan."

"Maybe I could lock him in the loo or something!" Gavin said, with an enthusiasm that seemed a little excessive. "With any luck they won't bother checking in there. Why would they want to search the caravan? I mean, look at us. Do we look like we've anything to hide? Do we look like drug mules? Do we look like members of al-Qaeda or the IRA?"

"I guess not."

"At the end of the day, the very worst that can happen is that we won't be allowed to board the ferry."

"Yep, you're right, Gavin. OK, let's do it. It's our only choice," Colin Draper said with authority.

"Cos there's no way I am going to leave him here in Holyhead. I mean, what else *can* we do? There's no other option," Gavin added.

"Alright, here's the queue. When we pull up behind that Audi A3, Gavin, you dart round to the caravan, coerce, shepherd or do whatever you've got to do to get Old Mr Cowie into the loo. And if anyone stops and asks what you're doing running in and out of the caravan, say you're looking for your driving licence or something. Then come back, get in and on we go. Simple."

Gavin Doyle pulled the Passat Estate up behind the one or two vehicles still approaching port security at the entrance to the ferry terminal. It was a relief to see that the gates were open and cars were still being directed onto the dock for boarding. Gavin just had time to dash over to the caravan, usher Old Mr Cowie into his toilet and return to the car before the queue moved.

The initial inspection of tickets and paperwork seemed pretty cursory; the two cars in front were processed and waved through without fuss. Then the Passat was called forward. Gavin pulled up adjacent to the port security guard who squatted down as Gavin lowered his window.

"Good afternoon, gentlemen."

"I'm so, so sorry we're late!" Gavin Doyle said through a beaming smile. "It's been a nightmare of a journey. We had a puncture somewhere near Conwy."

"Yes, you've cut that pretty fine, sir, but it would appear to be your lucky day after all. There's a delay due to the weather. Services are running about half an hour behind schedule. I'm afraid it's a bit choppy out at sea today."

"No problem at all. I'm just glad we made it."

"Good. OK, can I see your ticket printout please? Lovely. And your driving licence please, sir? Good. OK. And I take it we've all got appropriate ID then?" the security guard enquired cheerfully as he leaned in through the driver's window and scanned the interior of the car to make a quick head count. Everyone offered him a friendly smile and, for once, kept quiet.

"There's not too much time, sir, so could you please drive straight on to check-in over there. They'll want to see your tickets and some ID and will tell you where to go after that. Move along sharply, please, they've nearly finished boarding."

"Brilliant, thanks."

Gavin tried to pull away but stalled the engine. Then started the car whilst still in gear and stalled again. He gazed over at the guard who frowned, then grinned, then grimaced – an expression that seemed to combine pity, urgency and reassurance all in one.

At the third attempt Gavin got into first gear and accelerated off towards the check-in point, droplets of sweat running down his forehead. A hundred yards further on their ticket printout and ID were inspected by a steward from the ferry company who then directed them to park up in one of the lanes leading to the ship.

The ferry appeared an imposing structure from the dock. A plume of smoke was snaking skyward suggesting departure was imminent.

"I told you we'd make it, Drapes."

"But we're still not on the boat yet, Gavin. What about Old Mr Cowie?"

"What about him?"

"He'd better stay hidden. We can't risk him giving the game away. What we're about to do is akin to people smuggling. We could get locked up for this."

"Don't be daft, Drapes. This is Holyhead, not Calais. I'll check on Old Mr Cowie when we get parked up in the hold. I'll urge him to stay in the loo till we get to the other side."

"For Christ's sake, Gavin!"

"I didn't think you were allowed to blaspheme, Hugo."

"When I invoke the Lord's name, I can assure you that I'm not blaspheming, Gavin."

"Oh."

"But, listen, we can't leave Old Mr Cowie cooped up in his tiny toilet for two hours. He's not a battery hen."

"He was a submariner in World War Two, Hugo. He likes confined spaces."

"Good old Mr Cowie. We'll buy him a drink when we get to Dublin," Colin Draper enthused.

"No, Colin. Once we're underway, he'll join us on deck. I'll fetch him. Once we're on board I doubt very much they'll want to inspect our documents again. There's no need for him to stow away. He's not an illegal."

"But, Hugo—"

"No buts, Colin. No buts, Gavin. If we get caught, I'll take the blame. Whatever happens I am not going to leave that old man in the hold of a ship sitting on a toilet."

"Hang on! Here we go. We're going on board. Stay calm and look innocent. Drapes – you can do the talking."

"Why me, Gavin?"

"Because you're a public school wanker and sound authoritative."

"Oh, thanks very much."

The five fifteen fast service to Dublin Port was scheduled to arrive approximately two hours after departure, but since the ferry was late leaving Holyhead and going to be further delayed at sea, it wasn't due in now until sometime after eight.

Once at sea the swell made moving about the boat tricky and at times nigh impossible. With the lurching of the ship anything that was not strapped down slid or rolled about. Doors slammed whilst passengers braced themselves in their seats. The bar did good business whilst trade in the cafeterias was slack; a full stomach seemed a liability. Few ventured onto the passenger decks outside except for the hardened smokers.

The boys on tour sat at the end of the central lounge area ringed by a variety of bars and food outlets. With its blue and purple carpeting it reminded Draper of a classic Odeon cinema from the 1930s: a gilded lily in the art deco tradition. Not his favourite era.

"What's the matter, Drapes?" Gavin Doyle asked, clocking Colin Draper's glum expression.

"The ferry."

"What about it?"

"The interior."

"What's wrong with it, Colin?"

"Gaudy."

"Can't be."

"Can't be what?"

"Gaudí."

"*What?*"

"The interior. It can't be Gaudí. I don't think he ever turned his hand to boat design, Colin."

Draper shook his head.

"All the same, Drapes, I guess you're used to this kind of weather, being a sailor," Gavin continued after a short pause.

"Hardly, Gavin. When it gets like this we stay in the pub. The Solent can be pretty tricky at this time of year."

"You certainly wouldn't catch me going to sea in this."

"Mmm, funny that," Draper said, raising an eyebrow.

Hugo appeared with Old Mr Cowie on his arm.

"Sorry about the sea crossing, Mr Cowie."

"This is trifling, Colin. This is nothing compared to stalking a U-boat across the North Atlantic in the middle of winter. A couple of hours of this is a piece of cake to me."

"What time are we due at your cousin's?" Colin Draper asked, turning to Gavin Doyle.

"Any time. He's a restaurateur. He's like a hedgehog."

"What, prickly?"

"No, Hugo. Nocturnal. He only needs a few hours' sleep."

"Oh, God, for some intelligent company!" Draper muttered under his breath.

Colin Draper glanced at his watch then prised himself away from the group, struggling to make his way across the lounge using the backs of the nearest row of chairs for support.

"Hello, Mum?"

Draper was relieved to find he could still get reception in the middle of the Irish Sea in bad weather.

"Hello, Colin. Where are you? Sounds very noisy."

"It is, Mum, you'll have to speak up."

"It sounds like a launderette. Are you in a launderette, Colin?"

"No, Mum. The weather's playing up a bit, that's all."

"What?"

"It's the wind, Mother."

"Oh, OK. So, what have you been doing, Colin?"

"Running around like a blue-arsed fly, as usual."

"Ah, well, don't overdo it. You know what happened to your father."

"Yes, Mum."

"What's the weather like, dear?"

"Windy. But more to the point, did you have a nice time with Saffie today?"

"Saffie?"

"Yes, she told me you were all going out for lunch. She and Phil are staying over with you, aren't they?"

"Yes, yes, of course. Of course they are. Sorry, I always get a bit confused in the evenings. I'm tired, you know. What's the weather like?"

"It's fine, Mum, fine. Hey, if you're tired, I'll give you a call tomorrow. I'll have a bit more time then too."

"Right you be. Take care and give my love to Mary."

"Yes, yes. Bye, Mum," Draper said trying to sound cheery as he pressed the red button on his iPhone. But he felt guilty.

Didn't like to rush through calls to his mother. Knew it was wrong to use a lack of time as an excuse for cutting short their conversations. He was well aware that time would soon prove to be the most precious of commodities.

He tried Saffie.

"Hi, Dad."

"What are you up to, Saffie?"

"Out with Phil in Yarmouth. We're about to go back to Granny's."

"Having a good time?"

"Yes. Granny's very sweet. We had a lovely lunch. And she said she's really looking forward to coming to the wedding."

"Oh, good! And have you heard from your mum?"

"Yes. She's home tomorrow. I called her earlier. She wanted to know what you're wearing to the wedding."

"Are you serious?"

"Of course."

"What are Phil and his ushers wearing?"

"He's a Stewart. They'll be wearing the Stewart tartan, of course."

"Ah, kilts. That'll please your mother."

"What about you?"

"One thing's for sure, I won't be wearing a skirt. I've booked morning dress."

"Mmm, skirts. Yes, Dad. Phil will find that *very* funny. But you'd better be careful. Most of Phil's mates are at least a foot taller than you *and* they're all rugger buggers. I wouldn't mention skirts to them if I were you. Be warned: they really put the 'burly' into burly Scotsmen."

"Oh, don't worry. I'll be the soul of discretion."

"*Yeah, right!* Actually, Dad, I almost forgot. Phil's managed to book The Red Arrows."

"Bloody hell, Saffie, what's that going to cost?"

"About a hundred and fifty quid."

"What? For The Red Arrows?"

"Yeah. It's The Red Arrows from Cowes. They're a synchronised darts display team. They're supposed to be really entertaining. They'll be on before the dancing starts."

"Are you sure Phil's not having you on?"

"Phil? I don't think so."

"Well, it's your wedding. Hey, Saffie, got to go. Keep in touch."

"Dad, where the hell are you? It sounds very noisy."

"Yes, it is. It is, Saffie."

"Mmm, interesting. You're being very enigmatic these days, Dad. You know, international man of mystery and all that."

"Not at all."

"Whatever. Only don't forget to get in touch with the florist on or before Tuesday."

"No problem. Enjoy yourself at Granny's."

"Thanks. Will do. Take care, Dad. *Mwah.*"

"Bye, sweetheart."

Draper, who had been transfixed by the swell rolling past the windows, peered over to see what the rest of the party were up to. Hugo Saunders and Gavin Doyle were curled up like a pair of cats and appeared to be asleep whilst The Moose and Old Mr Cowie were staring out to sea as if searching for land, a glimpse of Howth perhaps, the sighting of which would be the first indication they were nearing Dublin.

Just then a message bleeped in: *Hi Colin. Glad you're around for Saffie. Thnx MaryX.*

9

Sunday, 8.00pm
Port de Pollença, Mallorca, Spain

"What about the wedding, Mary?"

"What about the wedding, Harvey?"

"Why didn't I get an invite?"

"Were you expecting one?"

"Dunno. Maybe. Maybe to the evening do."

"Why? You don't know Saffie *that* well, do you?"

"No, but I thought you might have fixed it for me."

"Why?"

"Oh, I don't know. I thought you might have wanted me to be there."

"You're not feeling left out by any chance, are you, Harvey?"

"No, no, of course not. Actually, as it happens, I'm going away again on Friday."

"Really? This Friday coming? End of next week?"

"Yes."

"Good. That's probably for the best then, isn't it?"

"Aren't you going to ask where?"

"Where, what?"

"Where I'm going. Where I'll be next weekend. You know, why I'm missing the wedding."

"Oh, go on then. I can tell you're dying to tell me. Where are you going to be next weekend, Harvey?"

"Barcelona."

"Oh! Business or pleasure?"

"Business."

"Good. Tennis business?"

"Yes. A tennis camp."

"I guess it can be, can't it, Harvey?"

"What?"

"Camp."

"What?"

"Tennis."

"Oh, very funny, Mary. Bloody hilarious. Actually, it's a training camp for teenagers. A holiday thing."

"So, even if, by chance, I could have got you an invite to Saffie's evening do – you couldn't have come?"

"No. And it's too late now. It's easier this way though, don't you think?'

"Probably, Harvey. Probably. But still, it's a pity we didn't think of it earlier."

"Yes, but there you go. Look, the camp's only for two weeks, Mary. I guess you can afford to skip your regular session till I get back."

"Let's hope so, Harvey. Though I can't guarantee that I won't have found another coach to play with by then. We'll just have to see. Let's face it, my tennis needs a lot of hands-on attention, Harvey – a lot of one-on-one."

"Indeed, Mary. Indeed."

10

Sunday, 8.15pm
The Irish Sea

The sky cleared, the wind dropped and the sea became calmer as the ferry slowed to make its final approach into Dublin Bay. After the rigours of the journey, the County Dublin coast seemed to possess a spiritual air, the lights from the city merging into an amber halo.

The two-and-a-half-hour crossing from North Wales had rendered many of the passengers speechless; stunned into silence by the relentless lurching of the ship. The procession down to the lower decks – as motorists were instructed to return to their vehicles – was performed in silence, the bedraggled parading down into the bowels of the ship in a zombielike trance.

"OK. Here's the plan, Colin," Gavin Doyle whispered as they descended to their car deck.

"What?"

"We go straight to the caravan and make Old Mr Cowie comfortable in the toilet."

"*Comfortable?*"

"Yes. As comfortable as we can. Get into the car and don't go near the caravan again till we're safely on dry land. You know, a few kilometres down the road from the port. OK? It's very important we look and act as though we're totally innocent as we leave the ship. The Garda Síochána—"

"Who?"

"*The Irish police* — aren't stupid. Friendly, but not stupid.

We have to give the impression that we've nothing to hide. We'll have our documentation ready, we'll make eye contact with them and we'll smile and look calm. I'll do the talking."

"*You?*"

"Yes. I'm Irish."

"Genius, Gavin. It's a pity you've lost your Irish accent then, isn't it? You sound like you're London born and bred to me. A South London wide boy. Lewisham perhaps. Somewhere off the high street, maybe. I'd say Welford Avenue. The right-hand side of the road. The odd numbers. Somewhere between eleven and nineteen. Possibly number fifteen," Draper teased.

They escorted Old Mr Cowie back to the caravan, climbed aboard the Passat and waited.

After ten or so minutes the vast bow door was raised, shuddering as the hydraulics strained to lift its great weight. Engines were engaged and those vehicles at the front – the artics first – were beckoned forward by a small army of deckhands and directed off the ship.

Before long Gavin was waved ahead and, without stalling the car, rolled the Passat towards the ramp, the dock and the distant lights of Dublin.

The line of cars in front of them was being channelled into a single lane that weaved across the dock towards the open road. Near the exit, however, was a barrier manned by a group of customs officers in peaked caps and fluorescent jackets brandishing clipboards. There were also police nearby.

It seemed to Colin Draper that the customs guys were stopping about one car in every four or five to inspect papers and quiz the drivers before waving the next three or four cars straight through. So far it seemed that only one vehicle, a transit van, had been ordered to move over into the adjacent lane for closer inspection. The driver was standing on the tarmac and being questioned by a couple of policemen whilst customs officers ducked in and out of the van's open doors to make a thorough search. They appeared to have emptied the van's contents onto the dock where one of them was sifting through the resultant pile of boxes with hands sheathed in blue latex. Meanwhile a dog handler was encouraging his spaniel to spring up into the van to sniff around the rear compartment.

Draper crossed his fingers and sat upright in his seat. Beside him, The Moose was gazing at the night sky.

"No moon tonight, Moose," Draper said quietly, leaning over and gently touching his arm.

The Moose gave Draper a quizzical look.

"There's a new moon, Moose. You won't see a thing."

The Moose rolled his eyes.

"You can't, Moose. The moon and the sun currently have the same ecliptic longitude. One's behind the other."

The Moose frowned.

"I know my astrology, Moose. It's all part and parcel of being a sailor," Draper said, adopting a pompous tone then feeling self-conscious when The Moose turned away – didn't smile, didn't blink.

"Right, here goes then!" Gavin Doyle said as they were within a car or two of the checkpoint.

"Phew, he's stopping the car in front. Boys, we're going to sail through this, it's going to be a doddle!"

They sat and watched as a customs officer approached the family saloon ahead of them. He leaned forward, rested one arm casually on its roof and bent his head down to the driver's window. He appeared to ask for and receive the appropriate bundle of papers to check. He was talking nineteen to the dozen but was amicable, laughing and making jokes. All seemed calm and relaxed. Within a minute or two he was slapping the car's roof to send it on its way. He then gesticulated for Gavin to drive up.

Gavin continued on at a steady ten to fifteen, confident they wouldn't be stopped and would soon be on their way. But the officer's demeanour suddenly changed, his face assuming a sterner expression as he brought the Passat and its passengers into sharper focus.

Surely there wasn't a problem? Surely he would wave them on through? Surely he needed to keep the traffic moving? Just as they were drawing level, the customs officer thrust up his hand. Gavin pulled up in the manner of an emergency stop which caused the car to jolt.

"Good evening, sir. Can I see your papers please?"

"No problem," Gavin said, gathering their various bits of ID. The others stashing away any empty cans by kicking them under the seats. Draper prayed the car didn't smell too much of stale beer.

The customs official stood upright and inspected each piece of paperwork then poked his head into the car and clocked each of their faces. He handed back their papers, moved away from the driver's window and walked to the front. There he glanced down at the car's registration plate then walked to the rear and started to inspect the caravan, kicking the tyres and peering under the tail end.

"Shit! He's trying the caravan door!" Gavin cursed as he watched the officer in his wing mirror. "Whatever you do, guys, don't turn round now!"

"Oh, fuck! We're screwed!" Colin Draper squealed.

"Sit up and sit still. Don't draw attention to yourselves. And for God's sake try and look innocent!" Gavin barked.

"What's he doing now?" Hugo Saunders whispered.

"He's only pulled the bloody caravan door open."

"Shit! Is he going in?"

"No, it's OK, he's wobbling it about on its hinges a bit. Doesn't seem happy, though. Ah, now he's shut it again. No, it's open. No! He's shutting it again. Phew, he's not going in. Oh, fuck, now he's called over a policeman. Ssh! Keep quiet! Shit! They're both coming over."

The customs officer and the policeman arrived back at Gavin's window.

"There appears to be a problem with your caravan, sir," the police officer snarled.

"Really, officer?" Gavin Doyle replied, trying to affect a little-boy-lost look: his eyes widening and cheeks flushed.

"Yes. There's something not quite in order, sir."

"Oh?"

"The catch on the door's faulty. It could prove hazardous to other motorists and pedestrians. You need to get that fixed. It should be locked and shut tight at all times when you're in transit. Must be secure by law. If it's not, the vehicle's not roadworthy, sir."

"Oh, OK, officer. I'm so sorry. I didn't realise."

"I'm afraid ignorance is no excuse, sir."

"No, no. Of course not."

"Get it fixed as soon as, eh? We don't want that swinging open and taking out some poor unsuspecting motorcyclist when we're bombing down the road, now do we, sir?"

"No. Certainly not, officer!"

"Where are you heading for?"

"Donegal."

"Golf, I suppose?" the guard asked, casting an eye over their clubs and smiling.

"Absolutely."

"Drive safely then, and make sure you get that door fixed before you go very much further, and definitely before you head up north, OK? Off you go then," the guard instructed.

"Thank you, officers. And don't worry, we'll get some gaffer tape on it at the nearest service station," Gavin Doyle said, wiping his clammy hands on his suit trousers before closing the window.

As he went to drive away Gavin stalled the Passat again. When he restarted the engine he slipped into second and took off at five miles an hour struggling to accelerate as he crawled towards the terminal gates, the harbour road and the motorway beyond, the car backfiring twice before they'd reached the exit.

In his mirror Gavin could see the customs officer chatting to the guard who was scratching his head, his hat tilted to one side, studying the rear of the caravan. The customs officer shrugged before scribbling something onto his clipboard.

Within a few minutes of exiting the ferry terminal Gavin was steering the Passat onto the dual carriageway heading north out of Dublin. They drove about six or seven kilometres before he thought it safe enough to pull over for a toilet break and to check on Old Mr Cowie. They stopped at a retail park near the main intersection with the N2, the route north-west towards Donegal. They found a secluded area beyond the bottle bank in a dimly lit corner of the car park. It was a few minutes before nine, there were few other cars about and it was quiet save for the constant hum of traffic drifting across from the main road.

They disembarked, staggering out of the car and stretching to their full height. Gavin popped over to the service station to buy some gaffer tape before going to see Old Mr Cowie.

"Tell me, Hugo, wouldn't it have been cheaper, and a lot less bother, to have *flown* to Donegal? I thought this was supposed to be a holiday, not the Dakar Rally. Bear Grylls would struggle to survive on this fucking trip."

"Yes. But Gavin made the car journey sound so attractive."

"Fucking salesmen!"

Colin Draper and Hugo Saunders strolled over to join The Moose who was having a piss beside the large privet hedge marking the car park boundary. They lined up to perform a pee in formation.

"It's refreshing to be somewhere different though, isn't it, Colin? Somewhere away from it all with clean air, green grass and friendly faces," Hugo said, staring heavenwards and gulping in deep breaths of dewy spring air.

"Yes, Hugo. Funnily enough, I think you're right."

The three walked back to the car. The Moose climbed in and sat and stared out the window whilst Colin and Hugo waited on the tarmac for Gavin to return from the caravan. Hugo rolled a cigarette and leaned against the bonnet.

"How much further is it to Donegal, do you think, Colin?"

"Oh, I don't know, Hugo. Three or four hours, say?"

"So, what's our ETA?"

"About twelve thirty, one o'clock-ish, I guess. Not too bad considering."

"Thank God we made that bloody ferry then."

"Absolutely. I don't care what time we get there as long as the bar's still open."

"What time are we playing golf tomorrow?"

"Gavin told me we're booked to tee off at midday. You up for it?"

"Sure. Why not?"

"*And* it's St Patrick's Day, so hopefully it'll be nice and lively in the bar later on."

The conversation lulled as Hugo Saunders lit his rollie whilst Draper reclined across the bonnet to gaze into space.

"Where are all the stars, Hugo?" Draper asked after a brief pause.

"Huh?"

"I guess when it comes to light pollution, Dublin's pretty much like any other European city," Colin Draper mused as he scanned the sky.

"Indeed, Colin, indeed," Hugo Saunders murmured, more interested in keeping his rollie lit in the breeze.

"Gavin's taking his time. Do you think we should go and check on him? I'd imagine we'd need to be getting under way pretty soon," Draper said, sitting up.

He regained his footing then set off towards the caravan. Hugo Saunders followed.

A dull yellowish light was shining inside. All was quiet. Draper tapped lightly on the caravan door.

Nothing. No response.

Draper tapped again.

Still nothing.

Draper looked at Hugo. Hugo shrugged.

Draper was about to give the door a hard thump when it creaked and started to swing open. Hugo and Draper stood rooted to the spot as Gavin Doyle appeared in the doorway, tears streaming down his cheeks.

"What? What is it, Gavin?"

"It's ... It's Old Mr Cowie."

"What's the matter? What's wrong, Gavin?"

"He's ... he's ..."

"What?"

"I think he's dead!"

11

Sunday, 8.50pm
Dublin

"Are you sure?"

"What are the symptoms of death, for fuck's sake, Colin?" Gavin Doyle scolded close to tears again. "Ah, let me see," he continued. "Has the patient stopped breathing? Is there a pulse? Can you detect a heartbeat? OK, how about we wait and see if rigor mortis sets in, Colin? Or maybe wait a bit longer for some flies to appear? Maggots maybe?"

"Alright, Gavin. I'm only trying to help."

"Fuck! *Help?* You? How the fuck can you help? He's fucking dead, Colin! It's a bit fucking late for that, isn't it, mate? This isn't something that a couple of paracetamol and a fucking hot-water bottle are going to make any better."

Colin Draper thought better of replying. Thought better of saying anything at all. Thought better of taking a dip into his imaginary tombola of comforting words in case he came up with something more inflammatory to say than he'd already said. He looked around at the others who thought better of returning his glance. They had their eyes fixed firmly on the floor.

A lengthy silence ensued occasionally interrupted by Gavin Doyle's sobs and sniffles.

Old Mr Cowie had been found slouched on the tiny plastic throne in the caravan's WC – more of a cupboard than a toilet. His head had rolled forward and was resting on his breastbone.

When The Moose arrived he took it upon himself to lift Old Mr Cowie very gently up into his arms like he was handling priceless china. So frail, it was as if the old man had the weight of a small doll. The Moose carried him into the main living area of the caravan. Old Mr Cowie now lay across the kitchenette table. Hugo closed the old man's eyes and then folded his arms across his chest. He appeared to murmur a prayer.

"What do you think we should do now, Colin?" Hugo whispered into Colin Draper's ear as they stood over Old Mr Cowie's corpse.

"Think. That's exactly what we need to do, Hugo. Think."

"With all due respect to Old Mr Cowie, maybe we should just get the hell out of here."

"And then what, Hugo?" Gavin said angrily, overhearing their whispers. "There are serious ramifications for all of us in this. Thanks to the gross neglect of everyone in our group, me included, we may well be responsible for Old Mr Cowie's untimely death. The journey was obviously far too much for him."

"What do *you* suggest we do then, Gavin?"

"Apart from making sure we cover our tracks, we need to work out a strategy that is best for Old Mr Cowie, Hugo. That is to say, one that honours his memory. One that second-guesses what *he* would have wanted us to do for him in these circumstances."

"He was a sailor, Gavin. Maybe a burial at sea would be appropriate? I could perform the rite."

"Are you completely mad, Hugo? You of all people must know that disposing of a body willy-nilly and unregistered is a criminal offence. That's why I say we need to think and act carefully."

"OK then, Gavin. But what? Hang around here and wait for the police?"

"Actually, I think we should drive on to Donegal as planned, Gavin," Colin Draper interjected. "And I mean now.

Immediately. And use that time to consider our options. Get to your cousin's place, park up, unpack and then in the morning make a group decision and agree on the most sensible course of action. But let's be serious for a moment, I'm not sure what the best solution is, but whatever course of action we choose to take, it's not going to pan out too well for any of us if we don't agree on a good story and stick to it. We'll have to handle this as a team, stay strong and pull together. What do you think, Gavin?"

Gavin Doyle didn't respond, simply sat and stared at the tabletop. The others eyed each other intermittently trying to gauge the mood.

"Gavin, you're the guy's son-in-law. Isn't there anything you'd like to say?" Colin Draper asked after a long pause.

"No. Except that maybe you've got a point. Maybe we should get Old Mr Cowie to Donegal. I think he'd want that. He loved Donegal. I don't think he'd like the idea of ending up on a slab in a Dublin morgue."

"Fair enough."

"And you're right. I'm his son-in-law. I'm responsible. There's no other family to inform or consult now. They're all dead. Karen was his only child. I'm all he has left and it's my decision to make."

"Really? And *you* think we should go on?"

"Yes. Because if we were to search for a positive in all of this, I think he'd rather have died on the open road than sitting on my bloody drive in Lewisham."

"I'm sure you're right, Gavin," Colin Draper said, placing an arm around Doyle's shoulders and pulling him in for a hug.

"Listen, why don't we lie Old Mr Cowie down on the banquette, make him comfortable and secure and get back on the road?"

"Alright, but what do you think we should do when we arrive in Donegal, Colin?"

"We can discuss that on the way, Hugo. If anyone comes

across us here and now it might look a bit fishy. I mean, four men and a corpse in a city car park? Who knows what spin the Dublin police would put on that? In Donegal we'll appear to be a group of poor, innocent tourists who have suffered a bereavement. Here we could be mistaken for a bunch of dodgy foreigners who're up to no good," Colin Draper suggested calmly.

Within a few minutes they had the caravan door taped shut, were all on board the Passat and manoeuvring out of the car park to take the road north for Donegal.

The first hour and a half of the journey passed in silence; there was no appetite for conversation. There was little to discuss that didn't involve Mr Cowie anyway. As they approached Aughnacloy, the first town over the border from the Republic of Ireland, Colin Draper coughed to clear his throat. The others sighed in anticipation of another announcement.

"Gavin, is there a Garda station in Ballyhanlon?"

"Yes. A two-man affair, Colin. It's about four doors up from my cousin's place."

"Good. That'll make this easier then because first thing tomorrow morning I think we should all go to the Garda station and tell them the truth. No beating about the bush. Simply come clean about everything that's happened since we left Greenwich. I mean, what's the worst that can happen?"

Silence.

"There's one thing we all need to agree on though. We need to agree on where and when we found Old Mr Cowie in his current state."

"He's dead, Colin!"

"Yes, *dead,* Gavin, obviously. Sorry. And it would be better for all of us if we agree on the time of discovery and stick to it. I think it's vital that we give the impression there was no delay in our reporting his death. And that would only be a small distortion of the truth in any case. So, when we report his death to the police, we report it not necessarily as though he has just died, but as though we have just found him – Old Mr Cowie that is – you know, dead."

"Why?"

"Because the police may want to establish the time of death. And if they do, they'll wonder why we didn't report his death closer to the time that it happened. Which is why we *have* to say we didn't know he had passed away until we checked on him the morning after we arrived in Donegal."

"You mean tomorrow morning then?"

"Exactly, Hugo."

"Sounds bloody complicated to me," Hugo cursed.

"It's not. It's simple. When we go to the Garda station in the morning we say that we've only just found him. And that before – when we last checked on him on arrival in Dublin – he was fine. We have to imply that he passed away sometime between our leaving Dublin and arriving in Donegal."

"Ah, and then, if asked, we say we're sorry but we don't know when."

"Exactly, Hugo."

"Is that it?"

"No, Gavin. To cover our tracks completely we have to come clean about how *he* insisted on hiding in the caravan when we embarked in Wales because *he* was travelling without a valid ticket and ID. We have to underline that it was *his* decision, *his* idea and *his* responsibility."

"But it wasn't really, was it? And why does it matter now?"

"In case they get suspicious, investigate our story in detail and find that Old Mr Cowie wasn't listed as a passenger on the ferry. It's a reasonable explanation and one that puts us in the clear."

"So we're going to make out that he sneaked himself on board then?"

"Well, he kind of did, didn't he?"

"I'm confused," Hugo whined.

"Leave it to me. I'll do the talking. All you have to do is back me up. Look, in essence, to any third party—"

"The police?"

"Yes. To the police ... I'm sure none of this will matter. It'll simply appear that an old man has passed away on holiday in Ballyhanlon and happened to be in our company at the time. Boohoo. Happens every day. And then, hopefully, they'll leave it at that."

"Shit, Drapes! That sounds a bit callous. He was my father-in-law after all!"

"Yes, I know, and I'm sorry, Gavin. And he was a very *lovely* old man, but we've got to be pragmatic. We need to be ready with answers in case, as I say, they get suspicious and question us further."

"So only one little white lie then, Colin?"

"Yes, Hugo."

"Two."

"What, Moose?"

"That's two," The Moose interjected.

"What?"

"Moose is saying that that's two white lies, Colin. The time and place of discovery and that Old Mr Cowie volunteered to hide in the caravan," Gavin explained.

"Yes. That's right, Moose. Two. But, Gavin ..."

"What?"

"Do you think Old Mr Cowie would disapprove of what we are doing?"

"I DON'T BLOODY KNOW!"

"Gavin!"

"OK then, no. Probably not."

"Thank you."

"I suppose he did have a spirit of adventure and he was no lover of authority. So, all things considered, I'm sure he wouldn't want us to get into any trouble on his account," Gavin added begrudgingly.

"Good! Agreed! That's all settled then."

After what seemed like an eternity, but was a little under four hours, the coastline at Ballyhanlon came into view over the loughs and inlets that pepper the far northwest of Donegal. The route along the causeway leading to the town passed through a plateau of farmland dotted with sheep and drystone walls.

As they approached an isolated sprawl of farm buildings, a pair of collies darted into the road beside them. The dogs were barking and charging at the wheels of the Passat sprinting alongside the car with their heads down, teeth bared and nipping at the tyres.

"Jesus, what's got into them?" Colin Draper shouted over the din, his shoulders hunched in alarm.

"Donegal sheepdogs do that kind of thing all the time. When they're not lying across the road to stop the traffic, they're chasing after all the cars. They like to show their human friends who's boss," Gavin Doyle replied.

"They look positively suicidal."

"Fucking mad if you ask me, Hugo," Draper muttered.

If they'd arrived in Ballyhanlon in daylight, they couldn't have failed to be impressed by the view across the bay towards the Derryveagh Mountains. Most noticeable in the dark, however, were the St Patrick's Day lights and decorations strung along the main street. It felt a little like Christmas.

At the top of the run of houses and shops they turned onto a quay. A small fleet of trawlers bobbed on their moorings below, rigging clanging in the breeze. On the far side of the harbour sat a stone building housing a pub and restaurant. To Draper it resembled an eighteenth-century coach house. A few doors up was the Garda station – a detached Georgian town house on three floors. It had a Garda lantern hanging over the doorway, a dim blue light creaking in the sea breeze.

"Here we are! Ballyhanlon. What do you think?" Gavin Doyle asked as he pulled up on the quay.

"It's hard to tell in the dark, Gavin. Truth be told I'm feeling a bit of an emotional wreck. I could really do with some alcohol-based refreshment if that's possible."

"If only, Hugo," Colin Draper moaned.

"Well, this is Donegal, that's the Harbour Inn and, technically speaking, it's St Patrick's Day," Gavin Doyle said with a hint of a smile. "Come on, let's go and find cousin Eugene."

"Gavin, lest we forget, first thing tomorrow we're going to see the local Gardaí. Agreed?"

"Of course, Colin! Goes without saying," Gavin Doyle sighed.

Gavin Doyle drove round to the rear of the bar and parked in the furthest corner of the car park. They clambered out of the Passat and ambled back to the front entrance.

"Right, a quick pint, if we can get one, and then we'll go and find our lodgings," Gavin said with a little more enthusiasm. "The staircase up the side there leads to the accommodation. As well as owning the bar and restaurant Cousin Eugene runs the upstairs as a B & B."

"He's almost as entrepreneurial as you then, Gavin."

"Almost, Drapes. Almost," Gavin murmured, choosing not to react.

As they neared the entrance, the door of the Harbour Inn blew open an inch or two, the sound of traditional music seeping out onto the street. Colin Draper could decipher fiddles, a tin whistle and what he guessed was a bodhrán all playing at a frantic pace.

A face appeared in the crack in the door which was immediately shoved open.

"Gavin Doyle! *Céad Míle Fáilte!* Where were you? I've been looking forward to seeing you all day. Come in, come in, the lot of you. You're all welcome here, lads."

"Thanks, Eugene."

"We're having a bit of a session. A bit of a private party. A lock-in, you might say."

Second cousin Eugene was a burly man nearly the size of The Moose, and noticeable for his oversized teeth – tombstones that played a prominent part in a near-permanent smile. His hands were the size of two bunches of bananas with a crushing handshake. He was older than Gavin – looked old enough to be an uncle rather than his cousin.

Eugene Doyle continued his welcome address without pausing for breath as he moved inside the pub ahead of them. Once they'd all reached the bar it was impossible to make sense of anything he was saying over the music and general hubbub – not that that stopped his monologue. They all grinned and guffawed regardless, taking their cues from his facial expressions.

"*Slàinte!* And I hope we're not going to go *too* mad tonight," Colin Draper said, raising his pint of stout.

"*Slàinte!* Speak for yourself, Colin. We're on holiday now. After what happened today I imagine we could all do with a bit of a lift. And I think it's probably what Old Mr Cowie would want too."

"How the hell do you know that, Hugo?"

"I know his type, Colin."

"That's very easy to say."

"With my professional experience of administering to the elderly, actually, yes, it is."

Hugo Saunders turned his back on Colin Draper, took a large gulp of Guinness and wandered over towards the musicians sitting in a circle on the far side of the room. Draper glanced round to check on the other two. Gavin was engrossed in conversation with an old-timer at the bar, whilst The Moose was staring into the embers of the peat fire.

An hour of music and drink and the musicians, who looked like they'd seen the better side of seventy, signalled they'd had enough and were packing their instruments away. The end of the music session was a cue for most customers to traipse home. Cousin Eugene continued to hold court from behind the pumps surrounded by a coterie of diehards.

Gavin nodded at Colin Draper, Hugo and The Moose and then towards the door. He walked over to the bar to return his beer glass, whispered into his cousin's ear and received a hefty slap on the back before being handed a fistful of keys.

The wind had got up out on the pier. The four men paused for a moment to breathe in the salty air. There wasn't much to be seen in the dark ahead of them but the house lights dotted along the coastline and the silhouette of distant hills.

"Are you OK?" Colin Draper asked, sidling over to Gavin Doyle and resting a hand on his shoulder.

"Shit, would you be?"

"No, I guess I probably wouldn't. And ... I'm sorry, mate."

"Don't be. Though to be honest, Drapes, I'm not sure what the hell we're doing here."

"Would you rather we'd gone home, Gavin?"

"That's a difficult one. But, no, not really. Coming here's probably what Old Mr Cowie would have wanted us to do. I guess we'll just have to make this trip a really special one to honour his memory."

"What was his name?"

"*His name?*"

"Yeah, I mean, what was his first name?"

"I'm not sure."

"Oh, come on, you must know!"

"Actually, it was Beverley. His first name was Beverley."

"*Beverley?*"

"Yes, Beverley. He didn't like people knowing."

"I'm not surprised."

"And, he preferred to be called Bev. Well, obviously."

"Obviously."

12

Monday, 9.05am
Ballyhanlon

Sergeant Seamus McIlhenny yawned loud and long as he tilted back in his chair and stretched his arms above his head. Regaining his composure he slumped back across his desk to resume shuffling papers, twiddling his fingers and contemplating the day ahead – the mindless activities that had been occupying him for most of his first hour on duty in the Garda station. The slowest of starts to one of the busiest days of the year: St Patrick's Day.

Kicking off in two hours' time, and like many other towns the length and breadth of Ireland, Ballyhanlon would be celebrating St Patrick's Day all day and long into the night. Sergeant McIlhenny would be required to police the event single-handed since Donal, his subordinate and sidekick, was off on stress-related sick leave.

There was some pleasure to be had during the morning, however, when the townsfolk were generally well behaved. Everyone would be in festive mood and preoccupied with either taking part in or watching the St Patrick's Day parade and the crowning of the Ballyhanlon St Patrick's Day Maid of Honour.

The parade comprised a cavalcade of floats: flatbed trucks decorated by, and representing, the primary school, the convent school, the fire brigade, the GAA club, the RNLI and the fisheries school. There would also be any number of tractors festooned with balloons and streamers and, bringing up the rear in its day-to-day livery, the local Spar shop refrigerated delivery van (though no one was ever quite sure why it was there).

Later there were other activities for Sergeant McIlhenny to marshal: the raft race around the harbour and the various running races on the green. His favourite events were the running-backwards race and the married couple's piggyback race. Not quite Olympic-standard sport, but both spectacular in their own light-hearted way with most entrants toppling over and ending up in a muddy, giggling heap well before the finish.

There would also be a funfair, some charity stalls, palm-reading, face painting and a fancy-dress competition. At any given point during the day some clown might try and dye the town's fountain green or add a squirt of detergent to get it to froth up, but the atmosphere would be a happy one and the festivities normally passed off without incident.

It was the evening and night that usually provided the fireworks. Drunkenness, disorderly behaviour and the odd punch-up were often the inevitable result of all-day drinking. Tonight Sergeant McIlhenny would expect to have company in the Garda station. Accommodation in the cells could be cramped. Most of the occupants being detained to sleep off the effects of drink and then released the next day to make their excuses at home, stumbling out through the station door blinking and tottering into the early-morning sun.

And should there be trouble, it was for Sergeant McIlhenny to stem the tide of antisocial behaviour alone and hold the fort until reinforcements could be summoned from Letterkenny, should they be available. If not, McIlhenny knew whom of the locals he could turn to for muscular support in his deputy's absence.

Sergeant McIlhenny peered down at his lapel, sighed and then lifted the shamrock his wife had bought him in the local greengrocers the previous week. It had been drowning in a glass of water on the office windowsill ever since. He fiddled with the greenery until the pin poking through the silver foil wrapped around its bottom was well and truly speared through the lapel of his jacket.

Sergeant McIlhenny looked up and out through the meshed window opposite his desk and gazed across the harbour. It was a fine day with a clear sky. Not even an occasional curmudgeon like the sergeant would wish for bad weather on St Patrick's Day. Anyway, there was no sign of rain and even the promise of a little sunshine. He hoped the local children would be well basted in sunscreen.

Just as his mind started to wander back to St Patrick's Days of the past and his enjoyment of the parade as a youth and the pranks he and his school friends got up to – the likes of which would annoy him if the local children indulged in them now – his eye was caught by a group of earnest-looking men strolling his way from the direction of the Harbour Inn. He didn't recognise them except for the one in a pink polo shirt whom he thought he remembered from summers past.

Yes, that's it. He's someone's cousin. A distant cousin. Yes, Eugene Doyle's. Yes, definitely.

They walked with heavy shoulders – looked like paperwork in the making.

"Right. Before we go in, let's go over the story one final time, OK? We simply tell it as it happened, only that when Old Mr Cowie realised he didn't have a ticket and had forgotten to bring any ID, *he* decided to hide in the caravan so he could make the ferry crossing. It was a suggestion *he* made and a decision *he* took. We saw him on board and then he returned to the caravan before we disembarked in Dublin. We presumed Old Mr Cowie was fine until we checked on him this morning and found him lying on the banquette, you know, indisposed."

"Dead, you mean, Drapes. Dead."

"Yes, sorry, Gavin. *Dead*. But none of us know precisely when he passed away. The last time we saw him alive was in

Dublin just after we got off the ferry. Now have we all got that?"

There was a silent pause.

"I hope so because if we stick to this story, we'll be fine. Otherwise? God knows! And I, for one, *have* to be home for Saffie's wedding on Sunday and that's written in stone."

Another pause.

"OK. So have you got that?" Colin Draper asked again, raising his voice a little.

"Yes, alright. We hear you, Drapes," Gavin Doyle groaned.

"Good. Then let's do this."

Being a man who liked to know and understand the detail of any case – he was a trained detective after all – half an hour later and Sergeant McIlhenny was still struggling to get his head round the boys' story concerning the demise of Mr Cowie.

"Now, lads, let me get this straight. You say the old man, Mr Cowie, was in fine fettle when you left London. Then when you arrived in Holyhead to catch the ferry you realised that he wasn't listed in the booking and had also forgotten to bring any form of ID."

Sergeant McIlhenny stared at each of the group in turn. They all nodded.

"So, in order to travel on with you to Donegal, *he* volunteered to hide in his caravan before you embarked on the ferry and again later when you disembarked. And you're saying this is something *he* offered to do. You didn't force him, coerce him, blackmail him and you weren't kidnapping him. It was his idea and he did this of his own volition."

Three of the four of them nodded again. The Moose stood impassive, seemingly unwilling to make eye contact with anyone let alone the sergeant.

"You say that when you arrived in Dublin you checked on him, saw that he was fine and then continued on your journey. You peeped in on him when you arrived here last night, but it was late and you thought he was asleep. And when you checked on him again this morning you couldn't rouse him and on taking a closer look found that he had passed away. Correct?"

The three nodded again.

"Right. So the reason you've come here now is to report that Mr Cowie is dead and also because you're worried that you might have committed, or be accessories in the committing of, an offence of some kind with regard to Mr Cowie travelling into Ireland without a ticket and ID."

Three more nods.

"You too, Mr Moose?"

The Moose nodded once, almost imperceptibly, and with little or no facial expression.

"Since he is, or was, a UK citizen, then, as far as I am concerned, he wouldn't need ID when entering the Republic of Ireland unless arriving by air. The ferries might like to see some proof of identity but that's for their security, it's not the law. However, travelling without a ticket might be deemed an offence, but, since Mr Cowie isn't here to answer the charge and won't be, I think we can avoid a lot of bother and forget that issue. Do you agree, gentlemen?"

They all nodded with enthusiasm.

"Good. Moving on then. Mr Cowie's death, you say you only discovered he'd passed away first thing this morning? I'm sorry, that must have been very distressing for you. You also say you don't know the actual time of his death?"

"That's correct, sergeant," Colin Draper replied.

"That's OK. We might not need to be sure of that precisely. We'll see. And you say he was in his early eighties? That's a quare age for any man. There's nothing unusual or suspicious about old-timers passing away in their eighties. Unless they're billionaires and someone's after their money, of course. I take it he wasn't a billionaire? No. Good. And it seems you've reported his death soon enough. And it looks as though there was little anyone could have done to help him."

"Sadly not, sergeant," Colin Draper said almost smiling.

"As far as I'm concerned, you've done the right thing, boys. You've reported his passing and told me all that you know in relation to that. Good. So what I think we should do now is go and inspect Mr Cowie's remains and then call for a doctor to come out. If they're satisfied Mr Cowie died of natural causes, they'll issue a death certificate. When that's done we'll call the local undertaker. With luck we'll catch him before he gets caught up with preparing his hearse for our St Patrick's Day parade."

"That's great. Thank you very much, sergeant. That's really very good of you."

"Now, hang on one moment, lads. I'm not finished yet. Listen, if any one of you did think it a good idea to transport an old man of Mr Cowie's advanced years in a small caravan for any length of time, you deserve to be horsewhipped. And should I find out that any of you did put pressure on him I will come down on you like a ton of bricks. Unfortunately, we aren't allowed to lay hands on the public here any more. More's the pity. A cuff round the ear is a very effective deterrent in my book. But don't you worry, if I find that you did force him to hide in the caravan, I'll be sure to think of some way of making your lives a living hell."

Sergeant McIlhenny paused for effect before continuing: "OK, gentlemen, I think it's time you showed me the vehicle in question and introduced me to Mr Cowie."

"Thank you, sergeant," Colin Draper mumbled half-heartedly.

Sergeant McIlhenny stood up, retrieved his cap from the coat stand behind his desk, buttoned his jacket and ushered the small group out onto the street. Gavin Doyle led the way back towards the Harbour Inn.

As they stepped round the corner into the car park, a bright shaft of sunlight burst through the cloud cover causing them all to shield their eyes. As they adjusted to the light and lowered their hands, the boys on tour let out a mixed bag of gasps, sighs and swear words.

"Shit!" Gavin Doyle cursed. "Shit, shit, shit!"

"Do we have a problem, gentlemen?" Sergeant McIlhenny enquired, straightening his cap.

No one spoke. Just stared across the car park in disbelief and shock, surveying a space which was empty save for Gavin Doyle's silver Passat Estate. The Passat Estate, but no caravan.

"It's, it's ... it's gone, officer. I don't bloody believe it! The fucking caravan's gone! It was here. It was here only a moment ago," Colin Draper stammered before clamping his hands over his mouth.

"Bastards!" Gavin Doyle screamed. "Fucking bastards!"

13

Monday, 9.45am

"Come on, lads. You know it's Paddy's Day and not April Fool's, don't you? You're not trying to take the mick now, are you? Cos if you are so, I wouldn't take too kindly to you wasting my time on the busiest day of the year. Wasting police time *is* a very serious matter, gentlemen," Sergeant McIlhenny warned whilst wearing his gravest expression.

The sergeant was sitting back behind his desk in the Garda station trying to take stock of a situation he feared could get out of hand.

"It's gone, officer. Stolen. Please believe me, it was there earlier."

"And you're quite sure?"

"Quite sure. Here one minute, gone the next."

"You're saying that someone has stolen your caravan."

"Old Mr Cowie's caravan."

"With Mr Cowie in it?"

"Yes, sergeant."

"The late Mr Cowie."

"Yes."

"Well, this *is* getting serious now."

"Absolutely."

"So, someone's stolen the caravan but left the car?"

"Yes, yes. The Passat Estate."

"And I suppose you've no idea who that *someone* is?"

"How do you mean, officer?"

"I mean, you have no idea who's stolen your caravan?"

"No. Of course not. No idea at all."

"Gentlemen, it might surprise you to know that I have a good idea who the culprit is. You see, I've seen this kind of theft – a caravan theft – occur before. Not often, but it has – does – happen."

"Really?"

"Yes. And I can make a pretty good guess as to who is responsible."

"Who?"

"There are prime suspects who immediately spring to mind. A group of people – a particular group of people, shall we say, who regularly borrow other people's caravans on a permanent basis. It probably wouldn't come as a complete shock to you if I mentioned them by name but I can't."

"What? Why?"

"They're an ethnic minority. It could be deemed racist, discriminatory and quite possibly against the law to put a name, or names, to this crime without any evidence, proof or known motive."

"And what do you think this ethnic group will do when they discover they have acquired Old Mr Cowie along with the caravan?"

"In my experience they'll find a quiet patch of land and burn the lot. Once they've stripped the caravan of anything valuable, parts for instance, the van will go up in flames with Mr Cowie in it. It'll be too risky for them to do anything else. I've seen it done. They'll torch everything to make sure their forensics aren't left. Not a trace."

Gavin Doyle, who was already looking pale, put his hands to his face and turned away, his shoulders starting to quiver.

"What can we do, officer?" Hugo Saunders asked in a small, childlike voice.

"I'll report this at once – I'll phone Letterkenny. We'll try and intercept the caravan on the road, but I expect they'll be miles away by now. If they stole it first thing, they could be well on the way to Dublin by now. It's St Patrick's Day, a national holiday, there'll be caravans all over the place. It'll be like looking for a needle in a haystack."

"Oh."

"How long are you staying in Ballyhanlon, lads?"

"Till Friday."

"Right. We'll need to fill out a crime report form. You'll need to give me your contact details here in Ballyhanlon and also how and where you can be contacted in the UK, and we'll take it from there. Oh, by the way, was there anything else of value in the caravan save for Mr Cowie?"

"No, not really. His medals, a bit of china and some photos, I think," Gavin Doyle said, gathering himself. "Karen would kill me for this," he added as tears started to roll down his cheeks again.

"Gentlemen, here's what we're going to do. I'm going to put out a general alert in the hope that one of my colleagues spots the caravan or its charred remains, then we're going to take care of the paperwork. It won't take long. It can't. I've got a St Patrick's Day parade to police."

Before long the boys were sitting in the Harbour Inn consoling themselves with a fry.

"I don't fucking believe it!"

"I'm sorry, Gavin. Old Mr Cowie didn't deserve this. He seemed a real gent."

"He was more than that, Colin. He was all I had left. I mean – all I had left of Karen. Old Mr Cowie and his caravan, that is. I've got nothing of her now," Gavin Doyle said in a tearful voice.

"What more can we do? Contact the papers?"

"What papers? Here? Where?"

"Offer a reward?"

"How? What's the point? He could be anywhere by now."

A quiet half hour passed with little interruption save the clatter of cutlery and the occasional squeak as Liam the barman polished the previous night's beer glasses.

"Have you told your cousin, Gavin?" Colin Draper asked after a prolonged silence.

"No, not yet. I've had enough fuss for one day."

"Do they ... I mean, did they know each other?"

"Maybe. Old Mr Cowie loved this part of the world. I'm pretty sure he's played golf here."

They turned to finish their breakfasts in silence.

"I don't suppose anyone's up for a game of golf?" Hugo Saunders asked when they'd finished eating and in a tone which sounded far too upbeat. "Aren't we booked in for twelve on The Old Course at Ballyhanlon, Gavin?"

Gavin Doyle picked up his coffee cup in a trembling hand, his face a picture of simmering rage.

"Golf? Are you fucking kidding, Hugo?" Colin Draper said, looking appalled and attempting to head off what he imagined would be a more extreme reaction from Gavin Doyle.

"But the show must go on, Colin. I'm sure Old Mr Cowie would expect nothing less. Isn't that so, Gavin?"

There was a nervous hush.

"OK. This is how I see it," Gavin said after a pregnant pause. "It's not for you or anyone else to suggest what we do or don't do today, Hugo. But, as it happens, for once I think you might be right. Old Mr Cowie wouldn't have wanted us to come all this way and not play golf. He loved his golf. I think he'd rather we played and played to honour his memory than not play at all."

"Maybe he'd rather we helped the police try and find his caravan?" Colin Draper queried.

"Judging from what the sergeant told us, Colin, there doesn't seem much point," Gavin added. "Let's face it, the caravan's probably been dumped on a beach and burnt to a crisp already. There's little else we can do but wait."

"He's right," Hugo Saunders said, giving Colin Draper a friendly nudge. "And even though I only met him a few times, Old Mr Cowie strikes me as the kind of bloke who'd want us to carry on regardless."

"Look, if and when the time comes, I'll be searching for somewhere to spread Old Mr Cowie's ashes."

"What ashes, Gavin?"

"His ashes – when we find them – and The Old Course is possibly as good a place as any to start searching for a suitable site."

"Jesus! I don't believe this ... *golf*? You really think we should be playing golf, Gavin?"

"Well, here we are then!" Gavin Doyle bellowed an hour later from the first tee box of the Old Course and projecting his voice as if onstage. His eyes were half-closed, his head tilted back, his chest pumped up and his arms stretched wide. He held his driver aloft like a broadsword; a stance which suggested that he might be about to be blessed with supernatural powers. "This is the real deal," he continued, "the alpha and omega of all golfing experiences. The hand of golfing history on our shoulders and guiding our feet."

And just as Gavin was concluding his speech his strawberry thatch was caught by a sudden gust exposing a gleaming pink forehead and a radiant smile that hinted at fanaticism.

"What the hell is he on?" Colin Draper murmured into Hugo Saunders' ear and, as usual, was overheard.

"As golfing experiences go, Drapes, you heathen, this is the real deal. We will be walking in the footsteps of the golfing gods," Gavin Doyle gushed.

"Who, for Christ's sake? Seve? Tiger? Rory?"

"Old Tom Morris for starters."

"Who?"

"Old Tom, Colin. The godfather of modern golf."

"Oh?"

"Yes. He designed this course. The original layout, that is. It's been remodelled a fair bit since, though."

"Yeah, yeah, very good. Blah blah blah. That's all very lovely, Gavin, but are you going to tee off or are we going to have to listen to you babbling crap all afternoon?"

"In other words, Gavin, Colin and I would like you to shut up and drive off. And any time now would be good," Hugo Saunders urged, not in the mood for prolonged shenanigans either.

As he waited for Gavin Doyle to take his drive, Colin Draper had time to look up and take in the broader landscape. Though he was loath to admit it, the setting *was* spectacular.

The view down the first fairway was of a typical links hole, an avenue of close-cropped turf rolling like carpet between high sandy dunes and on towards the green about four hundred yards ahead of them, ringed by a semicircular bank of grass. But beyond and above the dunes was a wild countryside, raw and untamed. Donegal at its most natural. Not picture-perfect – pockmarked as it was with a rash of eighties bungalows dotted across the landscape without plan – but a vast panorama all the same, of mountains and monstrous hills and sea and sandy beaches. The sky, a swathe of blue, alive with rolling white clouds and skylarks singing high overhead.

"You're right, Gavin. It's stunning here."

The four men drove off. They were to have a match-play competition. Colin Draper and Gavin Doyle versus the Reverend Hugo Saunders and The Moose. Judging by their drives at the first, low scores would be few and far between.

On the first hole, three of the four balls were quickly lost. Much effort resulted in moderate progress; more time was spent hunting for golf balls then playing golf shots.

Professional golfers drive the ball high and far, and if not dead straight then with a slight arc as suits the profile of the hole –

flights that resemble the paths of a cannonball or an Exocet; the ballistics, intentional and accurate. Cries of "fore" are seldom heard.

Colin Draper and his fellow golfers, however, were striking the ball in multiple bursts over short distances. Something akin to firing grapeshot: indiscriminate and inaccurate. Injury due to friendly fire seemed a possibility if not, at times, highly likely. There was much shouting.

Where the par for most of the holes was four, the boys on tour were taking at least four or five shots to reach the green. The occasional lucky putt might win the hole and keep the scores respectable, but the greens were of championship standard: hard, fast and undulating. Three, even four-putting was common on their round.

Other factors that weighed against the amateurs in their struggle to achieve a half decent score were the wind, a lack of practise, lack of fitness, lack of stamina, lack of basic ability, lack of strategic thinking, lack of mental strength – their confidence easily undermined – and lack of quality equipment; they were all playing with old and worn-out clubs, balls and shoes.

Interference from the local flora and fauna also hampered their progress. The flora: the long grass on the banks of the dunes which could swallow a ball whole never to be seen again, and the wiry grass in the semi-rough which clung tightly around their club heads to snaffle any shot that wasn't perfectly timed.

The fauna: the sheep on the third green who had to be played over and or round and the angry swarm in the gorse bushes running along the fifth fairway that caused much arm flapping and hopping about. Most annoying was the collie which appeared from nowhere on the seventh, darting onto the green to pick up Colin Draper's golf ball before hurtling back into the undergrowth with the Top Flite lodged firmly in its teeth.

"Effing sheepdogs! What the hell is their problem round here? No wonder there's sheep running around all over the fucking place if they can't do their job properly!" Colin Draper moaned, then felt his iPhone vibrate in his pocket.

"Hey, Drapes, I thought you said no phones!" Gavin Doyle yelled from the other side of the fairway as Colin Draper lifted his mobile.

Draper shrugged.

"Dad! Where are you?"

"Playing golf, Saffie."

"But I got an international dialing tone!"

"Yeah, there seems to be something funny going on with my phone. Weird! Look, sorry, but I can't really talk now, Saffie."

"The flowers, Dad. Don't forget to pay for them."

"Yep. No problem. Got it covered. As I say, I can't really talk right now. Sorry!"

"OK, but phone me later."

"Will do. Byee." Draper put his phone away. "Gavin! Sorry! Got to keep it on. It's Mum. You know, just in case."

Gavin Doyle peered over but didn't smile.

"Got any ammo? I'm almost out," Colin Draper called over.

Gavin ignored him, addressed his ball and played his next shot: a slashing three iron that duck-hooked viciously over the ridge of dunes to the left of the fairway and soared off into infinity. He tensed, froze for a moment and then slammed his club into the turf once, twice, three times as if to break it; stopped, swore, paused, then plodded over the ridge dragging his clubs behind him, shoulders hunched and head hanging low.

The round took four and a half long, laborious hours. Luckily the result was a draw; The Moose fluking a thirty-foot putt on the eighteenth to square the match. A fair result, and enough to placate four frail and exhausted egos. Next stop: the clubhouse to change their shoes.

Colin Draper stepped outside.

"Hi, Mum! It's me. How are you?"

"Ah, Colin! Are you checking up on me again?"

"Not at all. I'm only in from golf. Thought I'd call you."

"Were you playing with Taffy, dear?"

"No, Mum. Taffy died three years ago."

"Of course he did. Silly me. I get a little confused sometimes. What's the weather like?"

"Changeable, but when the sun's out, glorious. What's it like there?"

"Sunny and warm. Pretty good."

"Lovely."

"Is Mary with you, Colin?"

"No, Mum."

"Oh, well, send her my love when you see her."

"Have you been doing anything nice today, Mum?"

"Just the usual, you know."

"Seen anyone? Saffie?"

"No, Saffie's been out with Phil. It's been a quiet day."

"Good, good."

"What's the weather like, Colin?"

"Actually, I'm sorry, I have to go now, Mum. I'll call you tomorrow. Love you."

"Love you too, Colin."

"Bye, Mum."

"Bye, love."

Colin Draper hated when he failed to elevate their telephone chats above the mundane. He blamed himself for not applying the imagination required to spark a conversation based on his mother's longer-term memories. The London Blitz was always a good subject. She might talk about Paddy Finucane, their local fighter ace. The Finucanes lived on her street in Richmond. She might not remember the morning but could remember the war like it was yesterday – could remember Paddy Finucane.

"Pint?" Hugo asked with panache.

"Why not?" Draper replied, rejoining the group in the clubhouse. "Where do you fancy, Gavin?"

"The Harbour Inn? Dump the car. Get a bite to eat. It's St Patrick's Day, for God's sake. There's bound to be some kind of entertainment in the bar tonight. I'm sure it'll be heaving," Gavin Doyle enthused in a tone that would counter no dissent. "You up for that, Moose?"

The Moose said nothing. Colin Draper and Hugo Saunders exchanged glances, a relieved smile and a wink.

"Here, Colin. Your turn to drive," Gavin said, chucking him the keys.

14

Monday, 6pm

The drive back to the Harbour Inn was prolonged by the hordes participating in the festivities along the main street. Though the St Patrick's Day parade was long past there were still plenty of people, predominantly kids, milling about in the road. Most were either on their way to or from the small funfair or running in and out of the Spar shop with sweets and ice cream cones clamped in sticky hands.

As the boys on tour crawled along at five miles an hour through the crowds, they eventually chugged past Sergeant McIlhenny who was chatting to a family group; one child sitting in his arms, another trying on his cap. When the sergeant saw the Passat he smiled in their direction and then reached out to grab a bunch of overexcited children who looked like they might run across the road into the path of Gavin's car. They continued on through the town at a snail's pace and down towards the harbour, the sound of empty drinks cans, paper cups and crisp packets popping and crunching under their tyres.

"Shit, we should have booked!" Colin Draper moaned as they stood beside the PLEASE WAIT HERE TO BE SEATED sign at the entrance to The Harbour Restaurant.

The restaurant appeared full and was buzzing.

"Och, I should have thought," Gavin Doyle sighed.

"Not to worry, lads," cousin Eugene beamed as he stepped forward to greet them with an armful of menus. "If you're wanting steak and chips or a bowl of chowder – you know, something simple – we can serve you next door. Sure, you can eat in the snug bar. There'll be space enough in there. It's not too busy in the pub yet."

"Sounds good to me," Gavin Doyle chirped, looking round for a consensus.

"Sounds like we haven't got much choice."

"Sounds great!" Hugo Saunders interjected to counter Colin Draper's cynicism, realising that a speedy relief of hunger was dependent on an enthusiastic response.

"I was very sorry to hear about your father-in-law, Gavin. Terrible. Absolutely terrible."

"How did you find out?"

"The sergeant was in earlier. If there's anything ..."

"I know, Eugene, I know. That's very good of you. But what can you do?"

There was an awkward pause.

"OK. The snug's through here. I'll get Siobhán to come and take your order."

The boys sauntered through to the main bar. It was already starting to fill with those arriving for the night-time entertainment. There was a mix of locals and the regular blow-ins: second-home owners and weekend caravaners from Belfast.

The locals were fewer in number of late. There weren't many living in Ballyhanlon Monday to Friday due to the lack of work. Most of the young either left for university or to find employment elsewhere.

Gavin Doyle acknowledged those of the locals he knew as cousin Eugene shepherded them through to the snug. The small back bar was empty save for a couple of old-timers conspiring round a peat fire; regulars taking refuge from what they anticipated would be a raucous night next door.

The four found a table. Siobhán, the waitress, followed them in with eating irons and a pad.

"Gents, Liam will take your drinks order at the bar and I'll need to take your order for food right now, if that's OK. The kitchen's already starting to get flooded with orders," she said with a beatific smile, briefly switched on and then immediately switched off to imply a need for haste.

"Let's make this easy," Colin Draper said boldly, "steak and chips times four please."

"Sirloin OK for you?"

"Perfect."

"And how would you like those cooked, lads?"

"Rare."

"Rare for me too please."

"Rare."

"Medium to well done please."

"Jesus, Hugo. There's always one!"

Gavin got up and made a dash to the bar, seizing his chance when he noticed that Liam the barman, who'd been pouring pints non-stop next door, had popped into the snug.

"Four stout please."

Liam pumped away at the Guinness tap with an experienced hand. Whilst their drinks were settling, he passed through to the saloon to take another order. Gavin leaned over the counter and watched as Liam pulled another round of pints.

"I could eat a horse," Hugo Saunders said, drooling at the thought of a large serving of cholesterol, carbohydrate and animal fat.

"That can be arranged," Colin Draper responded drily.

Gavin Doyle pigeon-stepped the few paces back to the table balancing a pint in each hand. His mood had changed; he appeared strangely animated, his eyes wide as if in shock. He fetched the third and fourth pints, shaking slightly and spilling a little of the beer as he went.

"I love the way they always put a shamrock on the—"

"You are *not* going to believe who's drinking in the bar next door," Gavin exclaimed, beads of sweat popping up on his brow.

"The Pope? Bill and Hillary Clinton? No, don't tell me, the Dalai Lama?"

"Nadine Coyle!"

"Who?"

"Nadine bloody Coyle. You know, from Girls Aloud."

"Jesus Christ, Gavin. Have you lost your fucking marbles?" Draper moaned. "Anyway, who the fuck cares?"

"Gavin, pray tell, what the hell would Nadine Coyle be doing in bloody Ballyhanlon?" Hugo Saunders pleaded in a tone both exasperated and dismissive.

"I don't know. Apart from the fact that she's from Derry and that's only an hour away, but it's her alright."

"I wouldn't know one end of Girls Aloud from the other, but, please, do you really think any of them would be spending St Patrick's night in bloody Ballyhanlon?"

There was a pregnant pause.

"Sunset Beach."

"You what, Moose?"

"Nadine Coyle."

"What, Moose?"

"She lives in Sunset Beach, California. She's dating an American footballer and she's just had a baby."

"Jesus, Moose. How the hell do you know that?"

The Moose shrugged and sipped his pint.

"There you go, Gavin. She's in Sunset Beach, mate."

"It's her!"

"Gavin! It isn't! It can't be!"

"Maybe Gavin's right," Hugo Saunders interjected, employing a conciliatory tone.

"OK, let's consider all the evidence. Gavin, was this woman signing autographs? Was she being mobbed by fans?"

"This is Ireland, Drapes. People don't like to make a fuss."

"Did she seem at all self-conscious? Is she holding a baby? Is she with a tall, muscly bloke who looks like he could be an American footballer?"

"No. Maybe she's got a babysitter. Maybe she's here with her family from home."

"Gavin, if that *is* Nadine Coyle, everyone would be fawning all over her and buying her drinks. I don't mean to be disrespectful, but there are hundreds of Derry women with good looks and auburn hair who look like Nadine Coyle."

"Are there, Drapes?"

"Yes, Gavin. And you should bloody know. But what's of much more importance is discussing what we have planned for the rest of the week," Draper added, softening his tone a little and hoping to draw them into a more adult conversation.

"Oh, sod that, Colin. Let's get through this evening first. It's St Patrick's night, for God's sake, and we've had a rough ride. Let's let our hair down a little and enjoy the craic. Tomorrow can take care of itself. I know we've got off to an unfortunate start—"

"Unfortunate start? Old Mr Cowie's dead, Hugo!"

"Thank you, Gavin. I know we've got off to a bad start—"

"Bad start?"

"—in that we've lost a much-loved member of our group, but since we're here we might as well enjoy what Ballyhanlon has to offer. We've only got till Friday – just a few more days of golf and then home."

"Hold on a minute! What we *played* today, is that what you call golf, Hugo?"

"We're a little bit rusty, that's all, Colin. We can't all be as talented as you," Gavin countered. "Anyway, it'll be better tomorrow. The course at Portsalon's a little easier than Ballyhanlon, I seem to recall."

"It'd need to be, Gavin."

"Hey, here's the food. Looks delicious, thank you, Siobhán."

"Salt and pepper's over there at the bar, lads. Let me know if you need any mustard or whatever," the waitress said, when she'd set down the third and fourth plate and before rushing off lest anyone should ask for anything else to be fetched.

"Why don't we take it one day at a time. We've got food, we'll have some pints and then see what entertainment cousin Eugene has organised for us," Gavin said with a reassuring smile.

No sooner had they finished eating than Gavin Doyle was encouraging them to move into the main bar whilst there was still time to get a table. It was filling up fast and the hubbub rising in volume. Though lively there was no sign of rowdiness, however. The mood so far being celebratory and congenial. There was no sign of Gavin's Nadine Coyle lookalike either.

Within an hour the traditional musicians who'd been playing the night before arrived back, took their places in a corner of the bar beside the dance floor, unpacked their instruments and saw to some last-minute tuning. Then a deep breath, a nod and the music started. First, a lament – a lone violin, no drum, no tin whistle. The bar quietened to a hush. Not a word, not a cough; no sound bar the strings – haunting and atmospheric.

"It's to hush the crowd. Get their attention," Gavin whispered into Draper's ear.

Draper, who was entranced by the playing, raised a hand to pause the patronising commentary. Gavin appeared to be on the verge of tears as thoughts of Old Mr Cowie were given fresh resonance by the dirge.

One long last chord, held and held again through a slow steady sweep of the bow, and then, before the violin faded to silence, a startling yell from the bodhrán player. A gutteral cry to punctuate the end of the lament and signal a change of tempo as the playing of the bodhrán commenced; a light, rhythmic pitter patter at first, a scampering that built into an ever pacier and louder beat, louder still into a crescendo, preceding another sudden pause, unexpected, like a gasp.

Another nod, and, taking their cue, the rest of the musicians launched into a reel, the timing fast and furious. Throughout the bar hands clapped, feet stamped and tables were tapped, thumped and slapped in near enough time, the volume soaring as the hushed reverence was supplanted by a communal pounding rhythm of fingers and feet, strings and skins; the bar united as one.

All four of the boys smiled, drank and drummed and rocked and swayed in time to the music, drawn along on a pulsating wave of euphoria. And in that very moment no one could fail to feel the slightest scintilla of what it is to be Irish.

The bar was in uproar. A loud voice was required to be heard over the ruckus. Orders for pints were given on fingers like the odds at a racecourse passed over the heads of the crowd by tic-tac. It was easier for barman and punter alike when the order was stout – anything else involved complex pointing, gesticulation, lip-reading and mime. No cocktails tonight.

The harmony of the evening was then shattered when the bar door swung open crashing against a coat stand hurling hats, scarves, sticks and umbrellas across the floor, the sudden Atlantic gust that followed blowing life into the sleepy embers of the peat fire on the far side of the room, which instantly flickered into flame. The clapping abated. The musicians paused. Silence ensued. All was quiet.

A large ruddy-faced man, broad-shouldered and shovel-handed, staggered in through the door quivering with rage and short of breath. He stopped and swung what at first appeared to be a fur coat down onto the nearest drinks table scattering whatever bottles and glasses fell in its path. It scared the living daylights out of the couples huddled round who shrieked and pushed their stools back when it became evident that the coat was in fact the carcass of a dog revealed as its head rolled forward, eyes bulging and staring blankly and its tongue unfurling with a slap.

All eyes were on the wild man. A gasp rolled through the bar, a murmuring that resonated from the front to the rear of the room and fading like the passing of a Mexican wave.

"Mr McGettigan, how can we help you?" cousin Eugene called calmly from behind the counter.

"Someone has killed my fecking dog!" the farmer screamed, thrusting his free hand into the air. "With this!" he shrieked as he presented a small white object pincered between thumb and forefinger. As he rotated his hand it became obvious he was holding up a golf ball. "Would anyone like to claim it?" he hissed in a deep and menacing voice whilst scanning the room, his eyes resting on the four men from London for a moment longer than the rest of the company.

"Now, Willie. How could that be, so?" cousin Eugene asked in a soft voice, whilst moving slowly across the bar towards him.

"It's a Top Flite with the letter C drawn inside a circle," he continued, ignoring Eugene. "Anyone here's name begin with C? Any Colms or Cahals? Cormacs or Christies? Come on, must be someone's!"

The farmer tottered a little then swayed as he tried to regain his balance which, combined with his emotional state, implied he might not be completely sober.

Gavin and Hugo turned and stared at Colin Draper who dared do no more than shrug in response whilst hoping that nobody, especially the locals, noticed his reddening cheeks.

"My poor collie choked on it. It was stuck in its gullet."

"I'm very sorry about your dog, Willie, but, come on, let me get you a pint. I know you're upset, but we don't want any bother. Not on Paddy's Day."

"That dog was priceless," Willie continued, tears gathering in his eyes. "I've had her since she was a pup. Ten years. Hand-reared."

"Yes, but there's nothing you can do about it here and now. You'll need to see Sergeant McIlhenny in the morning. Was she running wild on the course again, Willie?"

Willie McGettigan ignored the question. He stood his ground, his head swivelling round like a security camera, rotating through one hundred and eighty degrees to register each face in turn.

"*Is Lá Fhéile Pádraig é, Willie ... Taitneamh a bhaint as féin nó téigh sa bhaile!*" Eugene added, staring at McGettigan, his smile receding.

Since it was obvious that McGettigan wasn't going to be given any clues or assistance in cracking the case, and not quite knowing what to do next, he leaned forward, spat on the floor, spun on his heel and marched out of the bar slamming the door behind him. He left the dog.

A murmur rolled through the room. Cousin Eugene gave a thumbs up to encourage the players to restart their music, walked over to the carcass, lifted it in both arms and retreated behind the bar cradling it as if it were a sleeping child.

"I bet you feel guilty now!" Gavin Doyle whispered into Colin Draper's ear.

Ignoring the comment, Draper was about to take a sip from his pint when Eugene sauntered over to collect some empties.

"Sorry about that, lads. Willie'll be OK. He's always been a bit of a hothead that one."

"What are you going to do with the dog?" Gavin Doyle asked politely.

"Maybe I'll get it stuffed – get it mounted in a glass box and display it on the shelf behind the bar," Eugene replied with a wink before carrying two handfuls of dirty beer glasses back to the counter.

"Why do you ask, Gavin? Professional interest? I imagine you've had a lot of experience with dead dogs," Colin Draper teased.

"So, are you going to talk to the farmer, Colin?" Gavin asked ignoring him.

"Are you mad? Of course I'm not, Gavin. That dog had it coming. That was my best shot of the day."

"Do you know how much a good sheepdog costs, Drapes?"

"No idea. Tell me."

"A well-trained dog? In the region of two-and-a-half grand."

"From what we saw of Shep there, I wouldn't give you two quid for that one."

"Jesus, Drapes! You're all heart."

"Thank you, Gavin."

"I'd keep a low profile for the next couple of days if I were you, Colin. And I'd alter that monogram on your golf balls too. It's a bit of a giveaway."

Cousin Eugene popped back to their table to give it a quick wipe, which was more an excuse to take a break and socialise than to tidy-up. He drew up a chair to sit with them for a while.

"Hey, you'll like what's coming up next, lads. Are you into Irish dancing?" Eugene asked during a pause in the music.

None of them replied, wary of cousin Eugene's demonic grin.

It didn't take long for the frenzied atmosphere to return once the musicians resumed their playing.

At the end of the next reel, and as the bodhrán player beat a steady rhythm, a pre-recorded backing track cut in over the PA system – a thunderous jig played at roughly the same volume as the live performance. And as the musicians put down their instruments, an all-girl troupe of Irish dancers emerged from behind the bar and took to the stage to an enthusiastic roar, the dancers springing across the floor in time to the music.

There were six, all clad in traditional Irish dancing costume: short, dark green velvet dresses adorned with Celtic motifs, black shoes, tights and tiaras, all worn with shoulder-length hair curled into ringlets.

"I thought Irish dancing was the preserve of the young? This lot look like they've seen the better side of thirty," Colin Draper bellowed into cousin Eugene's ear over the music.

"Ah, but these aren't ordinary Irish dancers, Colin. You wait and see."

Gavin Doyle, meanwhile, was wearing his wide-eyed and excitable expression again.

"What's the matter, Gavin?" Colin Draper shouted.

"Drapes. I don't believe it! The girl second from the left ... It's Nadine bloody Coyle!"

Colin Draper sighed and dropped his head into his hands. When he glanced up a group of the younger guys in the crowd were whooping and whistling as the dancers removed their tiaras and tossed them into the crowd. One landed in The Moose's lap. He picked it up and held it up to the light. Plastic. Cheap silver plastic studded with shiny paste gemstones.

As the backing music played on, Draper frowned when he noticed the dancers were all, in synchronised fashion, fiddling with their costumes behind their backs. He then gulped hard when they spun round so everyone watching could clearly see that they were slowly and seductively unzipping their dresses without changing expression or breaking step.

Gavin turned to his cousin and glared.

"What's wrong, Gavin?"

"You know what's wrong."

"This is modern Ireland, Gavin. Ireland in the twenty-first century," Eugene Doyle enthused.

"No, it's not, Eugene. It's ... It's like being in a working men's club somewhere in the north of England back in the seventies."

"Funny you should say that, Gavin. They're from Yorkshire."

"So?"

"Look, it's an Irish dancing-burlesque fusion. It's just a bit of craic."

"No, it's not Eugene, it's just tacky."

And as dresses dropped to the floor and lingerie was revealed, Colin Draper, Hugo Saunders and The Moose beat a hasty retreat to the snug bar.

The reaction of the audience was split between shock and enthusiasm depending on age, gender, taste and political sensitivity. The performers certainly thinned the crowd, at least a third of the customers opting for an early night. The remainder, who stayed to watch until the end of the performance, were loud and supportive. Gavin Doyle sat on amongst them, mute.

In the snug the others managed to reclaim their table. The old men by the peat fire looked up briefly before turning back to stare into the embers again. It was a room conducive to silent contemplation not helped by the din drifting in from the main bar.

Colin Draper got up and slipped outside onto the street when he felt his iPhone throbbing in his chest pocket. It was Mary.

"Hi, Colin, we need to talk."

"I agree. But you do realise that might involve us both having a turn to speak, Mary? Och, I'm sorry .... Let's start again ... Hello, Mary, how are you?"

"I haven't much time, Colin. Harvey's waiting in the car."

"I'm sorry if I'm keeping him up, Mary. It must be well past his bedtime by now. Remind me again, how old is Harvey? Twenty-three? Twenty-four? Does his mother know he's out this late with you?"

"Stop being a prick, Colin, and shut up and listen for once."

"*Jawohl*, Mary. Away you go."

"It's Saffie. I'm worried about her. She's getting very stressed. We need to do more to support her."

"Like what?"

"I'm not sure, but maybe we should meet up sometime tomorrow to discuss how we can best help her through the wedding. You know, reassure her that we'll show a united front."

"I can't tomorrow."

"Can't or won't?"

"Can't, Mary."

"When then?"

"Saturday morning? Yarmouth?"

"That's the day before! Is that the best you can do, Colin?"

"I'm sorry, Mary. I've got so much work on."

"Nothing changes there then."

"I'm sorry."

"Right. I'll meet you in the front bar of The Bull's Head. What time can you be there?"

"Eleven?"

"I guess that'll have to do then. OK, and don't be late."

"So, that's a date then?"

"No, and don't get any funny ideas either. This is for Saffie. We need to present a united front. I'll see you there, Colin," Mary said perfunctorily before putting the phone down without waiting for a response.

When Colin Draper returned to the snug bar, the mood seemed a bit brighter. The old men by the fire were chatting to Gavin, sharing their memories of his father when he was a boy in Ballyhanlon and talking of their own experiences in London. They'd both worked on the building of the Victoria line back in the sixties; a time when hard graft was Ireland's greatest export.

Liam, the barman, came into the snug with a round of drinks on a tray. Shorts. Looked like four double whiskeys.

"These are for you, gents."

"Cheers, Liam," Colin Draper replied, presuming they were on the house. "I guess we might as well be hung for a sheep as for a lamb. *Slàinte!*"

"*Slàinte!*"

A cheer erupted from those still in the saloon bar followed by whistling and the sound of tables being thumped which implied that the dance act had reached its climax. A more peaceful ambience began to permeate the bar, the live musicians striking up again but playing at a slower tempo. Ballads mostly.

"To Old Mr Cowie! God bless him," Hugo Saunders said, staggering to his feet.

"Old Mr Cowie," Colin Draper replied, and the three of them clinked their glasses and downed their drinks and settled in for the evening.

15

Tuesday, 3am

Sergeant McIlhenny sat on the front step of the Garda station and sighed. He removed his cap, set it down beside him and wiped his brow. Bowing his head he massaged the back of his scalp, raking his fingers through his thick brown hair, relieved his day was done.

It had been a quiet and unremarkable St Patrick's Day which, surprisingly, he found a bit of a disappointment. No fights, no broken windows, no reports of assaults, thefts or criminal damage. There had hardly been any drunken behaviour and no vandalism at all – the cells were empty.

He'd heard something or other about the farmer, Willie McGettigan, causing a bit of a commotion in the Harbour Inn, but that it seemed, and McIlhenny felt sure, was nothing more than a minor incident easily contained by the bar staff.

So possibly the quietest St Patrick's Day the sergeant could remember for many years. A bit of a let-down really and slightly worrying. It paid for him to be seen to be busy.

This train of thought made him laugh. As he chuckled to himself he retrieved a packet of rolling tobacco from his chest pocket, a pack of green cigarette papers and his cheap plastic lighter. Having laid them out neatly next to his cap on the step, he made himself a quick rollie. Just the one cigarette – a small treat. He would enjoy the solitude and this small indulgence before calling it a day. He never smoked at home. He believed his wife would be unlikely to allow him that luxury. She didn't know he smoked the occasional fag and probably wouldn't approve if she did.

He had lit up and was savouring the first drag when he heard the sound of a motor starting somewhere on the outskirts of the town, maybe a couple of fields away. It was definitely an engine of some sort – a whooshing, whirring sound – but not a car, tractor or lorry. There were no signs of life on the street and little other noise bar the constant splashing of the surf on the far side of the harbour wall, the clanging of rigging and the distant baaing of sheep from way beyond the golf course.

Naturally Sergeant McIlhenny was intrigued by the engine noise and so stood up to get a better view. As he did so the motor accelerated and increased in volume, and as he stretched to his full height and craned his neck he could make out a small whirlwind of leaves and grass in the moonlight rising in a twister from the field beside the Ballyhanlon Golf Hotel.

Ah, a helicopter!

It wasn't uncommon for helicopters to bring guests to and from the golf hotel. Irish links golf had had an international appeal for many years; rich American guests – Hollywood stars amongst them – had been making the pilgrimage to Donegal and Ballyhanlon since the thirties and forties. Then they might arrive by seaplane. Now they might come and go by helicopter. But who would be arriving or leaving at this hour? It was a large helicopter too. Judging by the silhouette it resembled one of those he'd seen used for air-sea rescue.

McIlhenny checked his wristwatch. Ten past three. Yeah, strange alright. He made a mental note, sat down and watched as the dark shape of the helicopter rose above the hedgerows. It hovered for a moment, the engine roar reaching a crescendo, turned and headed up the coast until disappearing from sight in the darkness.

McIlhenny leaned against the station door, stared up at the stars, brought the rollie back to his lips and took a puff. It was lifeless. There was no smoke and no fire. He retrieved the plastic lighter from his chest pocket and tried to bring a flame to the fag but failed to get a light in the breeze. He cupped his hands and hunched his shoulders to shield the lighter from the wind but still couldn't get a flame. He shook it, tried again, once, twice, three times, but no. No gas, no flame.

McIlhenny gave up, stood up, dropped his half-smoked fag on the pavement, stamped on it in disgust – twisting his foot to make doubly sure it was dead – and scurried home to bed.

16

Tuesday, 8am

Half asleep, disoriented and confused, Gavin Doyle fought the temptation to close his eyes again as he regained consciousness in the gloom. He would rather fall back to sleep but suspected that he wasn't alone in the bed. He stretched an arm across the mattress and wasn't surprised when his fingers bumped into something soft and warm. Flesh. Naked flesh.

The discovery provoked panic and instigated an immediate attempt to conjure up a memory of how he came to have company in whatever bed he was in. He rolled his eyes, blinked and looked up.

Of course! Ballyhanlon. Yep, Ballyhanlon. The Harbour Inn. And the body? Bloody hell! Nadine!

"Nadine?"

"Oh, for fuck's sake!" the naked body moaned after a short pause. "How many times? It's fucking Bernadette, you clampit."

Bernadette was lying face down, her curses muffled by the pillows.

"Oh, sorry."

"You were calling me Nadine *all* fucking night. Driving me fucking nuts you were. Well, until you conked out, that is."

"Conked out?"

"Yeah. Once we went to bed and had you-know-whatted, you pretty much went out like a light. It was a bit of a downer, to be honest," Bernadette continued, her voice increasing in volume as she rose from the pillow and turned to face Gavin Doyle. "And please get it into your thick skull, I am not Nadine fucking Coyle. I'm Bernadette McIvor from Leeds. And it's Bernadette, never Bernie. OK? Bernie makes me think of pipes, carpet slippers and string vests and that's not me. Got it?"

Gavin Doyle could detect Yorkshire in Bernadette's accent.

"My wife's got relatives in Leeds."

"What! You're married?" Bernadette yelled, sitting up.

"I was."

"Bastard."

"But I'm widowed now."

"Oh, I'm sorry!"

"It's OK."

"First things first. Where's the loo?"

Gavin Doyle flapped a hand in the general direction of the en suite then heard the patter of feet scampering across the room. His room? Yep, it was his room alright; the large one above the bar restaurant. Eugene had treated him to a family suite. He shuddered at the thought of the explaining he was going to have to do later. He flipped over just in time to catch a glimpse of a naked Bernadette McIvor disappearing into the bathroom.

As soon as Bernadette slammed the door to the en suite, Gavin got up and searched for his clothes. Spotting his trousers and boxers he wriggled into them as quickly as possible. He then waddled over to the dressing table, clicked on the kettle beside the complimentary tea and coffee tray and stuck out his tongue. Not a pretty sight. He bent down and picked up the crumpled polo shirt wrapped round one of the table legs and forced himself into it agitating his hangover as he wriggled and tugged to force his head through the neck.

Dressed, Gavin Doyle slumped into a sitting position on the edge of the bed and tried to recall the previous evening. He struggled. Couldn't remember any of it clearly. It was as if he'd been out cold. Then a memory, a sudden flashback, of Bernadette straddling him, thrusting her hips into his loins, of how she wouldn't let him kiss or fondle her and the frustration he felt that she wouldn't let him run his fingers over her body. That's right! She'd made him lie prone with his hands by his side whilst she rode him. Rode him like he was a mechanical bull. Mechanical but defective. Defective with a knackered motor; more dud than stud.

Hers was a steady and relentless rhythm. And every time he raised his hands to hold or caress her, she shoved them down again and rode on. Hadn't she slapped his face to fend him off? He ran a hand along his jaw but couldn't detect any bruising or soreness. Maybe not then.

"What's this bloody obsession with Nadine bloody Coyle anyway?" Bernadette asked as she emerged from the bathroom and walked back across to the bed. She was wearing a man's white shirt – one of his! – hanging loosely around her shoulders as if it was a light cotton dressing gown. She didn't seem at all self-conscious about her near-nakedness.

"I'm sorry."

"Don't be, mate. It's been happening a lot recently. Not nice though. Really quite irritating – a real turn-off."

Bernadette plonked herself down beside him, leant on one elbow and stretched her other arm over her head to retrieve a packet of Marlboro Lights from the bedside table.

"Want one?" she muttered, sitting up again.

"No, thanks. I've got a splitting headache. Feels like I've been hit with a hammer."

"Are you in a hurry, Gábhán Óg?"

Gábhán Óg? No one ever called him by his name using the Irish pronunciation and with the 'son of' bit tacked on the end except his parents, and they were dead. Even Old Mr Cowie had called him plain old Gavin or occasionally Gav. This worried him. That she called him Gábhán Óg must have been the result of some intense and delusional chatting up attempted the night before. A feeble effort on his part to enhance his Irish credentials, no doubt.

And what about the night before?

He ran through the fragmented snippets he could recall. The last thing he could picture with clarity was the big angry farmer arriving with the dead dog. Oh, and the Irish dancing. Yes, of course, he could remember the dancing. He'd watched that. Wasn't his kind of thing, but he couldn't take his eyes off the girl second from the left. That's right, he was spellbound by the diminutive auburn-haired dancer. And she, Bernadette, had appeared to notice him too.

Unlike the others in the crowd whose leers had a carnal intensity and who were baying like a pack of wild dogs: slobbering and scary, the older guy in the pink polo shirt seemed more reserved, softer, kind-faced and slightly embarrassed to be there, sympathetic even.

Gavin Doyle had a vague memory of how he'd mingled with the dancers when they reappeared in the bar after their performance – bought them a round of drinks. Made sure he was standing close to, and got into conversation with, Bernadette. Talked the usual tosh. Played his A game. Told her his best anecdotes but was thoughtful enough to ask her questions about herself too. Got a little tactile. Laughed at her jokes and touched her arm. Liked her northern humour. Wasn't too clingy – was sure to wander off and circulate with others then wander back again whenever he caught her eye.

Then the picture grew hazier. But he could remember how he was careful to stay close to the group and in their company when they piled into a minibus to go clubbing later on. They were driven to a hotel a few miles inland, the next town maybe; Bernadette sitting on his lap.

That's when Gavin took a gamble. Kissed her lightly on the nape of her neck. And that's when he could tell she was interested; the peck didn't faze her. She didn't flinch or lean away from him. A few minutes later he kissed her on the ear, and when she leaned her head against his and snuggled up, he knew for sure.

They arrived at the hotel to a fanfare of thumping drum and bass. A basement disco with a ridiculous name and a couple of overweight bouncers in evening dress. Bernadette held Gavin's hand. There was no more Irish dancing. The rest of the evening took on a pace of its own and drew towards an inevitable conclusion.

And where were the others all this time? Where were Draper, Hugo Saunders and The Moose?

"Gábhán Óg! I said ... Are you in a hurry?"

"Sorry? In a hurry? Why?"

"You got dressed pretty damn fast once I was out of the room."

"I was getting a bit cold, that's all."

"Well, fuck you. I guess you've got what you wanted and now you're going to fuck off."

"No, no. It's not that. It's, it's—"

Gavin Doyle didn't have time to finish articulating a reasonable explanation before she leaned over and kissed him. A huge kiss which enveloped his mouth and pinned him to the spot. Eyes shut, Bernadette tossed her unlit Marlboro over her shoulder and forced Gavin's face back till he overbalanced and was lying flat across the bed with her bearing down on him, their mouths sealed together.

Once on top her hand found his fly, unzipped it in one swift movement and delved inside. This time when Gavin Doyle raised his hands to cup her breasts there was no resistance.

But where were the others?

After napping for half an hour or so, Gavin Doyle slipped out of the bed. Bernadette was still snoozing. He covered her with a loose sheet, pulled on his trousers and polo shirt again and sneaked out of the room like a Comanche stalking deer whilst making sure the lock was left on the snib.

Gavin peered along the corridor to check the other doors.

They were all shut and none were displaying DO NOT DISTURB tags. He reached into his trouser pocket to retrieve his iPhone. It was nearly nine thirty. He rang the other three in turn. No one answered.

He approached the first door, tapped and waited a moment before tapping again.

"Psst, Drapes? It's me, Gavin. Are you in there, Colin?"

He waited a bit longer.

No answer.

Knocked more loudly.

Still nothing.

The Reverend Hugo Saunders' room was next door. Again, no answer. Gavin walked along to The Moose's room. Stood for a second, but then thought better of knocking.

Gavin strolled down to the door leading to the staircase at the end of the corridor, stared through the glass and gazed across the car park below. The Passat was there with their golf clubs still piled in the back. The others could have borrowed the car if they'd wanted. Gavin had left the keys tucked under a wheel arch.

Good, they're not playing golf then, he thought.

Gavin rang Colin Draper's mobile number again. It went straight to answerphone.

"Hello! Please leave a message after the bleep ... Bleep!"

"Shit! Ah, Drapes! It's me, Gavin. Please call me when you get this. Cheers."

To be doubly sure, Gavin also sent him a text message.

"Fancy a breakfast?" Gavin Doyle asked, sitting down on the bed and stroking the nape of Bernadette McIvor's neck.

"Fuck off!" Bernadette said groaning as if uttering her last words.

"Hey, maybe you should try this."

"What is it?"

"Orange juice."

"Any vodka in it?"

"What do *you* think? Here, have some. It'll help."

Bernadette leaned on one elbow, hair falling over her face, and waved a tentative hand in Gavin Doyle's direction.

"You seemed OK earlier," Gavin said, passing her the glass.

"Hangover's kicking in," she said between gulps.

"Come on, I'll take you to breakfast."

"Do I have to?"

"I thought you were supposed to be the dominatrix in this relationship. What's happened?"

"You. You've fucking poisoned me."

"Yeah, right. Look, I'm starving and I need to work out where my mates are."

"Mates? *You?* You mean you actually have some friends, Gábhán Óg?"

"Yes. Even I have friends."

"Really?"

"Yes, really."

"Where the fuck are they then?"

"*That* is a very good question, Bernadette."

"Are they staying here?"

"Yes. I've tried calling them on their mobiles – nothing – and I've checked their rooms and they're not there either. But the car's still here, so they can't be too far away."

"So, you *really* can't find them?"

"No. Don't know where they are. Haven't a clue."

"Oh."

"Obviously I'd like to know though."

"Are you worried?"

"A little."

"OK then!" Bernadette McIvor said leaping naked from the bed and springing across the room towards the en suite. "If they're anywhere round here, this will dig them out," she laughed, waving a hand towards the fire alarm beside the bathroom door. "Shall I?"

"No, no ... Better leave that to me," Gavin said walking over and then giving the glass a sharp jab with his elbow.

Within a minute or two a dishevelled Gavin Doyle and Bernadette McIvor – whose innocence was scarcely covered by Gavin's Puffa jacket – scurried out of the room, along the corridor and down the stairs at the side of the building to the car park where they joined a bemused crowd of guests and staff members fleeing from the din of the alarm bells and the dangers of the imaginary fire.

There was no sign of Gavin Doyle's missing friends.

17

Tuesday, 8am

A trickle of saliva sizzled in the heat a couple of inches from Colin Draper's mouth. A spider had just scuttled into the viscous pool and was struggling to find a footing, its tiny limbs thrashing to avoid a drowning. Finally, with exhaustion, the small insect was still, floating lifeless in the drool.

Why the hell had the poor bugger thought to wade in there in the first place? Draper wondered as he opened his eyes from a very deep sleep.

As he grew more alert he became aware of the heat of the wooden deck warming his cheek – not enough to burn it, but growing uncomfortable all the same.

That he was out in the open was obvious from the breeze ruffling his hair. That he was on a boat was evident from the rocking that was beginning to make him feel nauseous. It also had him imagining that he was on his yacht somewhere off the south coast of England. However, when he saw he was still dressed in his golf gear from the day before – the same black jeans, the same black polo shirt and V-neck – he quickly came to his senses.

What the fuck!

Colin Draper immediately sat upright to get his bearings, but was aghast when he saw that he was not only on a boat – a strange boat – but also adrift at sea and out of sight of land. He checked his pockets for his phone. It wasn't there.

"Shit, we're screwed!" Draper swore under his breath.

The last he knew, they'd been sitting by the peat fire in the snug of the Harbour Inn, Ballyhanlon, sipping pints and downing chasers, but then, nothing – a complete blank. A blackout.

He looked up and out to sea again then turned away blinking. The sun was up and strong. The sky a deep blue.

Irish coastal waters? He couldn't tell.

"Moose! Hugo! For fuck's sake, wake up!" Draper shouted.

And thank God the other two were there.

Hugo Saunders and The Moose were sprawled across the deck and out for the count as he had been a moment ago. But no Gavin. He couldn't see Gavin. He gave the other two a shake.

Draper found some shade and sat back to allow Hugo and The Moose time to gather their wits. He took deep breaths to try and prevent himself from being sick, which seemed a strong possibility.

But what the hell were they doing out at sea? Baffled, he had no memory of leaving land. Had no memory of leaving the bar, come to think of it, or of what they'd done after their last drink. It was as though he had been knocked out. Well, he must have blacked out as waking up felt more like coming round than rousing from sleep.

Colin Draper crawled back across the deck to where Hugo Saunders and The Moose were lying face down. They were side by side with their legs interlocking; they were nearly a pile. Draper gave them both another gentle shake and was relieved when their eyes began to flicker. They both yawned as they rolled onto their sides.

Draper got to his feet and leaned over the gunwale and, shielding his eyes, stared into the distance searching for anything that might give him a quick indication of where they were. But there were no landmarks, no ships, no trawlers, no signs of life. Nothing but broad views of sea and sky.

Colin Draper scanned the horizon checking for birdlife, a sure sign of land. There was none to be seen. Then he leaned further overboard when he felt nausea start to overwhelm him and the contents of his stomach racing up into his throat. The short, sharp expulsion that followed brought him some relief from the giddiness and the headache that were handicapping his ability to think straight, adjust to their new circumstances and conjure up a course of action.

And the boat? No sails were set and the engine wasn't running. It was bobbing aimlessly on its sea anchor.

The yacht reminded him a bit of his own – the boat which up until recently had been moored in the marina at Yarmouth Harbour on the Isle of Wight – up until Mary had sold it, that is. He hadn't agreed to the sale, she'd just decided that the money could be better used elsewhere.

His yacht, *Princess Leia*, was a bit smaller, but of a similar style and class: a classic ketch with a wooden deck. He'd always had plans for adventures that would have taken him much further out to sea than he was ever likely to go. He'd always blamed Mary for clipping his water wings – she wasn't keen on time spent at sea – but then he knew it was an easy cop out to blame Mary for anything he'd ever failed to achieve.

Colin Draper got up and walked the deck stem to stern. The stillness and quiet were spooky. It reminded him of the *Marie Celeste*.

"'*Where are the men who trod these planks, as their loved ones paced the shore?*'" Draper whispered as he made a cursory search for clues and to see whether Gavin Doyle was lurking somewhere unseen and as bewildered as he.

When he came back astern, Draper made a closer inspection of the cockpit, the wheel and the navigational equipment. A key was in the ignition. He tried the motor. It fired up. Relieved to find it working, he switched it off again thinking it better to conserve fuel. Last, he tried the radio. It appeared to be dead.

Then he noticed a white A4 envelope. It had been secured to a wooden shelf behind the wheel with gaffer tape. It was marked: *FAO Colin Draper*.

Draper peeled the envelope away from the ledge, being careful not to tear the sides. The silver tape was limpet-like in its grip. Inside he found a typed note.

Welcome aboard, Mr Draper!

You must be surprised to find yourself at sea. How you got here, however, is of no consequence now as you need to concentrate on getting safely back to the harbour at Ballyhanlon.

First of all, you would probably like to know where you are. If you go to the chart table you'll find an admiralty chart which will reveal all. It is the only one there. You will see that your position has been outlined in red pen along with a note of your present coordinates. These are approximate, as you have probably drifted a little since you arrived on board, but be assured, you are no more than a two-day sail away from the west coast of Ireland – maybe less. Even without the use of the navigational aids available to you on board this ship, if you were to sail due east from here you would easily reach land. However, we would like you to make harbour at Ballyhanlon. We know you are familiar with this class of craft and we know you have the competence to navigate your way there.

When you arrive you are to moor on the opposite side of the harbour to the trawler fleet and alongside the other pleasure craft. You will all immediately disembark and continue your golf tour as planned before travelling on to London.

Be aware, once you disembark in Ballyhanlon you are not, under any circumstances, to return to this boat.

If asked what your business is whilst at sea, you are to say that you are pleasure cruising. Nothing more. If documentation is requested there is paperwork in the chart table drawer that suggests that you chartered this craft in Calry, County Sligo.

You will have noticed that one of your associates is not accompanying you on this journey. Do not be concerned. He is quite safe and well and will remain so. If, however, you attempt to report anything regarding this trip to the authorities, i.e. contact the police, the coast guard, the Irish or Royal navies, the UK's Border Force or National Crime Agency or the Ballyhanlon harbour master, your friend's circumstances and safety will be subject to change.

If you do not sail directly to Ballyhanlon or fail to land within two days as instructed, your friend's circumstances and safety will be subject to change.

If you report the circumstances of this journey to any government agency at any point between now and your arrival back in London, your friend's circumstances and safety will be subject to change.

If you do not follow all of these instructions carefully and in full, your friend's circumstances and safety will be subject to change.

The weather is fine. You have favourable winds. Please enjoy your sail.

You are expected to disembark by 1800 hours Wednesday, 19 March 2014. This is non-negotiable.

Your mobile phones and passports have been left with your belongings in your rooms in Ballyhanlon. The ship's radio has been disabled. Do not attempt to signal to any other ships you might encounter. Your friend's good health and well-being are dependent on that.

Once you have read and fully understood the contents of this note you are to destroy it.

Colin Draper blew out his cheeks, folded up the A4 sheet and shoved it into his pocket.

"Fuck! They've got Gavin."

18

Tuesday, 10am
Ballyhanlon

"Your friends, Gábhán Óg, they do exist, don't they? I mean, they're not *imaginary* friends, are they?"

"Are you taking the piss, Bernadette? Anyway, before we go any further, would you please call me *Gavin*?"

"*Gavin*? Is that your real name? So why the fuck did you tell me it was Gábhán Óg, you dweeb? And, in any case, who said we were going any further? I mean, don't get your hopes up, big boy. I'm moving on soon. We're dancing in Ballybofey tomorrow night and then we're off to Sligo at the end of the week. After that, I don't know."

"*Dancing?*"

"It's classic Irish dancing with a modern contemporary twist."

"That's some twist alright."

"Well, you were lapping it up last night."

"Oh, hang on! We appear to be going in."

"So, if they're not here, where are your friends then?"

Gavin Doyle shrugged.

Gavin and Bernadette McIvor had been milling about in the car park behind the Harbour Inn for what seemed like ages waiting for the all-clear. A few minutes into what they both knew had been a false alarm, and once the incessant ringing had ceased, Gavin's cousin Eugene came marching across the tarmac offering smiles and excuses, clapping his hands and beckoning the guests back into the warmth of his gold mine.

"Sorry about that, folks. False alarm! But better safe than sorry! There's complimentary tea and coffee being served in the restaurant for everybody," he said beaming to all and sundry.

"Ah, Gavin. That false alarm ... It didn't have anything to do with you by any chance did it?"

"No, Eugene. Why?"

"Someone said it might have been set off in your room."

"Surely not! Must be a mistake."

"Yeah, right."

"Maybe it was faulty wiring or something. I'd get it checked if I were you, Eugene."

"You tell that to the fire brigade when they get here."

"Shit!"

"It's OK, I've called them off."

"Oh."

"And where have your boys gone? Aren't you supposed to be playing golf today?"

"No, it's a rest day."

"Rest day? What kind of golf tour are you on, son?"

"Oh, don't worry, Eugene, we'll be going out tomorrow."

"And the boys?"

"Don't know. Haven't seen them. Have you?"

"No. And, like you, they weren't down for breakfast. All the same, Gavin, it's good to see you're enjoying your stay," Eugene Doyle said nodding towards Bernadette, then winking and baring his teeth in a lascivious smile.

"Better be going," Gavin replied with a scowl, turning away to head back to his room. Bernadette avoided eye contact with Eugene Doyle as she strode past, head held high and with the grace, deportment and self-assurance of a Siamese cat.

"Can you give me a lift over to our guest house, Gavin? It's only up the road. The girls will be wondering where the fuck I've got to by now and a taxi would take bloody ages,"

Bernadette said climbing back into her dancing costume. When she held them up for inspection, her tights were riddled with ladders and torn at the knees. She scrunched them up into a ball and hurled them towards the bin under the dressing table.

"No problem. Where is it?"

"It's about four or five miles inland towards Letterkenny."

"What about something to eat? You hungry, Bernadette?"

"There's a convenience store that does food to go at the petrol station on the way. If you pull in there, we could get a sausage roll or something."

"Why? Do you like lukewarm horsemeat?"

"Very funny. In fact, almost as funny as your fancy-dress costume, Gavin. I mean, what the fuck are you wearing?" Bernadette asked whilst staring at Gavin Doyle's golfing attire.

"It's what men wear on a golf course."

"No. It's what men *wore* on a golf course in about 1971. I mean, turquoise slacks, a pink polo shirt and blue-and-yellow diamond V-neck? That get-up puts thirty years on you."

"And your Maid Marian outfit? I suppose that's typical everyday casual wear for a girl in her thirties."

"Don't be so fucking rude. It's my national costume."

"I thought you were from Leeds."

"I am. I was born there. But it doesn't mean I'm English. I mean 'McIvor', doesn't sound very Yorkshire, does it?"

"Right, are you ready, Bernie?"

"Yep, ready. And it's Bernadette. But then you know that, don't you, you dickhead?" she said pinching his arm hard enough to make him wince.

They shuffled out of the room and headed for the car park. They paid no attention to the Jag with tinted windows idling on the main street.

"OMG! What the fuck's this?" Bernadette demanded, holding up a CD she found under the Passat's passenger seat. They'd only driven a mile out of Ballyhanlon when she noticed it sliding around under her feet. She thrust it in the air as if it were incriminating evidence, her face screwed up with disdain.

"Girls Aloud? Are you some kind of pervert, Gavin?"

"Must be Hugo's. Probably belongs to his niece," Gavin replied, blushing.

Bernadette slid the window down and flicked the CD over the hedgerow as if it were a Frisbee.

"You do know that fly-tipping's a criminal offence?"

"Fuck off, paedo, I know your game—BLOODY HELL!" Bernadette suddenly shrieked, causing Gavin, who hadn't been looking ahead, to brake sharply and pull up just before they collided with a large ewe lying across the road.

"Jesus, Gavin!"

"Don't 'Jesus' me, I didn't put that fucking thing there."

"Drive on, Gavin. It's got nothing to do with—Hey! Don't get out! Hey! Don't get out of the fucking car!"

But Gavin Doyle had already leapt out and was dashing round to check on the stricken animal. Bernadette lowered her window.

"Is it ... is it ...?"

The sheep was lying on its side inches from the front of the car. Blood was oozing from its mouth. Gavin was kneeling beside it feeling for a pulse. He glanced up and shook his head.

"Must have been hit by a car."

"Gavin, look!"

Gavin Doyle turned and peered towards the roadside where a lamb was cowering at the bottom of the hedgerow.

"Shit! Poor thing!" Gavin said, spinning round to gauge Bernadette's reaction and wondering why her expression suddenly changed – her mouth dropping open and eyes bulging. He was unaware, however, of the large figure she could see charging through the gate of the adjacent field and bearing down on him wielding a shotgun as if it were a club, and barely heard the first utterance of her scream before feeling a thud on the back of his head as the lights went out.

19

Tuesday, 8.30am
Irish coastal waters

Colin Draper sat contemplating the instructions in the note. His first instinct was to get underway and make for shore immediately, but realised he'd have to carefully think through the procedures he'd learned for preparing a yacht for sea first. They couldn't afford to make any elementary mistakes and needed to make good speed in the prevailing conditions to find Gavin and ensure his safety before their deadline elapsed.

Draper cursed the loss of his mobile phone. Hated to be out of contact with his mother, or Saffie for that matter. That he wouldn't be able to call his mother or receive any calls should she have a fall was a major worry. Also that he wouldn't be able to pay for Saffie's wedding flowers on time as promised. But then his domestic responsibilities paled into insignificance when compared to Gavin Doyle's safety.

Colin Draper had found the admiralty chart mentioned in the note. A small red dot within a red circle had been drawn over the Atlantic to the west of the Irish coast. If that *was* their position, Draper estimated they were about one hundred and fifty miles offshore.

And more or less due west of Ballyhanlon Bay, he mused. *So even if we only average five knots, which should be very doable, that's, erm, five into a hundred and fifty, that'd be about a thirty-hour sail at the very most.*

There were still about thirty-four hours left to get back to shore before the specified deadline was up. So unless they were becalmed – which was highly unlikely in the North Atlantic in March – Draper reckoned they would make land in a little over a day, and that would allow for at least a four-hour margin of error. Even if the wind failed them, the ship's motor was working and the gauge indicated that they had a full tank of fuel.

Colin Draper turned to Hugo Saunders and The Moose, who by now were coming to their senses and sitting up but were shaking their heads and still looking a little dazed.

"What the hell's going on, Colin?" Hugo Saunders moaned.

"Oh, you may well ask, Hugo. This trip you dragged me on just keeps getting better and better," Draper replied. "I'm so, so glad you invited me to come along."

"Enough of the sarcasm, Colin, where the hell are we?"

"Never mind that – read this. You too, Moose," Draper implored them, getting the note out again.

The two men held the A4 page between them like they were sharing a hymn sheet.

"Shit! We're in the middle of the frigging Atlantic! And they've ... they've ..."

"Yep. They've got Gavin."

"Bloody hell!"

"Well, they say they have, Hugo."

"Why, for heaven's sake? And what the hell are we doing here on this bloody boat? I hate boats."

"We're obviously acting as couriers."

"Couriers for what?"

"Drugs, guns, explosives? I don't know. Take your pick, Hugo."

"What about Gavin? Do you think he's in danger?"

"Don't know. I'm sure they'll say anything to get us to sail this boat into Ballyhanlon. However, I guess it's probably best to assume they're holding him and that his life is in danger. And on that basis we don't have any choice but to follow their instructions to the letter."

"Oh, that's brilliant, fucking brilliant!"

"OK, let's not panic about this, Hugo. As long as we do as they wish, Gavin will be alright. And it's an easy sail. I can do it. I might need a bit of help from you two, but in essence it's easy. And unless we collide with some driftwood, a whale or a freight container, it'll be really quite safe."

"How do we know that Gavin's still alive?"

"We don't, Hugo, but let's be positive – let's presume so. And I can't see why he wouldn't be. After all, there's nothing as useless as a dead hostage."

"And how the hell do they know about us? That we're from London? How do they know about our golf tour? How do they know your name and that you can sail, Colin?"

"No idea. Social media? Maybe they've been tracking us. Maybe they hacked into the ferry company's database, picked some names at random and checked them out. I mean, I'm on Facebook. I'm sure there are photos of me sailing boats on Facebook. I don't know, Hugo, but what we've got to do right now is set sail for Ballyhanlon Harbour and get there ASAP."

"Are you sure you know what you're doing here, Colin? Can you actually sail this bloody thing?"

"Absolutely. I am a RYA-certified yachtmaster."

"That means bugger all to me, I'm afraid."

"It means, Hugo, that if you asked me to sail you from here to Bognor Regis, Bordeaux or fucking Buenos Aires I could do it."

"Ballyhanlon would be a good start then."

"Exactly."

"What about the weather? Please tell me there's no chance of a storm? Ever since I watched *Titanic* I've had a real phobia about the sea."

"Are you soft in the head, Hugo?"

"No."

"Good. Right. First we have to plot our course, set the sails and then get underway. We've got a good, steady northwesterly and a pretty calm sea, so I don't think conditions are going to be too testing. I'll tell you where to sit and what to do but please, please, listen to my instructions and do as I say."

"Aye aye, captain."

"That's the spirit, Hugo. Moose?"

The Moose nodded.

"Now, let's get the sea anchor in and get going. First of all, though, Hugo, can you do a quick recce and see if there are any provisions on board. Check the galley for food and drink. See what you can find. I imagine there won't be much though. I imagine they'll want to keep us lean, mean and keen to reach the harbour ASAP, but some water, any water, would be good in this sun."

"Aye aye, captain."

"And, Hugo. Please shut the fuck up with the 'aye aye, captain' bit. The joke's wearing a bit thin."

"Aye aye, captain."

Within half an hour of running around getting their bearings, setting the sails and going over the basics they began to make good progress – the yacht straining under the force of the wind and starting to cut through the swell at pace.

The Reverend Hugo Saunders and The Moose were sitting in the cockpit alongside Colin Draper sharing from a four-litre plastic tub of water.

"So, what happened, Hugo?"

"Last night?"

"Yeah."

"No idea. The last thing I recall is drinking in the snug bar."

"And what happened to Gavin?"

"Don't know, Colin."

"The last I saw of him he was watching the Irish dancing."

"And what do you think happened to us?"

"Someone spiked our drinks – Rohypnol or something."

"The date rape drug?"

"It has other uses."

"But which drinks? There were so many."

"I think it could have been the whiskeys, Hugo."

"Liam served that round."

"Yes. They were spiked," The Moose muttered.

"How can you be sure, Moose?"

"Because I could taste it, Colin."

"So, why the fuck did you drink it?"

"Because I wasn't sure what it was at the time."

"All the same, it appears we've probably got Gavin's family to thank for our present predicament, Hugo."

"You can't be sure of that, Colin."

"If this isn't their doing, then who, Hugo?"

"I can't see Eugene Doyle wanting to do anything to harm Gavin, Colin. He's family. He's his cousin, for God's sake."

"So, who then?"

"Whoever wants us to sail this yacht to Ballyhanlon, Colin."

"And how the hell did we end up on this fucking boat in the first place?"

Hugo shrugged. The Moose looked blank.

"Well, we didn't fucking swim or come by pedalo," Colin Draper continued.

"I remember hearing a loud whooshing sound. Reminded me of the opening scenes in *Apocalypse Now*."

"What! You think it was a helicopter, Hugo?"

"Yeah. I can remember some shouting and the sound of rotor blades. And what about the RIB? Do you remember that?"

"No! What RIB, for Christ's sake?"

"I remember being in a RIB. I remember the sea being rough."

"What! That's weird, Hugo, I don't remember a thing," Draper said, shaking his head.

"All the same, who do you reckon's responsible? Gunrunners? The RA? Drug barons?"

"Who knows, Hugo? But I would like to know what the fuck's on this boat that is *so* dodgy that they need *us* to bring it ashore?"

"Guns? Semtex?"

"Drugs, Hugo. Got to be."

"Maybe we've been set-up by one of your Eastern European builders, Colin."

"Don't be ridiculous, Hugo."

"Maybe we're smuggling illegals from Eastern Europe."

"So, where the fuck are they then? I haven't seen or heard anybody. They're either tiny or mute or both."

"Are you joking, Colin?"

"No. This *is* fucking serious, Hugo. They've got Gavin, we don't know if he's dead or alive, we're stuck out at sea and being forced to deliver God knows what into Ireland. Why the fuck would I be joking? This isn't fucking funny! And if we get caught red-handed with whatever it is they're making us sneak into the country, we could be going down for years."

"Oh, I'm sure that won't happen."

"What do you mean 'that won't happen'? Listen, Hugo, your reassurances count for nothing. Let's not forget that it's because of you that I'm here in the first fucking place. I told you I didn't want to go on this fucking tour. 'It'll do you good,' you said. Yeah, right!"

Hugo Saunders shrugged.

"Look, Hugo, if I don't get back across the water in time for Saffie's wedding, I will personally see to it that you never play golf again."

"Ivory."

"Sorry, Moose? Did we speak?"

"We could be carrying ivory. Or maybe elk antlers."

"What?"

"Elk antlers. They're rare. Very rare. A bloke dug some up in a peat bog in Ireland a year or two ago. They sold for thirty-five grand at auction."

"Yes, very enlightening, Moose. Thank you *so* much for that insight."

"Listen, Colin, I know, this is pretty serious, but it's going to be fine."

"Too right, Hugo. We're going to sail into that fucking harbour, we're going to dump this fucking boat, we're going to find Gavin and then we're going to fuck off back to London. End of."

20

Tuesday, 11.30am
Near Ballyhanlon

"Gavin, you OK? Gavin!"

Gavin Doyle shook his head to try and gain some sense of where he was and what he was doing. He would have raised his hands to rub the bruise on the back of his head but his wrists were tethered behind him, his skin burning from the rope that had him lashed hand and foot to whatever he was sitting on. Peering down it looked like an old kitchen chair.

Gavin glanced across to where Bernadette was lying trussed up in a heap on an old mattress in the corner. Judging by the smell, the dim light, the wooden planking, the dung, the straw and the miscellaneous agricultural tackle hanging from the posts and beams, they'd been dumped in a small barn.

"You OK, Gavin?" Bernadette hissed again when she saw him starting to move.

"Yes, I think so. How about you? What the hell happened?" Gavin whispered.

"The farmer. You know, the mad one from the bar."

"Eh?"

"You know, from the bar last night. The guy with the dead dog and the golf ball?"

"Oh, him."

"Yes. He spotted us at the roadside with the sheep. Thinks we knocked it down. You know, ran it over. Well, you, that is."

"I didn't."

"*I know.*"

"So?"

"So, I told you not to fucking stop."

"Too late now. What do you think he's going to do?"

"I don't know, but he's pretty mad. I think he's drunk. Are you OK?"

"A bit sore."

"I thought he was going to brain you."

"He did."

"Or worse. I mean, he's got a bloody shotgun!"

"Don't worry, all farmers have shotguns."

"Shh, I can hear someone coming."

They bowed their heads as the barn door creaked open. Then, as the farmer, Willie McGettigan, stooped to squeeze through the small aperture, they both peeped over whilst trying to avoid eye contact with him. His shotgun was broken over one arm.

"I took the precaution of bringing you in here to prevent you from driving away from the crime scene."

"But Willie—"

"Mr McGettigan to you."

"Mr McGettigan, I think you must be mistaken."

"I don't think so, son, I heard your car. I heard your brakes squealing, your tyres screeching and the thud when you hit my ewe."

"It wasn't us, mate."

"Wasn't you?"

"Yes. You've made a mistake," Gavin pleaded.

"Look, you fat bastard, I told him not to stop. I told him to drive on," Bernadette interjected, her expression growing fierce.

"Hit-and-run, aye?"

"No! Not fucking hit-and-run, you moron! He only stopped because he's a soft twat and wanted to see if he could help. And this is what he gets," Bernadette snarled.

"Listen here, lass," McGettigan said coldly, snapping his shotgun shut, stepping over to stand beside Gavin and raising the barrels until they were pointing at Gavin's brow. "I've been keeping an eye on this gentleman and his mates. It's them I reckon who got my dog killed yesterday. And now one of em's done away with my fecking ewe."

"I don't know anything about that, but who the fuck are you to go around tying people up and scaring them half to death?"

"I'll show you who the fuck I am, madam," McGettigan exclaimed, punctuating the sentence with a shotgun blast which he fired across the barn into the wooden planking on the opposite wall, peppering it with shot and punching a hole the size of a fist. Bernadette and Gavin squirmed and then stiffened, fear etched across their faces.

"I am a McGettigan," the farmer continued whilst slurring his words, his giant frame swaying slightly. "I'm the last of the McGettigans. We've farmed here since ... since ... the end of the last fucking ice age. And it's foreigners like you who want to drive us away. But you won't fecking get rid of me. I'm not going any-fecking-where. No. I'll make a stand and go under this earth before I get driven off my fecking land. No one's going to drive me away – no politicians, no bankers, no big city blow-ins and no bloody tourists, so I'd start praying if I were you, son."

"I might, but some would say that religion's not much more than a silly answer to a rather irrelevant question, sir," Gavin countered pompously.

McGettigan raised his gun to Gavin Doyle's temple again. Bernadette, for once, was speechless. Pale and speechless. Gavin had his eyes shut and was wincing, anticipating the worst. All three frozen. Bernadette and Gavin knew better than to speak, and McGettigan was too irate and inebriated to engage in any further dialogue.

The ensuing minute of silence seemed to last more like an hour until it was broken by a loud scraping as someone attempted to force the door open from the outside. McGettigan instinctively swung his shotgun away from Gavin's head towards the barn door then pointed it at the floor as Sergeant McIlhenny appeared.

"You took your time, sergeant. It must be a good hour since I called. Here, I've tied them up. Makes things a bit easier."

McGettigan was slurring his words but trying his hardest to speak coherently to the Garda sergeant.

"Right, Willie. First things first. Your gun please."

McGettigan swayed a little before breaking the shotgun – the spent and live cartridges springing out and bouncing across Sergeant McIlhenny's brogues – then transferring the gun from one hand to the other and holding it upright by the barrels as he passed it over.

"I think we'll untie these people now too, Willie. I think we might have overstepped the mark here a little."

"We don't want them running away, sergeant."

"No, Willie, but we'll untie them all the same, thank you. This man's had a tough time of it since he's arrived in Ballyhanlon. Let's not make things any worse for him," the sergeant added raising his voice.

"Any sign of the caravan, sergeant?"

"Nothing yet, I'm afraid, Mr Doyle."

"Caravan? What caravan's that, Gavin?"

"It's a long story, Bernadette. I'll tell you about it later."

"Now then, Willie. Let's get these two untied, shall we?" the sergeant continued.

The farmer leaned round behind the back of Gavin's chair and fiddled with the knotted ropes securing his hands, while Sergeant McIlhenny laid the shotgun on the floor, helped Bernadette to her feet and unbound her too.

"Willie, their car keys please," the sergeant said, holding out his free hand.

McGettigan produced a bunch of keys. The sergeant snatched them away from him and immediately passed them over to Gavin.

"Thank you, Willie. I think we can let these people go now. It's OK, you two, you have nothing to answer for. You're free to go. Your Passat's outside in the yard. I've checked the front of your car and there are no signs of an impact with a large animal such as a sheep. Also, the skid marks on the road leading to the point of impact wouldn't appear to match your tyre pattern. They're from a completely different type of tyre – a four-by-four's, I believe," the sergeant said to Bernadette and Gavin Doyle, ensuring that McGettigan could hear and was listening too. "Willie, as far as I am concerned you were mistaken about these people and I'm going to let them go, but before I do I think you owe them an apology. I did hear the sound of gunshot as I was approaching your farm from the road, but I imagine that was only someone trying to frighten off some crows somewhere. And whilst I realise you were probably trying to make some kind of citizen's arrest, I think we may have been a little bit overenthusiastic in the process. Wouldn't you agree, Willie?"

"I bloody would," Bernadette butted in.

The sergeant raised a hand to restore order.

"So, an apology please, Willie, to this couple ... now."

McGettigan stared back, mute and defiant.

"*Ná déan rudaí níos measa ná mar atá siad cheana féin, Willie!*" the sergeant whispered to McGettigan in Irish.

"Sorry," Willie McGettigan mumbled after a short pause.

"Louder."

"I'm sorry!" he barked petulantly.

"That'll have to do. OK, you two. Off you go," Sergeant McIlhenny urged whilst opening the barn door.

"What, that's it? Aren't you going to lock this nutter up?" Bernadette asked, exasperated.

"Mr Doyle, would you like to make a complaint?"

"No. Not if it means delaying my return to London."

"I thought you might say that, Mr Doyle. There you are, you see Miss ... Miss?"

"McIvor."

"There you are, Miss McIvor."

"Well, I'd certainly like to make one!"

"Miss McIvor, I see you're wearing a lovely Irish dancing costume, and very attractive you look in it too. And, I presume, you have bookings for your very tasteful Irish dancing up and down the west coast of Ireland this spring. Would I not be right? And in all kinds of respectable pubs and clubs and places of the night. Wouldn't it be a terrible shame now if you were to lose any of those bookings, Miss McIvor? But then these things can happen. And most unexpectedly. As you can imagine there's all manner of busybodies in Donegal who might object to your particular brand of artistic entertainment if it was brought to their attention. So, I think it best if you leave Mr McGettigan to me. He's in good hands. And we're going to have words, aren't we, Mr McGettigan?"

The farmer nodded.

"There you are, you see. No one's been seriously hurt and Mr McGettigan is very sorry for any inconvenience he's caused you. No harm done."

"*Bernadette*," Gavin hissed then turned towards the door, his appetite for a fight exhausted.

Gavin got the Passat on the road and away from McGettigan's farm without delay and without looking back. When they'd travelled a mile or two further along the road out of Ballyhanlon, he pulled over.

"You OK, Gavin?"

"Fine. I've got a bit of a sore bonce, but I'm sure I'll survive."

"Concussion?"

"Don't think so. I don't feel sick and I can remember my name. I've got a hard head, Bernadette. I think he just stunned me."

"You poor sod."

"Thanks. Anyway, where to now?"

But Bernadette didn't answer. She had her mobile clasped to her ear and raised a hand for quiet.

"Hi, Aoife. Yeah, it's me. Right. Yeah, right. Ballyhanlon. Yeah, I'm fine. No, no you go on. No, I'll see you when you get back. Yeah. See ya."

Gavin Doyle looked at her nonplussed.

"Apparently we've got the day off till six. The girls are heading into Letterkenny to go shopping."

"You going?"

"Me? Shopping? You kidding?"

"Oh."

"I'm getting a bit peckish, though. You?"

"A little. Pub? Any ideas?"

"Yes, The Singing Pub on the Atlantic Drive. It's just past Downings."

"The next village up the coast?"

"Yes. We played in one of the hotels there last year. Didn't go down too well, I'm afraid. There was nearly a bit of a scrap."

"In Downings?"

"Shit happens. Lovely town, though. Hey, I could do with getting a shower and a change of clothes first."

"OK. Then the pub?"

"Sure. But Gábhán Óg, let's not get too far ahead of ourselves, hey? One step at a time, as we say in dancing circles. One step at a time."

21

Tuesday, 2pm
Irish coastal waters

"It couldn't have been the ferry company."

"What? What couldn't have been the ferry company?"

"They couldn't have hacked and tracked me through the ferry company's database."

"Who couldn't have done *what*? What the hell are you on about, Colin?"

"*They* – our abductors – couldn't have hacked into the ferry company's database, found me and found out I can sail. I'm supposed to be travelling as Francis Devlin not Colin Draper and, as we all know, Fran's not a sailor."

"He was in the Sea Scouts!"

"Doesn't count. Sure, I wasn't coming with you until an hour before we left Greenwich, so I couldn't have been on the passenger list. Ergo, how did they know I was going to be here? It's like I'm the final piece of the jigsaw."

"Yes, that sounds like you, Colin."

"I guess the most important piece is always the one saved till last, Hugo."

"Actually, the last piece of the jigsaw is usually the most awkward. The one that no one understands. The one that's hardest to read, lacking in character and with no distinguishing features. The one that doesn't fit in. Yep, that's definitely you, Colin."

"Gosh, *thanks*, Hugo."

Six hours into their journey back towards the west coast and the sailing had surpassed all expectations. If it wasn't that they suspected they were carrying drugs or arms or Semtex, or that there might even be a bomb on board, the cruise would have made the perfect holiday activity. The wind was steady and constant, and since it was blowing northwesterly there was little work to be done on the sheets that Colin Draper couldn't handle himself. He did, however, encourage the other two to get involved and learn a little helmsmanship in case conditions changed and more assistance would be required later.

"What I mean is, it's obvious from the note that my sailing skills were thought to be key to this venture – an integral part of their strategy – whoever 'they' are. But how did they know I was coming to Donegal?"

"Maybe they didn't. Maybe they heard you bragging about your *sailing skills* in the bar last night. You do like to big yourself up a bit, Colin."

"Thank you very much, Hugo."

"So, where do you think this boat has come from, Colin?"

"Certainly not Sligo. I guess it depends on what we're carrying. If it's guns and ammo, could be North Africa. If it's drugs, could be the Caribbean."

"How the hell did it get here then?"

"The boat? Well, this class of yacht's easily big enough to sail the Atlantic."

"And what happened to the crew?"

"I don't know, Hugo. Taken off when we were dumped on board?"

"But why us?"

"Because we're good cover. We're tourists. We don't appear suspicious. We're mules – we reduce the risk for them. We fit the narrative."

"I have to say, this sailing lark looks a piece of piss, Colin."

"Thanks again, Hugo, but that's only because I make it look easy. I tell you what, though, I'd be enjoying this a lot more if

I weren't so damn worried about Gavin. I'm also worried about what the hell it is we're carrying. I don't want to be importing a bundle of shite that's going to put anyone in hospital."

"What's to stop us going straight to the police once we're ashore?"

"Because, Hugo, who knows what our masters are capable of doing to us or Gavin if we don't follow their instructions to the letter right up until we get home to London. They're probably playing for big stakes here. If they're capable of shanghaiing us out to sea, they'll be capable of doing much worse to us on dry land. Simple as."

"Shit!"

"Once we've got this boat to Ballyhanlon, there is the very real danger we could be accused of being accessories in the smuggling in of whatever shit we're carrying should any third parties be apprehended later. That's to say, our abductors could shop us. We might be acting under duress, but we're still accessories to a crime."

"Do you think we could fix the radio?"

"Why bother? You can try if you like, but there's not a lot we could do without compromising Gavin's safety if it was working in the first place. No, we'll just have to keep quiet, keep our heads down and keep going."

When it came, the sunset was spectacular. A three-hundred-and-sixty-degree panorama of luminescent pink and azure cloud stretching over them from the horizon and reflected back off a calm sea.

To pass the time and keep their spirits up the three-man crew had taken to singing: "Green Grow the Rushes, O" and "She'll be Coming Round the Mountain". They'd have sung sea shanties but didn't know any. Their voices blended into a natural three-part harmony – the Reverend Hugo Saunders singing falsetto, Draper tenor and The Moose a rich and resonant bass.

"Do you know why Mexicans call Americans 'gringos'?"

"I'm sorry, Hugo?"

"Do you know why people in Mexico call Americans 'gringos'?"

"Oh, go on. Why?"

"It goes back to the Alamo, Colin."

"What?"

"The Alamo. The settlers used to pass their time during the siege singing 'Green Grow The Rushes, O', you know, like every day. So much so that the Mexicans latched on to it and started calling them gringos."

"What a load of bollocks."

"I knew you'd be interested."

"You know, I could kill a beer," Draper moaned after a short pause.

"I don't – and I'm sure a little abstinence won't do you any harm either, Colin. I bet your liver's doubled in size since last night's binge."

"That sounds a little holier than thou, Hugo."

"What do you expect, Colin? I am a vicar."

"I'll tell you what though, Hugo, I'm bloody hungry."

"Fish?" The Moose said, reappearing from the cabin with a rod and what appeared to be a bag of fishing tackle.

"Do you know what to do with that lot, Moose?"

The Moose rolled his eyes, sat down in the cockpit and started rifling through the canvas bag.

"You didn't find anything else down there, did you, Moose? No white powder or putty-like substances, ammo or timid-looking foreigners?"

The Moose shook his head and continued to thread some line through one of the floats he'd found in the tackle bag.

"Why don't you go and see if you can find our cargo, Hugo?"

"I don't know that I really want to, to be honest, Colin. I think that's a hornets' nest that doesn't need kicking."

"Moose?"

The Moose was too preoccupied to answer.

"Shit. I'll go then," Colin Draper said, knitting his brow.

"What about the boat, Colin?"

"Easy, Hugo. You'll be fine without me for a few minutes. See that big star to port?"

"That one up there to the left?"

"Correct. Sit there and try and keep us on the path we're on now. Keep that star where it is in relation to you and the boat, and watch the compass. It's there right in front of you. See how it's set now? Keep it like that."

"Oh, OK."

"I'll be two minutes. I'll know if you do anything daft."

Colin Draper clambered forward imagining that there might be a hatch and sizeable storage area somewhere towards the bow. There was. The hatch was on the foredeck. However, when Draper got down on his hands and knees for a closer inspection he found it padlocked.

Draper tried his pockets in search of a handkerchief, found some tissue and lifted the lock to get a better look without leaving his prints. He was relieved that it was an old-style combination padlock, about three inches tall and a couple of inches wide, with a front-facing dial and a silver shackle – the U-shaped hoop at the top. He rotated the dial clockwise and then anticlockwise taking pot luck with a sequence of numbers. Nothing. He placed a finger through the shackle and pulled on it whilst twisting the dial clockwise. Then he released the pressure on the shackle until he could feel the point of least resistance whilst continuing to turn the dial in the same direction. This led to him detecting the first number in the combination which he committed to memory. He then knew to turn the dial anticlockwise while working the shackle against the lock until he could feel the dial free up again. This gave him the next number in the combination. Draper repeated this process until he had worked out all the numbers. Within a couple of minutes he'd memorised the number sequence and had the lock open. He set the padlock to one side and pulled the hatch open. There were no steps down, but the hold wasn't so deep that he couldn't swing down into it. There was little light to search by save for the moon and stars.

The idea was easier than the execution, however. As Draper levered himself over the side of the hatch and slid, he found himself stuck – his trousers caught on a pin or a nail.

Fuck it!

Pushing with his arms and wriggling his legs, his bodyweight was too much for the minor obstruction and he managed to force himself free but could feel the back of his trousers tearing on the nail in the process.

Bugger!

Draper crouched as he landed and put out his hands to feel his way around. Soon his fingers ran across a large hessian sack packed with something cold. He pulled at the top of the sack and managed to wriggle his fingers in through the drawstring. Inside he could feel small packages, about the same size as bags of sugar, wrapped in polythene and containing something soft and powdery. As he moved his hands around the hold he found many more sacks identical to the first.

"You took your time, Colin. How's our course?"

"Let me see," Draper said glancing at the ship's compass as he stepped into the cockpit. "Spot on! That's perfect. There you go, Hugo, we'll make a sailor of you yet."

"Well?"

"Well, what?"

"Did you find anything, Colin?"

"There was a lock on the hatch."

"Shit! You didn't break in or leave any marks, did you?"

"No. It was a combination lock."

"Never mind. But at least you tried."

"It's OK, I cracked it."

"Eh?"

"My Polish plasterer, Tomasz, he taught me how to do it. A tradesman we'd contracted left a combination lock on the back of our van once. You know, chained it up. He was being malicious. We were late paying him or something. I was going to take a hacksaw to it, but Tomasz showed me how to get the lock off by touch and feel. Simple really. Only takes a minute. It's quite easy when you know how."

"And what did you find?"

"Not people, not guns, not explosives. Actually, *it* has made me feel quite light-headed."

"Oh, God. You didn't sample the goods did you?"

"Had to, Hugo."

"What is it?"

"I'm not sure. It's a powder. Looks like coke. What coke looks like on the telly, anyway."

"Shit!"

"It's perked me up a treat."

"How much did you snort, you eejit?"

"I didn't snort any. I put a tiny dab on my finger."

"How much is there then?"

"I couldn't give you a weight or tell you its street value, but I'd estimate there's enough to fill Gavin's Passat about twice over."

"Shit, Colin! That's a hell of a lot. That's big league. But as you say, at least it's not guns or explosives. I take it you left it all exactly as you found it."

"Of course, Hugo."

"Didn't pocket a small supply for later?"

"Hardly."

"So, if it's coke, where's it from?"

"South America? Central America? The Caribbean? Well, obviously I can't say I know for sure, but I'd imagine this boat has crossed the Atlantic. There must be a fair weight of the stuff down there. It'd explain why we're lying a little low in the water."

"Could that be a problem? Isn't that a bit of a giveaway?"

"It could be, but they've probably repainted the sides of the yacht to create a dummy waterline. Let's hope so, anyway."

Suddenly they were interrupted by a thud as a large fish landed on board to the rear of the cockpit, writhing and slapping its head against the deck.

"Shit, Moose! What the hell's that?" Colin Draper and Hugo Saunders stuttered at the same time.

"Dinner."

Colin Draper didn't sleep much that night. Whenever the rolling of the ship started to rock him into a doze, a wave or the current would jerk the ship's wheel and jolt him awake again.

The Moose and Hugo Saunders had succumbed to tiredness and taken refuge below deck. They were lying flat out along the seating in the galley's dining area.

Colin Draper felt reassured that his friends were nearby and handy enough if he needed them in a hurry, but that was unlikely since the conditions at sea were so mild, the sail so very straightforward. Draper was almost disappointed by the lack of a challenge. However, he was alert to the likelihood that the waters around Ballyhanlon Bay might have some surprises in store – strange currents, sandbanks and concealed rocks being but a few.

22

Tuesday, 5pm

Sergeant McIlhenny was out and about in Ballyhanlon. He wasn't so much patrolling as wandering around trying to look busy. Whenever the paperwork was done and there was nothing else to do in the office, he thought it better for his reputation to be seen walking the streets rather than languishing indoors.

Crime in Ballyhanlon was pretty much non-existent; it certainly wasn't the Bronx. Sergeant McIlhenny felt he had more in common with the parish priest, Father O'Flaherty, than he did with any TV cop. A Jim Bergerac or a Dirty Harry he was not. It made him laugh a little when he considered how the townsfolk of Ballyhanlon seemed more fearful of Father O'Flaherty's fiery sermons than the tickings off of their local Garda sergeant. McIlhenny was a velvet glove to Father O'Flaherty's iron fist.

Drunken behaviour occasionally called for an intervention, but even that was rarely reported outside the confines of the Harbour Inn since Eugene Doyle was man enough to keep his own house in order. If the local grapevine suggested that any of his regulars were overindulging or stepping out of line at home, he would endeavour to solve the problem at source: persistent drunks were barred. Doyle feared for his licence too much to allow anyone or anything to get out of hand on his premises.

The height of Sergeant McIlhenny's police work generally involved minor parking offences, shoplifting and settling neighbourly squabbles. Ballyhanlon hadn't seen a murder in all his time there. Robbery was rare and only ever involved outsiders. There was a spate of joyriding one summer but that was a one-man spree – the work of a dysfunctional teenager from Belfast. It turned out that his parents had sent him away for the summer lest he be kneecapped by those residents of the city who have no patience for such activity.

The sergeant was pretty sure there was poaching and a little smuggling in the area, but that was almost impossible to detect unless someone were to make a complaint, and that would never happen in a community the size of Ballyhanlon. McIlhenny knew he had to tread carefully and employ discretion. The incident earlier in the day at Willie McGettigan's farm was a case in point.

In a large town or city, McGettigan's threatening behaviour with the shotgun may have resulted in him facing criminal charges. Things are different in Donegal, however. The incident had occurred on an isolated farm and McGettigan felt he had good reason to restrain the couple until the police arrived. Also, shotguns are rarely seen in towns and cities unless they are being used to hold-up banks. In rural Ireland they are common, and McGettigan held a licence for his.

Willie McGettigan was a son of Ballyhanlon, born and bred; a native of a dwindling community. Where others had left to seek a wage, McGettigan had stayed and worked the land. And he was typical of Sergeant McIlhenny's small flock. McIlhenny was well aware that further falls in Ballyhanlon's population could lead to cutbacks in government services. Cutbacks one day could include the Garda station. McIlhenny had a duty, therefore, to shepherd his flock with care – he certainly couldn't afford to have any of them carted off to jail if that could be avoided.

The disappearance of the old man and the caravan had been the first major incident requiring investigation for months. And yet there were few leads, if any, for Sergeant McIlhenny to follow. It was, to his mind, as close to an open-and-shut case as he'd come across. Frustrating. He'd have loved to get involved in some genuine detective work.

But the four English tourists left him puzzled. They were an odd bunch alright, even for Englishmen. His instincts as a detective suggested that they should be watched. That they had allowed an eighty-something-year-old man to travel in the back of a caravan all the way from London to Donegal was enough to rouse suspicion. He couldn't understand the callousness of such an act. And where were they now? They claimed to be on a golf tour but appeared to be playing very little golf. Odd.

One lap of the town and he was relieved to find that it was approaching five thirty. Time for a pint.

"Guinness, sergeant?"

Sergeant McIlhenny nodded.

"There you go. On the house," Eugene Doyle enthused, slouching over the bar taps.

"*Slàinte.*"

"Seen anything of those English lads today, Seamus?"

"I ran into your cousin up at McGettigan's farm. Got into a bit of a scrap so he did."

"I'm sorry, Seamus, Gavin didn't tell me anything about that! I hope he didn't get himself into any bother."

"No, not at all. Willie had some mad notion that the lad had run over one of his sheep. But then, you know what Willie's like."

"Actually, he's in here now."

"Who? McGettigan?"

"No, Gavin. He's round in the snug with his new friend. She's one of those Irish dancers we had in here last night."

"Dancers? I wouldn't call that dancing, Eugene, but I suppose it's good for business."

"It's just business, Seamus. We have to keep trying out new attractions and entertainment. It's not easy. Sure, you know how it is these days."

"Right enough. But don't let the entertainment get too *glamorous* or we'll have the church to deal with."

"Don't worry, I won't be putting on anything that'll have O'Flaherty sticking his nose in. That man's not good for trade."

"Now, you were asking about the rest of those lads."

"Gavin's mates?"

"Yes. Have you seen anything of them yourself?"

"No. Mad dogs and Englishmen, hey? They've probably gone hillwalking or something, Seamus. You know how those city types love going for long walks in their snoods, hi-vis anoraks and hiking boots and carrying those ski stick things."

"Don't know why they don't wear shorts and trainers. They'd be much lighter on their feet."

"Any sign of the caravan, Seamus?"

"You joking? It'll be a million miles away from here by now."

"Shit, that's a terrible business – oh, hang on, sorry, Seamus, I'll be back in a sec," Eugene Doyle said springing up to retreat into the snug to serve a customer.

23

Wednesday, 8am
Irish coastal waters

Colin Draper woke with a start. Could have been at home in bed – could have been anywhere. But then he felt something akin to a bucket of water being flung across his face that immediately brought him to his senses. It was the morning of their second day at sea. He'd finally nodded off but had only been asleep for a short while when he was woken by a God-Almighty thump. It scared the living daylights out of him, as it might easily have been the yacht hitting rocks or a collision with another vessel.

"Morning, Captain Draper," Hugo Saunders said sleepily as he climbed up into the cockpit.

"Very funny, Hugo."

"You OK?"

"Bit worried in case we drifted off course during the night."

The weather seemed to have deteriorated; the wind had picked up and the sea was growing choppier. It was the boat bouncing higher then smacking against the swell that had jolted him awake. That and the sea spray.

"Hold on. Let's take a look here," Draper mused as he peered at the yacht's instruments, and even though he wasn't an expert navigator he could tell they were still holding course. The sun was up too, which was reassuring. He puffed out his cheeks, glad that he had managed to complete his first solo night sail without incident. Draper stared out over towards the horizon then rubbed his eyes lest they were deceiving him.

"Moose! Hugo! Land ahoy!"

Draper had longed for years to have an opportunity to yell the clichéd phrase.

"You joking?"

"Look, way over there on the horizon, Hugo. See that? That hazy strip of grey?"

Within minutes a tern, exhausted and bedraggled, swooped down onto the foredeck as if to confirm their proximity to land.

They were moving faster through the water now and heeling at a sharper angle which indicated to Draper that he needed to adjust the sailing rig. The dark clouds ahead implied they were heading into more turbulent weather, maybe a squall, and he'd always been taught that it's safer to adapt a yacht's set-up in anticipation of worsening conditions than to react once you've hit them.

"Moose, Hugo, it looks like there's a bit of a blow coming on. We'll have to shorten sail and reef down."

"You what? What are you talking about, Colin?"

"We're going to have to reef in the sails."

"We?"

"Yes *we*. Reefing's fucking fiddly. You'll need to help."

"Really?"

"Yes. It's a matter of better safe than sorry. The good news is that with this wind we've picked up speed. At this rate we're going to get ashore ahead of schedule."

"Excuse me for asking but what the hell's reefing, Colin?"

"Reducing the size of the sails, Hugo. It's like taking in a pair of trousers to make it easier to walk on a windy day."

"Who the hell does that?"

"Oh, never mind, just follow my instructions. OK?"

"Yep."

"I'm going to explain a few simple hand signals for you. It'll save me shouting when we're further forward. It'll be easy enough if you do as I say," Draper said with confidence. "Hugo. You're as white as a sheet. Do you—"

But before Draper finished asking the question, Hugo Saunders made a lunge for the side of the ship.

Draper waited a couple of minutes to allow Hugo to compose himself.

"You OK, Hugo?"

"Shit! I really, really hate being at sea, Colin."

"But ...?"

"But, yeah, I guess I'll be fine. There's nothing left to come up now, for goodness sake."

"Good, cos we need to work fast."

Colin Draper was correct about the weather. Within ten or fifteen minutes the sky overhead darkened and the wind started to gust as a shower of rain came down. He was determined to keep them on course, though, and was enjoying the challenge. They'd been lucky that they'd hit the worsening weather in daylight and within sight of land.

Hugo didn't seem to be enjoying the experience quite as much as Draper, however, and spent much of the next while bent over the side of the ketch with his stomach in his mouth.

As they neared land, the bad weather started to pass over and, as they worked their way up the coast towards Ballyhanlon, the wind dropped, the sea became calmer, the sky cleared and they were bathed in sunshine.

They kept to a course parallel to the shoreline, about a mile out at sea. Draper placed Hugo at the wheel whilst he worked with The Moose to lower the sails and stow them away. With the change in conditions, Draper decided they would make the last mile or two into Ballyhanlon under engine power.

"Brilliant! It's going to be a breeze from here on in," Colin Draper enthused.

"Thank the Lord!" Hugo Saunders muttered.

"O ye of little—"

A loud scraping suddenly interrupted Draper as the yacht shuddered to a halt. It was if someone had pulled on a handbrake – the three men thrown to the floor by the force of the impact.

"What the hell was that?" Hugo moaned, staggering to his feet.

"We've run aground."

"How in God's name can we run aground when we're still out at sea?"

"Because we've probably hit a sandbar. There's hundreds of them up and down this coast."

"I thought you said you could sail this frigging boat, Colin."

"It's not my fault if the effing echo sounder's faulty. Christ! How the fuck do you think we've got this far, Hugo?"

"What if we start sinking?"

"We've run aground on a sandbar, we haven't crashed onto rocks or – since you're such a devotee of *Titanic* – hit an iceberg. We'll be fine."

"I'm sorry, Colin, but we're marooned out at sea, there's no one to help us and we can't seek help and you're telling me we'll be *fine*. What the hell are we going to do?"

"Stay calm. This is no time for a mutiny, Hugo."

"Hell, Colin! We're not on the effing *Bounty* and you're not Captain Bligh. We've got to be in Ballyhanlon by six o'clock or Gavin's in trouble. What if we can't get this thing shifted?"

"Don't worry. I reckon we've run aground pretty much at low tide. Once the sea level rises we'll catch the deeper water and be able to head in on the incoming tide. It's quite simple."

"Oh really?"

"Yes. We just have to sit here for a while and not panic."

"How long is a while?"

"I'm not sure. Three, maybe four hours?"

"Fuck, that's cutting it tight. And how do you know the tide isn't going out now?"

"Because I have eyes, Hugo, but we'll soon know if the boat starts to heel over."

"OK. But what if someone – the coastguard say – spots us and comes to help."

"That's a good question, Hugo, but you needn't worry on

that score. Firstly, they won't know we're in difficulties unless we send them standard nautical distress signals—"

"What?"

"You know, signal that we're in distress with a flare or a Mayday or semaphore or by flying flags or simply waving our arms like mad and shouting."

"Ah huh."

"And, secondly, we'll drop anchor and get The Moose to start fishing. Anyone who takes a blind bit of notice will presume we've tied up for a bit of rest and recuperation. If we don't ask for help, they won't think we need it and we won't get any. Simple."

"Won't they notice that we're lying a bit low in the water? Won't that make them suspicious?"

"We're on a sandbar. They won't notice. Tell you what, why don't you go for a swim, Hugo. I'm going to take a nap."

"Hang on, let's not forget about Gavin. We're not here to enjoy ourselves. I for one am not moving from this cockpit till we're underway again, Colin. I'm only interested in getting back to shore, getting off this effing boat and finding Gavin ASAP."

"Of course, Hugo. We all are."

As the conversation lulled, a voice could be heard crackling over the radio:

"Goldstar, Goldstar, Goldstar. This is Bad Boy. Over."

"Bloody hell, Colin! What's that?"

"It's the VHF."

"The what?"

"The radio."

"I thought it was broken."

"It was. Well, that's what they told us, but apparently it would seem not."

"Goldstar. This is Bad Boy. How do you read? Can we have a working channel? Over."

"I guess we're Goldstar, Hugo. Hang on ... *Bad Boy, this is Goldstar. You're loud and clear, go to Channel 72. Over,*"

Draper replied, picking up the handpiece and switching to Channel 72.

"*Goldstar, change of plan. End your cruise at Downings Harbour. Over.*"

"*This is Goldstar, copy that, Bad Boy. May be a bit later than scheduled. Over.*"

"*Then the cat will chase the canary. This is Bad Boy ... Out.*"

The radio went dead.

"Bastards! Fucking bastards! FUCK YOU!" Colin Draper shouted into the handpiece before flinging it down.

"Colin, Colin, calm down."

"Shit! But they've got us just where they want us, Hugo."

"Where is Downings from here, Colin?"

"Hold on," Draper said, running a finger up and down the chart. "It's about another ten or fifteen miles up the coast. Don't worry, we can still meet their deadline."

"God, I hope you're right, Colin. Anyway, what do you think that accent was over the radio?"

"Hard to say. It wasn't South American, Hugo, that's for sure. Why, what do you think?"

"I don't know. I couldn't make it out either."

The wait for the incoming tide was a nervous one. There was little to do and the worry of missing the deadline spoiled any enjoyment of the natural surroundings. Aground on a sandbar under a strong sun and suffering from pangs of hunger made for an uncomfortable intermission.

The Moose was preoccupied with fishing and achieved some success, not that he demonstrated any great excitement. Hugo Saunders finally bowed to temptation and contemplated going for a swim. He imagined that the sea would be freezing but the water looked calm and inviting and the ambient temperature made the prospect of a quick dip attractive. Hugo pulled off his polo shirt and was loosening his cargo pants when he spotted a vessel approaching at speed.

"Colin!"

Colin Draper was snoozing in the cabin.

"Colin!" Hugo yelled through the hatch again.

"Colin!"

"For fuck's sake, Hugo, please stop shouting. Sound travels a long way over open water, you plank," Colin Draper hissed whilst making his way up to the cockpit.

"What the hell's that boat doing?"

"Fuck! It's coming our way. Looks like the Irish Naval Service to me, Hugo. So, please, please quieten down or they'll think there's something wrong."

"How do you know, Colin?" Hugo Saunders whispered.

"How do I know *what*?"

"How do you know that that's the Irish Naval Service?"

"Because it appears how I would expect an Irish Naval Service vessel to look. It's battleship grey, has a small cannon on the foredeck and is patrolling off the coast of Donegal. That kind of tells you something, doesn't it?"

"And why do you think they're headed this way?"

"Simple. Because they're patrolling, they've seen us and these days they suspect that everybody's up to no good."

"Bloody hell! What are we going to do, Colin!"

"Keep it together, Hugo. We're going to keep calm. They may or may not come aboard but they certainly will if we make a fuss."

"What'll happen if they come aboard?"

"They'll want to check our papers."

"What papers, Colin?"

"Exactly."

"Oh."

"And what's worse, Hugo, is if and when they come aboard they may well want to conduct a search and if they do, then I'm afraid we're totally screwed."

"Oh, God!"

"Exactly."

The patrol boat powered back as it neared. Almost immediately a RIB was deployed and sped across the short distance between them. As it got close an officer in a navy jumper and beret stood and addressed them.

"You guys alright? Have you run aground?"

"Yes. But we're OK. We're waiting for the tide."

"What's your business here?"

"We chartered this yacht in Sligo. We're just cruising around the west coast. You know, a bit of R&R," Colin Draper yelled back.

"Where are you headed?"

"We're mooring overnight in Downings."

"Fair enough. We *were* going to come on board and check your papers but we've just picked up a call from a trawler with engine difficulties off Tory. I take it you've not got a large stash of drugs hidden away on board or anything, sir?" the sailor asked with a smile.

"No. Absolutely not, officer. Just a few cases of semi-automatics."

"Yes, sir. Very funny."

"Look, if I throw you a line, is there any chance you could tow us off this bank?" Colin Draper asked with a nervous laugh.

"No problem. If you look lively, we'll get you off in a jiffy."

With a rope attached the yacht was dragged off the sandbar in seconds. The RIB doubled back alongside before leaving.

"As you head north, sir, keep west of that promontory and no closer to the beach before the next low tide and you'll avoid any trouble between here and your port of call. Good luck!" the officer shouted.

"Cheers!" Colin Draper yelled back and gave an exaggerated double thumbs up as the officer opened his throttle and turned to head back to the patrol ship.

"That, Hugo, was a very, very close call. Those guys don't fuck about."

"Sure, but what if someone was watching us from the shore, Colin? You know, one of our druggie friends," Hugo Saunders asked as they got underway and the naval vessel became but a black dot on the horizon.

"Well, if they were watching carefully, they'd have been able to see exactly what went on," Colin Draper replied, exasperated.

"Which was?"

"Damn all for them to worry about, Hugo."

Within an hour of cruising north along the coast, Ballyhanlon Bay came into view. Another twenty minutes and they were rounding the head into Downings Harbour; the infrastructure comprising little more than a single concrete pier. As they approached the quay Colin Draper put the motor into reverse and brought them alongside. He scanned the pier wall for suspicious-looking characters but the place appeared deserted.

Hugo Saunders and The Moose jumped onto the quay. Hugo kissed the ground before helping The Moose secure the yacht fore and aft. Colin Draper then followed them ashore, checked their work and ran up the pier, the other two trailing in his wake. Next step: find Gavin Doyle.

"Shit, I'm scared, Colin," Hugo wheezed whilst trying to keep up.

"You should be."

"What now?"

"We'll head straight for that bar up the road, see if Gavin's answering his phone, then call for a cab and get back to Ballyhanlon PDQ. Hopefully we'll be able to find him somewhere around there. But, let's face it, he could be being held anywhere between here and Dublin by now."

"God, he'd better be OK."

"Yep. Better had," Draper replied, panting and picking up the pace.

The tiny harbour was eerily quiet. No other boats. No other people. Those houses they past – mostly weekend holiday homes – seemed dark and inhospitable, every window threatening a pair of eyes.

The bar was about four hundred yards uphill from the quay, and by the time they reached the pub forecourt they were all gasping for air. They didn't have time to notice the magnificent view across the bay or care to. They were about to dash in through the front door when they had to stop and stand aside for the large figure walking out.

"Good morning, lads. Did you enjoy your cruise now?"

"Yes. Very much, thank you, sergeant," Colin Draper replied, looking sheepish.

"Your friend, Mr Doyle, I take it he hasn't got sea legs then?"

"Sorry?"

"Mr Doyle ... You didn't take him sailing with you? Seasickness, is it?"

"Yes! Very much so. He hates the sea."

"Well, I don't think he's been missing you too much," Sergeant McIlhenny said with a wry smile.

"Oh? So you've seen him then?" Draper stuttered.

"Of course."

"Oh, thank God!"

"Why, is there something the matter, lads?"

"Oh, no, not at all ... But you've seen him recently? Today?"

"No, not today, as it happens. Not yet anyway."

"But as far as you know he's OK?"

"Of course. Though he did have a bit of a run-in with one of our local farmers yesterday."

"Oh?"

"We got it sorted, sure. It was nothing much. I'll let him tell you all about that."

"And he's OK?" Draper asked again.

"Yes, he seems to be. Why do you keep asking? I mean, why wouldn't he be? Especially now he's got a new friend to play with."

"A friend?"

168

"A girl. You know, one of those Irish dancers from the Harbour Inn."

"Oh, OK. Yes, of course."

"All the same, he seemed happy enough the last time I saw him."

"Oh, good ... fine, fine."

"What about you? What were you doing on the boat?"

"Part of our holiday itinerary, sergeant. A charter. Colin's a keen sailor. He's been dying to take us out on an excursion for ages. Hasn't stopped talking about it for months."

"But Mr Doyle's not so keen?"

"No. And as you say, he gets very seasick. Very."

"Anyway, did you enjoy yourselves?"

"Yes! It was great fun, sergeant. We had a great time, didn't we, boys?" Draper enthused.

"Yes. Brilliant," Hugo Saunders replied through gritted teeth.

"Any sign of the caravan, sergeant?"

"Nothing, I'm afraid."

"Pants."

"Don't worry, I'll let you know the moment I hear anything."

"Thanks."

"You're welcome, boys."

"Err, sergeant, I'm sorry, but we'd better be going. Lovely to see you," Colin Draper splurted out after Hugo gave him a nudge in the ribs.

"How are you getting back to Ballyhanlon, lads?"

"We're going to call a taxi."

"Don't be daft. I'll give you a lift. I'm going there now."

"That's very kind of you, but we were going to have a quick pint here then call for a cab."

"A cab? Round here? You must be joking. That'll take all day to come. No, if you can wait for your pint till you get to Ballyhanlon, I can give you a lift right now."

"No, honestly, that's far too much bother."

"No, I insist."

"But Hugo here needs to make a quick call in the bar."

"What, here?"

"Yes."

"Not got mobiles?"

"They're out of charge. Forgot our chargers."

"But there's no payphone in the bar, lads. Sure, Hugo can use my personal mobile. It's in the car."

"Really?"

"Yes, and it's no bother."

"Oh, OK, thanks."

"I'll give you a lift, then so."

"Thanks. Thanks very much."

"I don't do it for everyone, mind. Well, unless they've done something very naughty of course. All the same, we have to take care of our visitors or they won't come back."

"Thank you, sergeant," Colin replied whilst frowning at the others.

Hugo Saunders grabbed Colin Draper by the sleeve and pulled him out of earshot as they crossed over the road to the pub's car park.

"Are you mad? There's no way we can risk getting into his car," Hugo hissed. "If they, whoever they are, see us riding in a bloody police car, Gavin could be toast."

"What the hell can we do, Hugo? I don't think we have any choice."

"OK, gentlemen, are we ready to go?" Sergeant McIlhenny said, a slight impatience creeping into his voice as he waited for The Moose, Colin Draper and Hugo Saunders to catch up.

"We don't want to be any bother, sergeant."

"You're not. It's no bother. I'm giving you a lift now and that's final. Unless of course there's some reason you don't want to come with me – something you're not telling me."

"You're very perceptive, sergeant, but, no, of course not," Colin Draper said through a forced smile.

24

Wednesday, 4pm

The drive to Ballyhanlon was a quiet one. Sergeant McIlhenny seemed determined to conduct an investigation in the guise of casual conversation, whilst the boys were determined to give nothing away. Not that McIlhenny had any real suspicions they'd been up to no good, but over the years his nature had become an inquisitive one. He was an old-school policeman and thought it his business to know everybody else's.

As they drove, Hugo tried calling Gavin on the sergeant's mobile. He hunched his shoulders, cupped a hand over his mouth and whispered when Gavin's phone went straight to answerphone.

"*Gavin, it's Hugo. We're heading back to the Harbour Inn. Call me and leave a message as soon as you get this, please. It's urgent.*"

"No good?"

"No. No worries. I'll try again later, thank you, sergeant," Hugo said, handing back McIlhenny's phone.

"You alright, Colin?" Hugo mumbled into Colin Draper's ear beneath the sound of the car's engine. They were both sitting in the rear of the police car, The Moose up front.

"I'm just wondering who the fuck this dancer is, Hugo."

"Do you think we should be worried?"

"Definitely! I don't think we can trust anyone round here. In fact anyone we've met since we got off the ferry."

"I know what you mean. It's a pity."

"It's a necessity."

"So, you think the girl could be involved?"

"Absolutely! Sure, she could easily be one of the bad guys. They needed a hostage and maybe she got them one."

"Really?"

"Let's face it, Gavin's hardly Brad Pitt, is he? How come he's managed to hook up with an attractive thirty-something like her? It doesn't ring true to me, Hugo."

"Animal magnetism?"

"Too much animal, not enough magnetism."

"Let's hope he's not being held in some despicable hellhole."

"But the sergeant's seen him. I just hope we've fulfilled all the conditions they specified in the note."

"We got the boat ashore, Colin."

"And are we being watched now? Did they see us get into this fucking police car? If we've got involved with dissidents, there could be any number of eyes watching us round here. We'd be sitting ducks."

"And what about you-know-who, Colin?" Hugo whispered nodding towards Sergeant McIlhenny. "How do we know we can trust him?"

Colin Draper put a finger to his lips.

"Better save it till we get to the pub, Hugo," he murmured.

"Weren't you due to play golf today, gentlemen?" Sergeant McIlhenny asked, trying to break another awkward silence as they approached Ballyhanlon.

"You've got a good memory, sergeant," Hugo replied in a friendly tone.

"Goes with the job."

"We would have played if we'd got back on time, but then we didn't know Colin here was going to run us aground."

"Sandbank?"

"Apparently."

"So, only the two rounds of golf on this trip then?"

"Yes, only two rounds."

"That's not much of a golf tour then, is it?"

"It's enough for us, sergeant, believe me."

"Or is the golf just an excuse?"

"Well, it's always good to get away from the daily grind, so, yes, you're quite right, the golf's a bit of an excuse."

"Interesting," Sergeant McIlhenny said, his comment sounding like an accusation. "Right you be, I'll drop you here then, boys. I have to pop into the station now and then a quick pint before home," McIlhenny added as he performed a U-turn in front of the bar.

"Thanks, sergeant," the three of them muttered as they clambered out of the car.

"Be good now, lads. And stay out of trouble," McIlhenny added, as Draper swung the door shut.

They watched Sergeant McIlhenny drive off then dashed into the Harbour Inn.

"Moose! Hugo! Come on, we'll check the saloon bar first," Draper urged.

"What is it about Sergeant McIlhenny that always makes me feel guilty the moment I see him?" Hugo Saunders asked as they burst in through the front door.

"Boys! There you are! Where have you been? What have you been up to?"

"Don't ask, Eugene."

"But whatever it was, I hope it was fun," Eugene Doyle said enthusiastically.

"Eugene, have you seen Gavin?" Hugo Saunders asked.

"Yes, and he's been wondering where you've been too. I think he was starting to get a bit worried."

"But he's OK? And you've seen him today?"

"Yes. He was in having a spot of lunch earlier."

"Do you know where he is now?"

"No."

"But he was OK the last time you saw him?"

"He appeared to be happy enough."

"Are you sure?"

"Put it this way, he had company."

"Who was he with, Eugene? The dancer?" Hugo interjected.

"That's the one."

"Do you know her? Do you know anything about her?" Colin Draper asked quietly.

"Only that she's travelling with the troupe that came over from England, Colin. Seems like a nice girl to me, though. Well, Gavin certainly seems to think so."

"And you say you don't know where Gavin is now?"

"You seem very concerned about him."

"No, not really. But, as you know, we haven't seen him for a while and weren't expecting to be away for quite so long."

"So, where were you?"

"Sea cruising."

"What!"

"Yes. Colin made us."

"Very good. Anyway, I've no idea where Gavin is at present. As I say, he was in here with the girl earlier at lunchtime, but I haven't seen him all afternoon."

"Shit!"

"Is there something wrong, Hugo?"

"No, no, it's fine, Eugene," Hugo Saunders replied calmly. "There was something I wanted to tell him, that's all. I guess it'll keep."

Colin Draper dandered over to one of the bar tables and sat down. The others followed, pulled up chairs and leaned in so as to speak in hushed tones.

"Do you lads want anything to eat?" Eugene Doyle enquired heading back to the bar.

Draper shook his head.

"Right, Colin, what's the plan?"

"We'd need to phone him again. At least leave another message. The note said that our phones were left in our rooms. We'd better go and check. See if Gavin's left any messages too. We can call him from there, sure. Keys, Hugo?"

"I left mine in reception."

"Moose?"

The Moose nodded.

"Good. Me too."

Upstairs they found their phones and passports had been left on their bedside tables as stated. They reconvened in Colin Draper's room.

"Everyone got battery power? I've got twenty per cent. You two?"

The Moose shook his head.

"Yep, about the same as you," Hugo Saunders replied.

"Any messages, Hugo?"

"No. You?"

"Let's see. Yeah, loads of texts and voicemails from Saffie and my mum. And, bingo! Here we are, a text message from Gavin."

"Brilliant! What does it say?"

"*Give us a ring whenever you get this – G.*"

"Shit!"

"Here, I'll try his number, Hugo. Hang on, it's ringing. Bugger, it's gone straight to voicemail again. *Gavin, it's Colin. Call me. It's really urgent. Really urgent.*"

"Call him again!" The Moose shouted.

"Why?"

"Actually, come over here and do it!" The Moose urged from beside the bedroom door. "You come here too, Hugo."

"OK, Moose," Draper said, shuffling over and holding his phone out ahead of him.

"Right, here goes."

Colin Draper tried the number again.

"Did you hear it ringing that time?" The Moose asked.

"What, next door?"

"Yep."

"Gavin's room?"

"Yep."

The three men dashed into the hallway and knocked on the neighbouring door. There was no answer. Hugo Saunders tried the handle. The door opened a fraction but the security chain was on. Draper and Hugo glanced up at The Moose.

"Moose?"

The Moose leaned forward, put his shoulder against the door, leaned back four or five inches and then gave it a shove; it was no contest. The door popped open.

Inside the curtains were drawn making it hard to see anything clearly, but there was enough light to make out the two figures sprawled across the bed.

Draper tried the light switch.

"Shit! Who the fuck are you?" a girl's voice immediately screamed in a Yorkshire accent.

"It's OK, they're with me," Gavin replied sleepily.

Bernadette McIvor grabbed the top sheet and yanked it up to protect her modesty. They both peeked over the hem like an adulterous couple caught in flagrante; two sets of startled eyes peering over a veil of Egyptian cotton.

"Gavin! Thank Christ!"

"Afternoon, Colin."

"Glad to see you're having fun, Irish," Hugo Saunders commented drily.

"Where the fuck have you three been? I nearly got shot yesterday by that fucking mad farmer with the dead dog. I've been through hell since you all pissed off."

"Well, it doesn't look like it from here, Gavin," Draper countered.

"Are these your so-called mates, Gav?" Bernadette asked, growing irritable. "Can't you three gimps see we're busy?

Why don't you switch that light off, piss off and close that fucking door behind you?" she barked.

"Gavin, we need to talk to you. It's serious. We think you could be in danger. Extreme danger. Life-threatening danger."

"What, from moral turpitude, I suppose?" Bernadette moaned.

"Danger? Are you fucking nuts, Colin?" Gavin said wearily.

"Look, we'll talk to you downstairs."

"When?"

"You know, just as soon as, Gavin."

"Bloody hell! Give me a minute or two and I'll see you in the bar."

"Alright, in the bar then. In about ten minutes?"

"Or so!" Bernadette grunted.

The light was switched off, the door pulled shut; the room quiet once more.

"Now, where were we?" Gavin cajoled as he stretched out an arm, found Bernadette McIvor's waist and pulled her gently towards him.

"Shit, Gavin. There's no time for that now," she said, taking a peep at her watch then shifting away again.

"Why, what time are you performing tonight?"

"Ten o'clock."

"Where? Ballybofey?"

"Yeah, 'fraid so and it's nearly five now. I really *do* have to get a wiggle on. Can you give me a lift back to the guest house? It might be a day off, but the girls will kill me if I'm not there by six."

"Yep, no problem. Will I see you before we go home on Friday?"

"Maybe, maybe not. We're staying at the guest house the next two nights and then we're off to Sligo Friday afternoon. What are you doing tomorrow, Gavin?"

"We're supposed to be playing golf."

"Scintillating."

Gavin kissed her neck then started to nuzzle her earlobe in an attempt to scupper her plans.

"Stop that! I can't be late!" Bernadette shrieked, leaping from the bed and heading for the shower.

By the time Gavin and Bernadette McIvor ambled into the bar, The Moose and Hugo Saunders had changed out of their two-day-old golfing togs, showered and were already halfway through their second pint. They jumped out of their seats to greet Gavin Doyle.

"Gavin! Thank God you're alright!" Hugo shrieked.

"Hey, steady on, guys. And where's Colin?"

"Outside calling his mum and dealing with wedding stuff."

"Any news of the caravan?"

"No. Nothing I'm afraid. But fuck me, Gavin, we thought you'd been kidnapped!"

"Kidnapped?"

"Yeah. It's a long story."

Gavin sat down and signalled for Bernadette to join them. She stayed standing.

"Jesus, Gavin, you won't believe what we've been through."

"I'm sorry, Hugo, I'm dying to hear, but first I've got to run Bernadette here over to her lodgings. She's running late. Listen, I won't be long."

"Is that a good idea?"

"Why the hell not!"

"Well, be bloody careful and don't get out of the car."

"*And don't take sweets from strange men.* Come on, give us a break, Hugo!"

"Just be quick – and come straight back."

"Why? What's going on?"

"It's big. We'll tell you later. But, please, please don't be too long."

"Oh, I'm sorry, by the way, this is Bernadette. Bernadette, Hugo, The Moose … And Colin's the one outside."

"The posh one?"

"Yes, the posh one."

"Gavin, we're going to order some grub. We're starving. Feels like we haven't eaten for days. Actually, we haven't, apart from Moose's sushi. What about you?"

"I'll order something later, Hugo. I'll only be about fifteen or twenty minutes. Unless there's any sheep blocking the road, of course."

"What?"

"Oh, nothing, that's a long story too. Look, better go."

"OK, see you. But, Gavin ..."

"What?"

"Be careful. Be bloody careful. And, as I say, please come straight back, don't stop and don't get out of the car for anything or anyone. There's something fishy going on."

"Colin!"

"Mum, hi! Have you missed me?"

"No, why?"

"Oh, nothing."

"What's the weather like, Colin?"

"To be honest, Mum, I haven't had time to notice."

"You work too hard, Colin. How's Mary?"

"She's fine, thanks. Are you looking forward to Saffie's wedding, Mum?"

"Saffie's getting married?"

"Yes, Mum. You know she is. It's on her birthday."

"I don't think I know, do I? No one tells me anything."

"Well, it's on Sunday."

"This Sunday coming?"

"Yes. It's in your diary."

"Then of course I'm coming, Colin."

"Good, good."

"What's the weather like, Colin?"

"It's lovely, Mum. Lovely."

Colin Draper rang off, sighed and then spotted Gavin driving past in the Passat with the Irish dancer in the front seat beside him.

"Where the hell's he going now?" Draper asked, standing in the bar with his arms outstretched and staring wide-eyed in amazement.

"He's gone to drop the girl off, Colin."

"She's called Bernadette."

"Thank you, Moose. Yes, *Bernadette*," Hugo replied.

"Jesus! Why the hell did you let him go, Hugo? He's in danger, for fuck's sake. We've already lost Old Mr Cowie – we don't want to lose Gavin too. We don't know anything about that girl. She could be one of them, for all we know."

"Look, if he's not back within the hour, we'll go straight to the sergeant, Colin."

Since it was nearing the end of the working day, the Harbour Inn was starting to fill with regulars. The boys on tour were too preoccupied with food to take too much notice of who was and wasn't in the bar, but they all felt more self-conscious in the company of the locals than they had done previously. To make matters worse any sound or movement they made seemed to induce a mass mumbling amongst the locals behind them.

Before long, Gavin returned. He went straight to the counter and ordered a round, picked up a snack menu and rejoined the others. Colin Draper leaned forward, fixed Gavin with a stare and began in a hushed voice.

"Gavin, we have got ourselves into some really deep shit."

"What kind of shit?"

"I don't know where to start except to say we've just been at sea for two days."

"*You what?*"

"Somehow, and I don't know how, but it appears we've got ourselves caught up in the middle of a major international drug-smuggling operation."

"Congratulations! I didn't know you were into drugs."

"I'm not and this isn't funny, so please shut up and listen."

The boys hung about the Harbour Inn for the rest of the evening. They didn't dare venture out. Sergeant McIlhenny dropped by for his regular pint before home but kept out of their way. Willie McGettigan popped in too but came and went as soon as he saw that the sergeant was in residence. Draper wondered whether the farmer had come to spy on them.

"Are you not going to make a night of it, lads?" Eugene Doyle called over from behind the bar when he saw them making a move for the door.

"Not tonight, Eugene. It's been a long couple of days and we've got to play golf first thing," Colin Draper replied.

"Got to?"

"Yes. *Got to.*"

"What time are you playing?"

"About ten."

"Jeez, that's not first thing. Why don't you take yourselves off to Ballybofey and go see those dancers again? I'm sure you'd love that, Gavin."

"I'm sure he would too, Mr Doyle, but it's early nights all round for us."

"Can I tempt you to have one for the road? It's on the house."

"No. No, thanks," Colin Draper replied smiling nervously.

25

The Old Course, Ballyhanlon

"OK. This is it!" Colin Draper announced loudly on the first tee box at Ballyhanlon to attract attention, then put a finger to his lips to encourage silence.

"Remind me. Why are we playing golf here again and not Ballyliffin as planned?" Hugo Saunders whined.

"You sound tired and irritable, Hugo."

"That's because I am tired and irritable, Colin."

"Well, that's why we're playing here. We're all tired and we're all irritable and Ballyliffin's a bit too far. We've played here already. We know the course a little, and we can't play any worse than we did the last time. I thought you loved Ballyhanlon, Hugo. 'This is the real deal, the alpha and omega of all golfing experiences' isn't that how you described it on Monday?"

"No. That was Gavin. Anyway, I thought we had an itinerary and if we have one, we should keep to it."

"So far we've failed massively on that score, Hugo – ever since we left Greenwich, in fact."

"I don't know why we're even bothering to play golf."

"Where have you been, Hugo? Firstly, because we're on a bloody golf tour and secondly, and most importantly, because our hosts on the boat instructed us to. Personally, I don't fancy upsetting our drug barons before we get out of bloody Donegal and safely back to London, do you?"

"OK, OK. Let's get on with it then, shall we?"

"Right, a return match. You and me, Gavin, versus The Moose and Hugo. The first match was tied, so it's winner takes all."

"How much are we playing for, Colin?"

"The stake? How about a flat fifty quid for the match, Hugo?" Draper proposed poker-faced.

"Each?"

"Done," Draper replied, spitting on his hand and offering it to Hugo Saunders.

The Moose rolled his eyes and frowned.

"Good luck, gentleman," Draper said, addressing his ball. He took a long backswing, paused at the top and then made a slashing swipe. The ball sailed a hundred yards straight down the first fairway and was looking good until it veered off to the right as a bit of slice kicked in and, aided by a crosswind, carried the ball off into the grassy dune beyond the semi rough. The other three also failed to land a ball on the fairway.

"So, who do you think set us up, Hugo?" Colin asked as they walked down the first hole pulling a couple of hired golf trolleys behind them.

"As you said yesterday, it could be any number of people, Colin. I mean, who knew we were coming to Donegal apart from Gavin's cousin Eugene? Having said that, Eugene's got a big mouth on him. He could have quite easily tipped someone off about our trip in the bar without thinking."

"Maybe he's in financial diffs, Hugo."

"Could be. I mean, why else would he hire those sleazy dancers? And he's in the perfect location to facilitate a bit of transatlantic smuggling."

"But his bar and restaurant business seems to be thriving."

"True."

"The good news is we docked that bloody boat in Downings without getting caught by the Irish police or customs. But now I keep racking my brains to try and think if there's anything we might have left on board that would incriminate us."

"I'm pretty sure that most of my forensics went over the side, Colin."

"Yes, I noticed that, Hugo," Draper said, taking out a five wood on finding his ball sitting up nicely in the rough.

Hugo stepped back and waited for Draper to play his second shot. Draper made a good connection and drove the ball another hundred and fifty yards towards the green, landing the ball about sixty yards short. Draper paused, smiled with satisfaction and walked on.

"What worries me is that we were spotted on the boat out at sea, Colin."

"The Irish Naval Service?"

"Yes."

"Well apart from towing us off the sandbank they didn't appear to pay us too much attention in the end."

"But what about the sergeant? What about McIlhenny?"

"What about him?"

"He watched us tie up and come ashore, Colin."

"But he's only the local bobby, Hugo. He's more Clouseau than Columbo. I hardly think we need worry about him. And let's not forget, we haven't actually done anything wrong."

"You're right, Colin, we're totally innocent."

"Well, apart from smuggling Old Mr Cowie and a huge shipment of cocaine into Ireland, that is."

"Shit. Poor Old Mr Cowie. Hey, you don't think there's a link there somewhere, do you? You don't think it was our drug guys who pinched the caravan?"

"I can't see it, Hugo. I mean, nicking a caravan? It's not in the same league as international drug smuggling, is it? One's worth a few quid, the other a few million."

"I don't think I'll ever forgive myself for my part in Old Mr Cowie's passing though."

"It wasn't your fault, Hugo."

"Yeah, but that is precisely where each of us let him down. No one spoke up or took responsibility."

After a protracted search they found Hugo Saunders' golf ball lying in the semi rough, a yard off the fairway. He tried a six iron and topped the ball which then proceeded to run along the ground stopping short of a greenside bunker. A terrible shot, but a reasonable result.

Draper glanced over to the opposite side of the fairway in time to see Gavin Doyle take an air shot, missing his ball completely, and then slam his iron into the turf in frustration. The Moose looked on, a picture of patience.

After a flurry of chipping and putting, The Moose sank a twelve-foot putt to win the first hole with a creditable five.

On the next tee they all settled down to concentrate on the golf. Thereafter the standard of their play proved higher than on their previous round but was hampered by a brisk wind.

The second, a par three, was played without incident: no lost balls, no scores in double figures. The hole was won by Moose in par. It was with some nervousness that Colin Draper tackled the seventh following his run-in with the sheepdog during their previous round.

Maybe it was that they were distracted, or maybe because there was money riding on the result, or maybe because the last round had offered them a chance to practise, but there was a marked improvement in their play; an improvement that was reflected in their scoring. As the competition grew in intensity, the less they chatted and the more their concentration levels rose. The match was nip and tuck. Playing a bad shot seemed to matter more. Playing a good shot – and there were more of them – seemed to bring greater pleasure and mutual respect.

As the match neared its end, four and a half hours after they'd teed off, the rivalry intensified. Coming to the eighteenth and last hole, the match was all square. The eighteenth was a long par five that ran uphill back towards the clubhouse and a statue of Old Tom Morris which stood above the green – Old Tom staring out over the course, club in hand and frozen in perpetuity.

The Moose had the best drive. The other three, a bit wayward. He was on the green in three shots and then putted out for a par to win the hole and the match.

The Moose slowly raised his putter high above his head and, twitching muscles that had lain dormant for years, produced a modest grin which then burst into the broadest of smiles to expose a huge rack of teeth and gums. The others ran over and hugged him.

"Shit, you're not going to cry, are you, Moose?"

"Jesus, Moose, I know you're tight, but did you need the fifty quid *that* badly?" Colin Draper laughed, patting him on the back.

"Hi, Saffie. How's the wedding planning?" Colin Draper asked in a genial voice from the clubhouse car park. The others, as usual, were still fiddling about with their golf gear inside.

"Really great, Dad."

"Good, good. Now, I know it's a bit late, but have you ticked off all the one-week-to-go things on your planner?"

"Don't tell me you're carrying it around in your head?"

"Of course."

"Go on then."

"Going away outfit purchased?"

"Yep."

"Currency ordered?"

"Check."

"Hen night?"

"Yep. Done. The yacht club. Ouch!"

"Final checks with caterers and photographer?"

"Done."

"Been wearing in your wedding shoes at home?"

"Yep."

"Men's suiting booked and date circulated for collection?"

"Done."

"Relaxing massage booked for the day before?"

"Done."

"Packed your honeymoon suitcase?"

"Yep."

"Where are you going again?"

"Portugal. The Algarve."

"Lovely. OK, that's it then. A clean bill of health. You're good to go."

"Thanks, Dad, you've been brilliant."

"Aw, shucks. It's nothing."

"What about poor Old Mr Cowie?" Colin Draper asked Gavin as they were walking back to the Passat.

"Shit, Drapes. I mean, what can we do?"

"I think we need to talk through our next steps with Sergeant McIlhenny. Make sure everything that can be done is being done. You know, make sure the police are on the case, make sure he's been listed as a missing person and that the local papers have been alerted."

"It makes me feel like shit to suggest it but, if what Sergeant McIlhenny says is true, it'd probably be easier to track down Lord Lucan than Old Mr Cowie at this point."

26

Thursday, 8.30am

Thursday was not Sergeant McIlhenny's favourite day of the week. For most nine-to-fivers Thursday is the day when the weekend seems within reach and a break from the daily strife a tangible possibility. But for Sergeant McIlhenny Thursdays were the low point of his week and were dreaded.

McIlhenny's Thursdays were dedicated to filing reports and crime sheets and uploading crime statistics to head office. A dull desk-bound activity but essential, he'd been cautioned, to justify his role out in the sticks. The justification, however, required a fair amount of creative writing, massaging of figures and an embellishing of the truth. When it came to criminal activity, he needed to portray Ballyhanlon as though it had more in common with downtown Chicago than Connemara, and it was with this that he struggled.

Sergeant McIlhenny was not a natural pen-pusher. He saw himself more as a man of action, was happier patrolling his patch by car and on foot, and if not actually solving crime then at least being proactive in preventing it.

It was with a deep sigh and heavy shoulders, therefore, that he worked his bangle of keys around the various locks securing the entrance to the Garda station early on the first Thursday morning following St Patrick's Day. Once the doors were unlocked there was always a mad rush to tap in the code on the keypad in the lobby to prevent the beeping that greeted him on opening the front door from suddenly switching to a pulsating foghorn loud enough to wake the dead as the alarm tripped. He could be doing without the embarrassment this would bring as the rest of the neighbourhood would inevitably spill out onto the street to see what the hell was going on and then mock the red-faced officer.

To make matters worse, as soon as he entered the premises McIlhenny thought he could hear the landline ringing over the beeping, and once he'd typed in the alarm code – his birthdate – made a dash to pick it up.

"Yes, this is Sergeant McIlhenny. Good morning to you too, sir. How can I help? Oh ... Oh, I see. Good, good! Where? The car park at Ballybrack Beach? Tell me, is it an old one? Pretty decrepit, you say? Yep. How long? Oh, you don't know. Right, right. Never mind. And you? Right. Out with the dog. OK. What was that? Aha, the door's been left open. Dodgy. Yep, looks a bit dodgy, you say. Did you look inside? Oh, OK. No. And please don't. Yeah, I'll be down to check it right away. No, no, it's OK, you don't have to wait. Oh, and what's the make? A Lightning. Good man! Excellent. Right you be. Oh, and can I take your name, sir? Hello, hello. Hang on, you're breaking up ..."

But they were gone. McIlhenny put the receiver down slowly and firmly, straightened his back and smiled. This Thursday was starting to look up. The filing could wait.

Ballybrack Beach was about seven or eight miles up the coast from Ballyhanlon. The next cove along. It was quite a deep inlet, but not much more than a slit in the landscape and well hidden. In short, it was miles off the beaten track and not much used by anyone – tourists or locals – apart from sea anglers and courting couples. Ramblers might pass through but rarely stopped. It felt inhospitable. Like Glencoe it had an aura that suggested only bad things ever happened there.

The beach at Ballybrack was but a handkerchief of sand that appeared at low tide and was accessed from the main road by a small, dark lane: a dirt track fringed by gorse bushes; so narrow that the branches would brush up against the side of any car and have the owners worried about scratched paintwork.

The beach at Ballyhanlon Strand, on the other hand, was a large stretch of golden sand that wrapped round the coast for a couple of miles with dunes behind, ideal for picnics. Cars could drive directly onto the beach. In a popularity contest there would be little competition.

Above the beach and rocks at Ballybrack, where the cove opened out a little, there was a small grass-covered car park about the size of a tennis court, corralled by a drystone wall and home to a wooden bench, a large metal bin – a sanctuary for wasps, seldom emptied – and an abandoned telephone box that always smelt of urine.

Sergeant McIlhenny drove down to the car park, his detective's senses warning him that something was amiss. Whether it was the isolation combined with the dewy morning mist or his overactive imagination, he wasn't sure, but there was definitely something in the air that raised his hackles.

And there was the caravan just as the caller had described it. And, yes, the door was open. And, yes, it was a Lightning with a British registration plate. Now McIlhenny dreaded the possibility of coming across a corpse.

He pulled up on the far side of the grass, opposite the caravan, and wheeled his car round to face the exit in case he should need to get away in a hurry. He felt for his baton and wished he had a firearm. Firearmed is forewarned, as one of his colleagues in the Emergency Response Unit always said. Usually McIlhenny would disagree, today he wasn't so sure.

Sergeant McIlhenny had a good look round him as he eased himself out of the car, then started to think about backup. Who would come and how long would it take them to reach him? Would he be able to get into radio contact with anyone from this frigging cove deep in the rocks anyway? He wished he'd taken the precaution of leaving a note or emailing someone to let them know where he was going before he'd left the station. But then the anonymous caller would know where he'd be, if he could be traced, that is.

Good, good, that's alright then, he thought.

McIlhenny breathed deeply as he approached the vehicle. As a young officer he had never had a problem with corpses. For years he'd only ever had to deal with the dead bodies of old people who'd died at home. They usually appeared to be at peace. He'd always admired the quiet dignity they achieved in death – the calmness on their faces. But later, as local traffic increased, cars got faster and accidents became more common; the horrific scenes of teenage drivers and their passengers lying mutilated beyond recognition in crashed vehicles had turned his stomach and left him scarred with a lingering fear of death.

McIlhenny gulped when he reached the caravan's open door. He leaned in and peered around the living area. The contents were undisturbed and it was dry – the weather hadn't got to it – and it smelled clean. It certainly didn't smell of death and decay.

"Hello?" McIlhenny called out tentatively. He didn't expect a response and didn't get one.

Mr Cowie. Where the hell is Mr Cowie or what's left of him? he wondered. *Probably dumped. And, if so, he could be anywhere between here and the Ring of Kerry.*

Gaining in confidence, McIlhenny entered the van and tried the bathroom door. It wouldn't budge at first and required a bit of force, but brute force was Sergeant McIlhenny's forte. Given a thump, the door swung open easily. McIlhenny peered in, but Mr Cowie wasn't to be found there either.

Never mind, Sergeant McIlhenny thought. His life would be easier for not finding a corpse on his beat.

McIlhenny walked to the front of the caravan, hopped out onto the grass and sat down on the doorstep, pushed his cap to the back of his head and rolled a cigarette. Lighting up he pondered how – if he had found the body – he would have had to radio in for backup. Then, within hours, he would have had a swarm of detectives from Letterkenny descending on him, plus the forensics team, the pathologist and the crime-scene photographer – the works.

It could still happen if Mr Cowie's remains were to show up, but, no, he couldn't see that happening at this stage. No, now he would only have to write a crime report about the theft, inform head office that Mr Cowie was still missing and tell the golfers that the caravan had been found and help them recover it. He'd show them the way to the cove. They could follow in their estate, hook up the caravan and tow it back to Ballyhanlon. Following that he could slip back into his usual routine and still be home in time for tea. Job done.

But then he thought he heard something. Alone in the cove, whatever it was was enough to spook him. He froze. Dropped his fag. Grasped his baton. He couldn't tell what the noise was over the sound of the surf smashing onto the rocks below, but, yes, he had heard something – was convinced of it. He stood up. Felt vulnerable. Swallowed hard. Then he heard whatever it was again. It sounded like groaning. The noise was coming from the direction of the shore. He couldn't see anything, but knew he should investigate. Then, as he walked down towards the sea, he spotted a pile of clothes dumped in the undergrowth beyond the car park wall. He gasped when he saw the bundle had human form – had feet and shoes. As he neared it he could make out a man lying in the bracken rolled into a ball. Looked frail. Skin and bones. And since there had been sound, Sergeant McIlhenny presumed there must be life. He paused for a moment, checked to make sure there was no one else there, ran to the man's side and immediately felt for a pulse.

"Mr Cowie? Is that you? Can you hear me, Mr Cowie?"

"Yes, yes. I'm Mr Cowie. I'm he. But, young man, please, there's no need to shout. I'm not deaf."

"Are you alright, sir? Are you OK? I had it on reasonable authority that you were dead."

"Do I look dead to you?"

"No, but are you OK? Do you have any injuries? Are you hurt in any way?"

"No, no, I'm not. Well, I don't think so. Would you mind helping me get to my fee— Oh, I see you're a police officer, young man."

"Garda Síochána, sir. Sergeant McIlhenny. And, perhaps, not quite *so* young."

"Lovely. Could you help me get up, please?"

"Are you sure you're fit to walk, sir?"

"Of course, of course. Please, help me up, young man. I've been lying here long enough, thank you."

McIlhenny helped the old man to his feet. Mr Cowie was short, slight and as light as a feather. McIlhenny reckoned he could easily have picked him up and carried him in his arms.

"Now, how's that? Can you walk?"

"Yes, yes, I can walk," Mr Cowie said, tottering along on the sergeant's arm.

"Would you like to come back with me, find your friends and get checked out by one of our local doctors, Mr Cowie?"

"Gavin?"

"Yes, Mr Doyle and the other three."

"Yes. Yes, please, I'd like that very much, thank you ... But I don't need a doctor."

"Are you sure?"

"Absolutely positive. I'm as tough as old boots, you know."

"Alright. Come on then, we'll go and find them."

"Where are they? Where are we going?"

"Ballyhanlon. It's about ten or fifteen minutes up the road."

"Oh, yes, yes. Of course it is."

"We'll go in this, Mr Cowie," the sergeant said pointing to his car.

"But what about my caravan?"

"It'll be safe enough here. Sure, we'll shut the door, make it nice and secure and get your boys to come and pick it up in a wee while."

"So, what's been happening, Mr Cowie?" Sergeant McIlhenny asked as they sat in his squad car with its engine idling. The sergeant wasn't for moving until he'd asked a few basic questions.

"I'm not sure. It's all a bit of a blur. I remember the ferry crossing. And I remember falling asleep a lot. The next thing I remember clearly is waking up to find I'm being towed behind a transit van. A Ford I think it was. An old one. Blue. A bit of a surprise when I was expecting to see Gavin's silver estate car out in front."

"Did you get the registration number?"

"It was foreign. I know that. A European plate."

"Irish?"

"Could have been. I'm not sure."

"Oh, OK."

"Then we stopped and these three fellers jumped out of the transit and tried to get into my caravan."

"Where were you?"

"Sitting at the kitchen table of course."

"I mean, where was the van, Mr Cowie? Did you see any town names? Any clues as to your whereabouts? Do you remember seeing any landmarks?"

"No. I've no idea where I was. I could see water though."

"The sea?"

"Yes. Then they managed to get the caravan door open and saw me. And, obviously, I saw them."

"What did they look like?"

"Bloody scruffy they were. Unkempt. Yes, Mrs Cowie would have said that. Yes, unkempt's the word. I feared for my life, Mr McIlhenny."

"It's Sergeant McIlhenny."

"Then they started talking, Sergeant McIlhenny. I couldn't understand a word they were saying, but – as it turned out – they were very friendly. Nice lads they were. Except, of course, they were trying to nick my caravan."

"Then what, Mr Cowie?"

"I think they felt sorry for me. Could see I'm an old-timer. God bless them, they drove me here, parked me up and left me to it. Meanwhile, they scarpered."

"Can you describe them? Would you recognise them if you saw them again?"

"Blimey, I don't know, sergeant. They were just a bunch of young men with long hair and jeans. Looked foreign, I suppose. I don't know. My eyesight's not what it was."

"So, how did you end up down in the bushes there?"

"I was out taking a breather and slipped. Banged my loaf. I'd have been OK in a while. I'm as tough as old boots."

"We'll have to get that bump checked, Mr Cowie."

"There's no need. I'm pretty sure I'm OK."

"Even so."

"I'm fine, I tell you."

"How long have you been here, do you think?"

"A couple of days."

"And you had no way of getting in touch?"

"I have a portable telephone but then it doesn't appear to work down here, and that bloody phone box is out of order, so I couldn't call anybody on that either."

"What about walking?"

"I wasn't going to risk walking. I knew someone would come along sooner or later. I've got milk, bread and a bit of tinned grub, you know, baked beans and spaghetti hoops, and the view out to sea's lovely here. It's been really quite pleasant."

"And you didn't see anyone? No passers-by?"

"No. That was a plus point too. Nice and quiet it is here."

"Now, Mr Cowie. Your young associates, Mr Doyle, Mr Draper and so on, they seem to think you're dead. Now, why would that be?"

"So, you've met them then?"

"Yes, of course. They came to the station to tell me that you'd passed away – to report your death."

"Well, what do you think of them?"

"They're nice enough boys, Mr Cowie."

"Thick as two short planks, eh, sergeant? I'd probably passed out, that's all. I imagine they were being a tad overdramatic." Old Mr Cowie continued in a hushed voice: "I'm afraid they wouldn't know their arses from their elbows."

"I couldn't possibly comment."

"Say no more, sergeant," Old Mr Cowie said, tapping the side of his nose and winking.

"One final question. How old are you?"

"That's very personal."

"The boys said you were in your early eighties."

"There you go, you see. Thick as two short planks. I'll tell you this much. I went into the submarines in 1943. I was seventeen. We were operating somewhere out there actually," Mr Cowie said, waving an arm towards the North Atlantic. "You work the rest out for yourself. Early eighties, my arse."

"OK, Mr Cowie. Shall we get you back to civilisation?"

"Do we have to?"

"Yes, I think we should."

"Really?"

"Yes, Mr Cowie."

"Sergeant, do you think I'm in any danger here?"

"No. I wouldn't have thought so."

"So, why don't you leave me here whilst you fetch my boys?"

"If you're sure, I suppose I could go and round up your lads whilst you stay here. It's only ten minutes up the road."

"In that case, yes, I'd rather wait here. I like the peace and quiet. I think I'll stay and enjoy it here for a bit longer while I can."

"I think your lads are in for a bit of a shock when they see you though, Mr Cowie."

"Let's hope so, eh? Tell you what, please don't tell them I'm here. I'd love to make them jump when they get here. It would serve them bloody well right."

27

Thursday, 4pm

Shafts of sunlight were flooding through the arched windows of the Harbour Inn. Dust swirled in a fine mist, visible where caught in the beams. The only other movement the lazy rhythm of the drinkers' arms as they took an occasional sip of stout, eking out the dregs to fill an hour or so before home.

When the boys on tour arrived back from the golf course, they caught Sergeant McIlhenny snuggling up to a sly glass of Guinness at the counter whilst deep in conversation with Eugene Doyle. The sergeant glanced up and smiled when he saw them, then downed the last inch of his stout in one gulp.

"Ah, gentlemen, I've been waiting for you. I was wondering if you'd care to accompany me to Ballybrack. I've found something that I think might be of interest to you," he said, assuming a superior tone, straightening his jacket and raising an eyebrow as he stood upright.

"Ballybrack?" Colin Draper queried.

"It's a cove a few miles up the road," Gavin Doyle replied.

"I think it's best if you tag along behind me in your own car this time."

"What exactly is the *something*?"

"You'll see when we get there," the sergeant replied, donning his cap and turning to walk out the door.

The boys stared at one another quizzically and, without further comment, started to follow. Halfway to the door Colin Draper coughed to catch Sergeant McIlhenny's attention.

"Is this anything for us to be concerned about?"

The sergeant ignored him.

"Do I need to call my lawyer?" Draper murmured with a hint of sarcasm.

"That'd be a waste of time in your case, Colin. Yours only does divorces," Hugo Saunders whispered.

"I'm sorry, Sergeant McIlhenny, but why are we going to Ballybrack?" Gavin enquired politely.

"You'll see soon enough," the sergeant replied sternly.

Stepping outside into the bright sunshine induced a mass squinting.

"Come on, this way. Keep up!" Sergeant McIlhenny bellowed before easing himself into his car and slamming the door.

"Any ideas?" Colin Draper asked the others. Hugo frowned, Gavin Doyle shrugged and The Moose blinked two or three times and continued to look blank.

"He's found the caravan, Drapes."

"How do you know that, Moose?"

"Because it's bloody obvious."

The boys scrambled into the Passat and sped off to catch up with Sergeant McIlhenny who was waiting for them on the main road out of Ballyhanlon.

When he was sure they were following, Sergeant McIlhenny drove north along the coast, the road rising and dipping across the headland. The boys trailed after the sergeant in silence.

They'd been driving for no more than ten minutes when they came upon the battered brown road sign for Ballybrack Beach. Gavin, who was at the wheel as usual, kept a discreet distance as the sergeant slowed and steered off the coast road to tackle the overgrown lane.

Having rattled down through the tunnel of prickly vegetation and survived its many potholes, they came upon the cove, the road opening up to offer a panoramic view of the sea, the grassy car park in the foreground and Old Mr Cowie's caravan.

The four men in the Passat gasped and exchanged wide-eyed stares.

"Christ Almighty!" Gavin Doyle screamed as they drove into the car park. He flung the driver's door open, stepped out and was about to make a dash for the caravan when he thought twice, paused and peered over to Sergeant McIlhenny who was already halfway across the grass.

"Mr Doyle, please wait a moment," McIlhenny urged, panting.

Gavin stopped and turned.

"Mr Doyle ... Gavin, I think we need to have a quiet word," the sergeant cautioned, walking over and placing a hand on Gavin's shoulder.

Sergeant McIlhenny leaned over and whispered something into Gavin's ear which caused him to sink to his knees and raise his hands to his head as though it had doubled in weight.

There was a moment or two of quiet before Gavin leapt up, sprinted the rest of the short distance to the caravan, grabbed at the door – yanking as hard as he could – and squeezed in.

Colin Draper, Hugo Saunders and The Moose looked over to the sergeant who smiled back and nodded for them to follow.

"Mr Cowie!" Colin Draper exclaimed the moment he caught sight of the old man sitting in the shadows. "But ... but ..."

Gavin was hugging the old man seemingly incapable of speech and with tears filling his eyes.

"How, how—"

"Sit down, Colin," Old Mr Cowie said with a calm authority. "You too Moose and you Hugo."

They joined the old man and Gavin at the table, squashing up on the banquette as if grouping together for a selfie.

"Whatever happened to you, Mr Cowie?"

"I guess you might say I was stolen, Hugo," Old Mr Cowie said, speaking softly. "Me and the caravan both."

"Yes, yes, we know, but what happened to you in Dublin when we got off the ferry? We thought you were dead. When we reached Dublin, you *were* dead. Really dead. In fact, very dead indeed."

"Well – and no thanks to you lot – I'm not. As you can see, I'm very much alive."

"But you were. You were *dead*!" Gavin Doyle exclaimed. "I saw it with my own eyes."

"Never mind that. Let's just be grateful he's here now and still in one piece."

"Thank you, Colin," Old Mr Cowie said with a benign smile.

"So, what's been happening since we last saw you, Mr Cowie? Did anyone try and hurt you?" Colin Draper asked.

"No, no. Nothing like that. As I said, the van and I were stolen. That's all."

"Who by?"

"A bunch of lads."

"Lads?"

"Yes! Young lads with curly hair."

"From where? From round here? Locals?"

"No idea, Colin. They spoke English – not that I could understand half of what they were saying – not that that amounted to any more than a few words. But they were very nice about the whole thing."

"And at what point did you come round?"

"When I was getting towed away."

"Being stolen, you mean?"

"Yes, and they were going like the clappers. Their driving was worse than yours, Gavin!"

"Why didn't you call me on your mobile?"

"Och, you know how it is, Gavin, I can't stand the bloody thing. If the battery's not flat, then I can't get service. In fact, I don't really use it. Rarely charge it. Hate it."

"And what about you? We really did think you'd kicked the bucket. I mean, has this happened to you before?" Hugo asked calmly.

"What, the passing out? Yes, maybe once before."

"Have you seen anybody about it?"

"Yes, Hugo. Apparently I suffer from catalepsy."

"Cata-what?"

"It's to do with a glitch in the nervous system, Hugo."

"Oh, thank you, Dr Colin."

"It's something that can affect people suffering from Parkinson's," Colin continued.

"And you suffer from ...?"

"I suffer from the early onset of Parkinson's, Hugo."

"So, how come you appeared dead, Mr Cowie? I mean, we were sure that you were dead."

"Because of the symptoms."

"Symptoms of catalepsy?"

"Yes, Hugo."

"Which are?"

"Rigid limbs and muscles, slowing down of breathing and heart rate."

"Does that actually happen?"

"Yes, Colin, it happens. It happened to me. There was a case once where a person suffering from catalepsy woke up in the morgue."

"No!"

"Yes."

"And are you OK?"

"Apart from the slight bang on the head I got earlier, yes, I'm fine. It's passed. And I have my medication."

"Why didn't you say anything before we left London?"

"Because I didn't think you'd bring me with you, Gavin. And in my condition I don't like being left on my own for very long. But sure, you know now."

"Mr Cowie, you gave us one hell of a fright. We thought we'd killed you."

"What can I say, Colin? I'm sorry, but I guess I'm not as fit as I once was. Anyway, how was the golf?"

"What? Golf! Mr Cowie, who cares about the bloody golf?"

"It was very enjoyable, thank you, Mr Cowie," Hugo Saunders replied calmly.

"Gentlemen, I'm sorry to break up the party, but I'm afraid I've got other matters to attend to," Sergeant McIlhenny announced at the door. "Right, now, lads, can I trust you to escort Mr Cowie safely back to civilisation? Well, at least to Ballyhanlon? It strikes me that you've done a pretty average job of taking care of him so far on your holiday. Can I take it that you're capable of hitching up the caravan and towing it back to the Harbour Inn in one piece?"

"No problem, sergeant," the boys replied in an upbeat tone that implied success was a given.

The drive to Ballyhanlon was far from straightforward, however. No sooner had they hitched up the caravan and got the Passat started than its wheels started to slip and spin on the grass. Colin Draper and The Moose had to jump out and push until the estate got some traction. But even when they'd got the car and caravan rolling, the Passat struggled to climb the narrow lane with the extra weight of the caravan on the back and its sides scraping against the hedgerows. It was a bumpy ride up a steep incline made worse by the stench filtering into the car as the clutch started to burn. It was also cramped in the estate as they'd thought better of letting Old Mr Cowie ride in the caravan.

The journey got easier once they reached the top of the lane and turned onto the coast road. And as the drive went smoothly on the short run into Ballyhanlon, a mood of renewed optimism spread through the group; a sense that maybe the worst was over. However, Colin Draper still couldn't shake off the feeling that there might be dark forces watching their every move.

Within ten minutes of leaving the lane they were approaching the outskirts of Ballyhanlon with the Harbour Inn in view. And no sooner had Gavin Doyle given a loud cheer in celebration than the car swerved and then stopped abruptly with the caravan listing to one side at a precarious angle.

Gavin peeped into the rear-view mirror just in time to see one of the caravan's cream wheels weaving down the road and wobbling away into the distance.

"Shit! She's lost a wheel!" he bellowed.

The others looked round.

"Fuck this fucking golf tour!"

"It's OK, Drapes. Calm down. It's probably going to be easy enough to fix."

"Yeah, right, Gavin. Easy. Really bloody easy."

By the time Sergeant McIlhenny spotted the boys and their broken-down caravan, the five of them had been standing around for a good ten minutes staring hopelessly at the offside of the Lightning and taking it in turns to inspect the axle and then offer a diagnosis. But none of them could agree on why the wheel had fallen off or what was wrong with the axle and what to do about fixing it. No one came up with a practical solution until, that is, Old Mr Cowie nudged Colin Draper and nodded towards the chrome AA badge on the front – a 1960's edition. Colin Draper took a peek and then nodded back.

"Mr Cowie, is that badge part of the retro look or are you actually an AA member?"

"Been a member man and boy, Colin. Since I first owned a car, in fact. An Austin-Healey. A lovely little motor she was—"

"Good. I'll call them then."

Colin Draper stepped away and started tapping at his phone.

"I'm afraid you can't leave the caravan there, gentlemen," Sergeant McIlhenny bellowed as he quick marched across the road towards them from the Garda station.

"We kind of assumed that, sergeant."

"So, could you reattach the wheel and tow it up to the car park please, boys."

"It's the axle, sergeant."

"What about it, Mr Doyle?"

"We think it's banjaxed."

"And I suppose you can't fix it yourselves?"

"No, 'fraid not. It'll probably need replaced or welded or something and that's way beyond our capabilities."

"Can't you get it fixed at a garage?"

"Possibly. But then we've got to catch a ferry tomorrow, sergeant."

"I hope you're not thinking of dumping it here, gentlemen."

"Scrap the caravan? Good God, no! That would break Old Mr Cowie's heart."

"I've called the AA. Mr Cowie's covered," Colin Draper interjected.

"In Ireland?"

"Yes. Something to do with a reciprocal arrangement. They're getting back to me, but I think they're going to put her on a flatbed."

"Right. Any idea when, Mr Draper?"

"That's what I'm waiting to hear, Sergeant McIlhenny. But, subject to confirmation, they seem to think tomorrow should be OK. Probably be in the morning before lunch."

"Good."

"Since we can't move her, will she be OK here overnight, sergeant?"

"Overnight? Here? I don't think we've got much choice, do we? I'll get the cones out," Sergeant McIlhenny said with a heavy sigh before wandering over to the Garda station to dig out whatever accident paraphernalia he had in his store.

"Pint, Mr Cowie?" Colin Draper asked the old man with a smile.

"Don't mind if I do, Colin," Mr Cowie replied.

28

Thursday, 8pm

Margaret McIlhenny wasn't a big fan of Daniel O'Donnell. This, she knew, set her apart from many of the middle-aged women of Ireland. There was something about the Irish country singer that made her want to give him a good shake.

"I'd love to see that one running with the bulls of Pamplona, so I would. That would soon sort him out. Could be the making of him," she said as Daniel softly crooned a ballad to a bewitched studio audience. He was the guest star on an RTÉ country-music television special.

It surprised Margaret McIlhenny that there was no response from her spouse sat at the other end of the sofa. Her catty remarks usually irked her Seamus who never had a bad word to say about anybody except for hardened criminals, sex offenders, paedophiles and wife beaters. He would normally counter her malevolence with a mild and uncontroversial observation: "Come now, Margaret, wee Daniel's not a bad lad, and he's got a lovely singing voice. Sure, he dotes on his mother, and his Majella's a saint," being the kind of comment she might expect from him, but tonight he wasn't taking the bait. She wasn't sure if he'd even heard her.

"That Daniel's a bit of a plonker, don't you think, Seamus?" she asked, giving it another shot.

But nothing. No reply. Not even a little rapid eye movement.

"Seamus! Daniel O'Donnell. Complete tit or what?"

"Mmm. Yes, Margaret."

Margaret thought she'd give up on conversation altogether and fetch the papers from the kitchen. On walking past she paused and ran her fingers through her husband's hair.

"Seamus, are you OK? You're very quiet."

"What? Err, yeah. No, no, I'm fine. Yes, sorry, Margaret, I'm fine," he finally answered as he arrived back in her orbit.

"Something troubling you at work, love?"

"Yeah. I can't really talk about it though, Margaret. You know how it is."

"Of course."

"But it's those British boys."

"What about them?"

"I think there's something fishy going on. I can't put my finger on it. But there's something fishy."

"Fishy?"

"Yeah. There's something about their story that doesn't quite ring true. Either that or they're very unlucky or just plain stupid or ..."

"Or what?"

"I don't know. Tell you what, I think I might pop out and make sure their caravan's OK."

"The one keeled over in the road?"

"Yes. Don't worry, I won't be long. Will you be OK for a minute or two?"

"Me?"

"Yes, you, sweetheart," he replied, giving her shoulder an affectionate squeeze as he got out of his chair.

"Course I'll be OK, I've got Daniel to keep me company."

"What? Oh, oh, right ... Daniel."

Sergeant McIlhenny tutted and pulled on his cap.

As he strolled down to where the caravan had been abandoned at the side of the street, McIlhenny searched his pockets for his rolling tobacco and cigarette papers. It was a calm night, warm and balmy, the air heavy with the salty smells of the ocean.

A faint sound of traditional music was drifting down the high street from the Harbour Inn, increasing in volume as he strode towards the caravan. As the bar came into view it was hard to resist the lure of the warm yellow glow in the windows and the tantalising promise of a pint of the black stuff.

He lit up a rollie.

The music would be a useful diversion and mask any sound he might make, Sergeant McIlhenny thought as he neared the caravan, not wanting company or attention.

"What time do the AA reckon they'll be here tomorrow, Drapes?" Gavin Doyle asked. He had to lean over and shout to be heard. Old Mr Cowie was sitting with them, oblivious to their conversation.

All of the boys were downing pints of Guinness in the saloon of the Harbour Inn and enjoying the music. Colin Draper and Gavin Doyle were drumming their hands on the table in between gulps, and forcefully enough to make their collection of empty glasses wobble, jump and clatter. Old Mr Cowie watched the glasses with a wary eye, twitching at every clink.

"What?"

"What time will they be here tomorrow?"

"The AA? They said around eleven or twelve. Twelve at the very latest. What time's our ferry, Gavin?" Draper shouted over the din.

"Five fifteen. If we miss that one, there's one at eight."

"So we'll be fine then," Colin Draper concluded as the current jig drew to a close.

"Don't you worry, Colin. We'll get you back in time for Saffie's wedding," Hugo hollered just as there was a pause in the music.

"You making a speech, Drapes?"

"Doesn't he always, Hugo?" Gavin interjected.

"I'm father of the bride. I have to."

"Saints preserve us!"

"Oh, thanks very much, Hugo, but I'm sure it'll be a lot easier to follow than one of your sermons," Colin Draper countered, smiling and then sinking his lips into a fresh pint.

"They were always much appreciated by the insomniacs in our parish," Hugo added with a smile.

"Hey, you don't think you should report the yacht business to the authorities before we set off? You don't think we should tell Sergeant McIlhenny about the drugs?" Gavin whispered into Draper's ear.

"Look, the instructions were quite clear: to play golf and then leave tomorrow as planned. We don't know anybody here well enough to trust them with this and, on that basis, I'm certainly not going to open up to Sergeant McIlhenny. I mean, would you, Gavin? Really? It was one thing going to him about Old Mr Cowie dying on us, but this is something completely different."

"Actually, I agree with you, Drapes. I know it sounds selfish, but I think we should just get the hell out of here, and as soon as."

"Exactly, Gavin. Especially since they said that if we don't fully comply with their instructions, *you* could be in danger."

"Yeah. Well, I'm here and I'm fine and I want to keep it that way."

"I won't feel comfortable till we're on that friggin' ferry tomorrow afternoon."

"Yeah, I think the safest option now is to stay in the bar here tonight and head off as early as we can tomorrow. There's no point in wandering off somewhere and getting into any more trouble."

"Have you've noticed anybody watching you or following you around over the last couple of days, Gavin? Anything or anyone suspicious?"

"No. Not really."

"What about the farmer?"

"He's just a farmer. A bad-tempered farmer, but just a farmer."

"McIlhenny?"

"He seems OK. I think he has his suspicions about us, but then that's what he's paid to do."

"What about your dancer friend?"

"Bernadette?"

"Yes, her."

"Why don't you ask her yourself? Here she comes."

The rest of the evening was spent in the confines of the bar and with drink taken there was also a little dancing. Bernadette McIvor gave the tourists a beginner's lesson in Irish dancing and soon had the boys staggering through a four-hand reel. It was not a pretty sight.

Having struggled through a couple of set dances, Colin Draper stepped outside to use his iPhone.

"Hi, Saffie, it's only me. How's it going?"

"Yep, all good, Dad."

"Are you excited?"

"Of course."

"Me too."

"Why are you panting, Dad?"

"Oh, I've been doing some aerobic exercise."

"What? You?"

"Why not?"

"Where are you, Dad? I don't know why you bother with your landline, you're never there when I call."

"I've been popping in and out. Got a lot on, Saffie."

"When are you arriving here?"

"I'm aiming for tomorrow, late evening."

"Jesus, Dad! You're cutting it fine."

"Don't you worry, Saffie."

"I'm sorry but I am worried. It's what brides do."

"What about your mum?"

"She's back."

"Good. That'll keep you on your toes then."

"Oh, stop it!"

"No, it's good that she's going to be around to help you. I'd only get in the way. Sure, it'll be lovely to see her at the wedding."

"Yeah, right."

"OK, I've got to go, Saffie. Take care and call me if you need anything. Anything. And if I don't speak to you before, I'll see you tomorrow evening."

Outside in the dark, Sergeant McIlhenny was on his hands and knees bending under the caravan to inspect the axle and chassis by the light of his police torch. The pencil beam could find little that made sense through the congealed stew of mud and rust caking the underside, but the axle was twisted alright, although he couldn't work out whether that was the cause of the wheel falling off or as a consequence of it.

The sergeant sat down on the tarmac, rolled onto his side and then wriggled his way underneath the side of the van to get a closer look. He poked about with a bit of stick, prodding here and there, whilst trying to dodge the flakes of dust and dirt dislodged falling about him. He jabbed at the wheel hub to test the bearing and see if there was much lateral play but jabbed a little too hard causing the stick to slip and pierce a hole through the underside of the floor and across into the side panelling. Sergeant McIlhenny blinked as he was immediately showered in a fine plume of powder that began to drain through the hole and pour onto his face.

Fucking asbestos! he thought, wriggling back out into the open air, springing to his feet, shaking his head and flapping his handkerchief to brush off any residual dust.

He'd leave the caravan well alone now. There wasn't an investigation he would follow if it meant coming into contact with asbestos. He might smoke the odd fag, but he wouldn't willingly expose his lungs to asbestos dust. He loved his job, but not even *he* was that dedicated. Fuck the caravan! He'd complete his lap of the town and then go home to Margaret, even if it meant further exposure to Daniel O'Donnell.

On passing the Harbour Inn, he peeped in through the window and watched as the four British golfers hopped round the room in a ragged formation that suggested that they might be attempting to perform some kind of traditional Irish dance. Even Mr Cowie seemed to be giving it a go.

Sergeant McIlhenny raised his eyebrows, tutted and walked on.

29

Friday, 9.30am

"For fuck's sake, Benny!" Maureen O'Hara cursed as she steered her yellow flatbed round the winding wastes north-west of Letterkenny. But no one was listening; no one could hear. Her enjoyment of the drive across the vast and desolate moors of west Donegal was being compromised by the sprawl of empty fag packets, drink cartons and takeaway boxes left scattered across the dashboard by her colleague, Benny McCreary. These were now sliding back and forth and spilling onto the floor every time Maureen negotiated a bend.

Maureen was scrupulously tidy – a legacy of her three years of army service – however, Benny McCreary, with whom she shared the use of the AA Ireland flatbed, was a waste disposal disaster. And he smoked. And even though he smoked outside the cab and never actually in it (on pain of disciplinary action), a nicotine fug seemed to follow him everywhere and settled on everything he came into contact with.

Thus Maureen O'Hara was charging along the high road over the moorlands with the windows wound down and the fresh morning air billowing through her hair in order to shift Benny McCreary's stench. OK, it was spring but, still, it wasn't the warmest of mornings.

Maureen was to be in Ballyhanlon by noon. She reckoned she'd be there by half ten.

Her first call-out of the day, a flat battery up the coast in Burtonport, had been abortive. Whoever had called the AA from the small catering business there had already got their van started and away by the time she'd arrived. They'd needed to, since they required their van to be available for deliveries at all times.

The office manager was embarrassed then when Maureen arrived at the industrial unit to find the problem had already been solved. This scenario always made Maureen laugh – that AA members thought she might give a damn about false alarms, that she might object to the free time created or that the next customer would be overjoyed when she arrived earlier than expected. Often it was easier to manage the public's expectations than cope with Benny McCreary's sloppiness.

However, apart from Benny's crap veering across the dashboard, it was a beautiful morning with a blue sky and the promise of a sunny day. The air wafting through the cab was fragrant and dewy and she had a panoramic view across the peaty glens towards Mount Errigal in the distance. Then Maureen spotted a sign for a lay-by. She reduced speed, drove in and pulled up beside a large black dumpster. Benny's crap was binned. Gone. Oh, the relief!

Maureen liked the sound of her next assignment. It involved a long drive to Ballyhanlon – a quiet town with attractive scenery on the way – a pickup, then on to one of the ferry terminals at Dublin Port, back to base in Sligo and then home. The travel time indicated that today looked like becoming a one-job day: straightforward and simple, though she wouldn't relax until she had the caravan safely secured on the flatbed.

From the information she'd been given the caravan was an old model, ancient some would say, and when winching it on to the back of the flatbed there was no guarantee that it would survive the procedure in one piece. She'd give it her best shot though. It was nothing she hadn't handled before in her ten years with the AA.

Colin Draper, Hugo Saunders and The Moose were up early, breakfasted and packing their gear into the boot of the Passat by the time the AA lorry arrived. They would all be pretty much ready to leave for Dublin just as soon as the caravan was loaded, not wanting a repeat of the panic they'd had on the previous Sunday. The only worry was Gavin, who was yet to show his face.

"Morning, gentlemen!" Maureen O'Hara beamed through the cab window as she pulled up next to the Passat in the car park. "Maureen O'Hara. Now which one of you gentlemen is Mr Cowie?" she asked theatrically as she swung the cab door open. Maureen enjoyed an audience.

She bounced down onto the tarmac brandishing a clipboard and extending a hand towards one of the four men, the one who seemed most likely to be in charge. The Moose took her hand, shook it gently and turned to Colin Draper for support.

"Err, Colin Draper. Thanks for coming to help us, Maureen. Here's Mr Cowie," Colin Draper said, ushering Old Mr Cowie forward.

"Mr Cowie, we'll get you loaded and on your way as soon as we've done a little paperwork."

"Maureen O'Hara. That's a fine name," the Reverend Hugo Saunders interjected whilst Maureen got Old Mr Cowie to sign a form.

"Thank you," she mumbled.

"And you've got the flaming red hair to go with it. Fine looking woman, Maureen O'Hara."

No one smiled. Maureen paused, glanced up, glowered and then waited for the usual boorish references to John Wayne and *The Quiet Man*.

No one dared speak.

"Right, let's get your caravan loaded, shall we?" Maureen said, seizing back the clipboard, spinning round on her heels and marching off to find the caravan.

"Sorry about my friend there, Maureen. He can be pretty witless at times for a man of the cloth," Colin Draper said as he followed in her path struggling to keep up.

"It's OK, Mr ... Mr?"

"Draper, Colin Draper."

"I come across all sorts in this job, I can assure you."

"All the same—"

"Don't worry, Mr Draper, I'm used to it. I'm afraid some of the older male drivers tend to pigeonhole me. Obviously not everybody is used to, or comfortable with, getting roadside assistance from a woman. I simply ignore them and pigeonhole them right back. I'll leave you to guess as what."

"In any case, thanks for coming all this way."

"Well, we don't want to miss that ferry, do we?"

"Look, can I get you a cup of tea or something?"

"No need, I've got my own flask, thanks," Maureen O'Hara replied, striding towards the caravan and leaving Colin Draper dawdling in her wake.

When Draper peered back towards the pub car park he caught a glimpse of the others peeking round the corner of the Harbour Inn like naughty school children. He failed, however, to notice the curtains twitching in the bedroom window above.

"What's so interesting out there, Gavin, that's keeping you from this lovely warm bed?" Bernadette McIvor purred from her pillow whilst stroking the top of the duvet.

"Shit! I'm sorry but I've really got to get my act together," Gavin Doyle said turning away from the window.

"What's up?"

"The AA's here. We'll be heading off as soon as they've loaded the caravan," he replied, bending down to hook his boxers on over one foot then the other with all the poise of a punch-drunk boxer. He overbalanced and toppled backwards across the bed.

"Jesus! I didn't think you were leaving till lunchtime."

"I'm sorry, Bernadette. They must have got here early or something," Gavin cooed cupping her face in both hands so as to give her an affectionate peck.

215

"So, you're buggering off then?" she said, jerking away from his clutches. "Well, fine. Just as long as you drop me off at the guest house when you're passing. I don't want to be stuck in this bloody place any longer than I have to," she snarled whilst sitting up and jerking the duvet over her bare shoulders.

By the time Maureen O'Hara had inspected the caravan and fetched her truck round from the car park, Sergeant McIlhenny had emerged from behind his desk in the Garda station. The sergeant was still wiping away the residue of his last cup of coffee with one hand whilst buttoning the top button of his tunic with the other as he bustled across the street.

Maureen was manoeuvring the truck with well-practised precision. Colin Draper was guiding her in, helping her to reverse up as close as possible to the front of the caravan.

"Whoa! OK, that's enough!" he yelled stepping forward and brandishing both palms above his head as if surrendering to enemy forces.

Parked and with the engine idling, Maureen trotted round to the rear of her rig to attach the winch to the caravan performing the whole operation as though competing in a time trial.

"Anything I can do to help?" Sergeant McIlhenny called over as he approached.

"No, I'm getting along fine, thank you, sergeant. I guess there won't be much traffic coming through this way whilst I'm fiddling about here, will there?"

"No. Nothing much happens at this time of day. But I'd keep your hazards flashing," he replied, nodding towards the lights on top of her cab.

"Will do."

"Oh look, here comes trouble," Sergeant McIlhenny added as the Passat rolled round the corner at the speed of a hearse.

Gavin Doyle pulled up a good fifty yards behind the caravan and waited, engine running. He switched off the motor when he saw Maureen O'Hara approaching and lowered his window. She leant in.

"OK, I want to jack up the caravan and see if I can reattach the wheel before I start to winch her on. Do you have the wheel?"

"We left it inside the caravan," Gavin replied.

"Is there anything more I can do to help?" Colin Draper asked, trailing around after Maureen.

"Not really, sir. But please make sure you're ready to hit the road whenever we've got her loaded."

"No problem."

"And please stay close once we're underway, I won't be going too fast," she said, turning to Gavin. "Try and stay behind me the whole way to Dublin if you can, please."

Gavin nodded.

"Actually, Maureen, our car's going to be a bit cramped. Any chance you could take our elderly friend here and possibly one other with you?" Colin Draper asked politely.

"Absolutely. There's plenty of room in the cab. I'd be glad of the company. I presume neither of them smoke?"

"No, no. Of course not."

"Good. Right, let's get this show on the road."

Within half an hour the caravan was loaded, strapped down and ready to go.

"Be sure to come and visit us next year, lads, won't you?" Eugene Doyle called over from the front door of the pub when he realised they were about to set off. The boys strolled across the road to say their goodbyes.

"Go on now. Make sure you head straight down to Dublin. And don't be frigging about on the way. I wouldn't want you to miss your ferry," he added with a final flash of his teeth and some hefty backslapping.

Before climbing into her cab Maureen ensured everybody was where they should be. Gavin helped Old Mr Cowie up into the front of the truck beside The Moose, before running back to drive the Passat.

Maureen started up the flatbed and idled the engine as McIlhenny slid his line of traffic cones out of her path. As the small convoy rolled passed, the sergeant offered a fixed grin and a nod to anyone whose eyes he met, trying to suppress any facial expression that might reveal the relief he felt that they were finally leaving Ballyhanlon. He watched as they headed inland, glad to see them gone.

Colin Draper gazed out of his passenger window. He had to wipe condensation off with his sleeve to better see the hedgerows as they passed by in a blur. Before they'd driven much further he glanced over his shoulder and watched the town shrinking from view, the Garda sergeant still standing in the road to follow their progress.

As they were nearing McGettigan's farm, Colin Draper looked round again just in time to catch a glimpse of the surviving sheepdog dart into the road ahead and chase the tyres of the flatbed for fifty yards or so. Maureen didn't slow down or waiver. As they approached the farm buildings, Draper caught sight of McGettigan standing at the roadside, stock-still and staring as they passed. Draper shuddered a little when he caught the farmer's eye and clocked his sinister smile.

Sergeant McIlhenny watched the Passat Estate until it was but a small speck in the distance, and then, when it had disappeared altogether, turned his attention to the area on the high street where the caravan had been sitting overnight and the debris left behind. As he surveyed the mess with his hands on his hips, sighing and wondering whether he could be bothered to fetch a broom from the office, he noticed the remnants of the pale powder that had fallen on him the previous night. The pile had congealed into a small pancake in the early morning dew. It was off-white and easily spotted amidst the flecks of rust and mud.

The sergeant stepped a little nearer and, bending down, reached into his left chest pocket to retrieve his reading glasses.

The powder – that at night he had thought to be asbestos – now appeared to have a paleness that he thought at odds with his previous identification. Confident he had been mistaken, he licked a finger, dabbed it onto the pat, raised it when he was satisfied he had harvested enough and held it up to the light. Reluctant, and with great care, he touched his fingertip lightly onto the end of his tongue, closed his eyes and braced himself to make a quick analysis of whatever it tasted of, but all the while knowing what to expect.

30

Friday, 12.30pm

"I guess this is it, then," Gavin Doyle muttered to Bernadette as they were getting out of the car opposite her accommodation in Carrigart. She gave him a quick peck on the cheek and started to walk off.

"Bernadette!"

"What?"

"I guess ... I guess ..."

"What?"

"Oh, nothing."

Bernadette shrugged, continued on a step or two then spun round, a frown crossing her brow.

"What the hell is it, Gavin? What do you want?"

"It's ... it's ..."

"Listen, I've got your number. If I need you, I'll call," she said, then turned away and headed off at a brisk pace without looking back.

When they left Ballyhanlon the weather had been summer-like, but by the time the convoy reached Carrigart the wind was gusting and a bank of grey cloud was moving in. Shortly after, the heavens opened. Rain. A persistent downpour that looked like it could be settling in for the rest of the day.

"Och, well, lads. It's not as if we were going sightseeing. Sure, if we can keep to a steady pace, we'll be in Dublin in no time," Maureen O'Hara enthused.

No answer.

She could have done with a little banter to enliven her day, but her travelling companions, Old Mr Cowie and The Moose, weren't the chatty types she'd hoped for. In fact they both seemed quite sullen if not a little tetchy. So while she couldn't resist making a comment every now and then, she didn't hold out much hope of being entertained with lively conversation any time soon.

The others following in the Passat didn't have much to say either. The strains of the golf tour were starting to tell. Colin Draper was rummaging around in the glove compartment for some music to play and found a couple of CDs that they hadn't already heard. One: another from Gavin's collection of eighties hits, the other: a recording of Mozart's Requiem Mass.

It was in sombre mood, therefore, that they progressed through the rainstorm with the Mozart at full volume.

"Gavin ... How long do you think till we get there?"

"Jesus Christ, Hugo! I hope you're not going to start asking me that every ten minutes, are you?"

"I was only asking."

"You're like a frigging child. You're worse than a kid."

"Sorry."

"OK, just this once, and just this once, mind. We're about an hour from Strabane and that's roughly three hours from Dublin give or take a puncture, mechanical breakdown, traffic jam or a motorway pile-up."

"So, we're early?" Colin Draper asked

"On time, Drapes. We're on time."

"Did you get a chance to add Old Mr Cowie's details onto the booking for the return crossing?"

"Of course."

"And mine?"

"Naturally."

"Good. Here's Fran's passport then."

"Cheers."

"And you're sure you changed the booking?"

"Relax, Colin. It's done, OK? All you have to do is sit back and enjoy the music."

"Yey! The Mozart Requiem! Party time! Tell you what, why don't we have a singalong?"

"Look Colin, if you want some entertainment, why don't you phone your mum? Must be at least ten minutes since you last spoke to her. Actually, don't bother. Just sit there and shut the fuck up and listen to the effing CD."

"Culture, Gavin? I didn't know you did culture."

"As I say, shut up and listen."

And so they drove on through the cloudburst, the opening chorus demanding – and finally receiving – the attention, respect and decorum Gavin Doyle thought it merited.

Meanwhile Hugo Saunders hummed along in the back.

The rest of the drive to Dublin was pretty uneventful. Dour, but uneventful. Hugo Saunders and Colin Draper slept fitfully for most of the journey south: their heads lolling from side to side and then flopping forward to startle them awake again.

Gavin Doyle enjoyed the peace and quiet this brought him. When they were thirty or so miles from Dublin and he thought his travelling companions were showing signs of stirring, he switched on the fan and fired hot air through the car at full blast in an attempt to stupefy them back to sleep.

An hour from Dublin and Maureen O'Hara's male companions had still barely spoken to her or each other. The Moose was happy to stare out the window whilst Old Mr Cowie slept for most of the way. Even when she asked if she could get them anything for lunch, they had merely grunted.

No thanks, she'd believed they'd said, but couldn't be sure.

This breakdown recovery had become just another job to her now, best completed and best forgotten.

"Do you mind if I switch the radio on?" she had asked a couple of hours into the journey. She took their mumbled responses to be affirmative, but when she couldn't find anything worth listening to had started to hum and then to sing a variety of show tunes, her full repertoire. The Moose sat impassive gazing through the rain-dotted windscreen as if in a trance. Old Mr Cowie snored.

"Well, here we are then," Maureen announced when the ferry terminal came into view.

They had arrived half an hour earlier than planned and way before the ferry's scheduled departure time. By now the wind had dropped and the rain had eased.

Maureen pulled up at the security post, showed her ID, explained their circumstances and was promptly waved through onto the quay, as were the boys in the Passat.

"OK, Mr Cowie. I need you to sign this form with regard to the recovery of your caravan to this point. There, please, and there, and then there," Maureen instructed as they all stood on the quay. Mr Cowie looked at the form, hesitated for a second or two and then signed.

"Right. Got all your tickets and ID ready?"

"Yes."

"Good, and we're here nice and early. Since you'll be getting off last when you arrive in Holyhead, they'll be loading all the other traffic onto the ferry ahead of you here. When it's your turn, I'll drive you on board and offload you at the rear of the car decks. Then I'll get out of the way and skedaddle back to base."

"I take it someone's going to meet us at the other end, Maureen?" Draper asked.

"Of course. When the ferry docks, your own AA will be there to come on board, load you up onto another flatbed and transport you on to London."

"Brilliant, Maureen. Thanks, you've been a gem," Colin Draper enthused.

"What's got into you, laughing boy?" Hugo Saunders hissed into Draper's ear.

"What?"

"What's made you so bloody happy all of a sudden?"

"Because once that ferry leaves with us safely on board, we'll have fulfilled all the demands made of us in that bloody note. Fingers crossed but somehow, and thank Christ, we're all safe and in one piece, including Gavin. So it looks to me like this fucking nightmare is nearly over and we can get the hell out of here and forget about the whole damn thing."

"You don't think we should report what happened when we get home to London? You know, tell the police about the drugs run?"

"No. Absolutely not, Hugo."

"But doesn't that make us accessories?"

"How can we be considered accessories if we didn't know what was being carried on the yacht?"

"Because we *did* know. Because *you* couldn't resist sticking your nose in. If you hadn't gone poking about on that boat, we would never have known what she was carrying."

"But no one needs to know about that, Hugo. Anyway, we had to find out. What if we'd been smuggling guns or explosives? There's a hell of a difference between guns and recreational drugs."

"Is there? They both kill, Colin."

"The point is, we survived and we're going home. As I say, no one needs to know."

"So, what? We lie?"

"We won't lie because we won't be asked. We simply keep quiet and return to our boring humdrum lives. And, look here, Hugo," Colin Draper said glaring. "I am not going to risk missing Saffie's bloody wedding for anyone or anything. And if that means not getting caught up in a drugs bust, all well and good!"

"OK, OK. I understand."

"I hope you do, Hugo."

"I wanted to sound you out, that's all, Colin."

"As I said before, let's forget that the whole damn thing ever happened."

The ferry crossing wasn't as rough as they'd feared. By the time it was leaving port, the storm front had passed. It was dark when they sailed into the harbour at Holyhead, but the promise of one last drive and then home lifted their spirits. They were relieved when a ship's officer could be heard over the tannoy asking motorists to return to their vehicles. When they regrouped back at the Passat, however, they were informed that the AA wouldn't be coming aboard until all the other cars, passengers and freight had disembarked. Rather than hang around on the car deck they were asked to wait in the caravan.

"What are you planning to do when you get home, Mr Cowie?" Colin Draper asked to pass the time.

"If Gavin will let me use his facilities, I think I might like a hot bath and a whiskey."

"I'm sure that can be arranged,' Gavin replied with a smile.

Half an hour later, there was a knock on the door. The Moose sprung up and shoved it with his shoulder.

"Good afternoon, gentlemen. Stephen Calow, AA. I'm here to get you to London. My flatbed's on board and we're ready to lift you off," Calow announced with a flourish. "First I have a little paperwork for you to sign. Now which one of you is Mr Cowie?"

"That's me."

"I need you to sign here, here and here," he said, crouching down beside the old man at the kitchenette table.

"Good, good. Thank you, that's fine. Now, if you gentlemen would like to come with me," Calow said, clipping his pen onto his chest pocket, getting up and turning to leave.

The five of them followed him out of the caravan, peering through the shadows for signs of the AA recovery vehicle. For some reason the deck lights had been switched off and it was too gloomy to see too much more than each other. The car deck appeared to be empty though, the clanging of their footsteps echoing around the bare metal interior.

Suddenly there was a series of loud clicks as a blanket of brilliant white light flooded down the deck. Startled, they froze, stunned by the halogen, a light so dazzling that they had no option but to close their eyes and turn their backs to it. Then came the din of stampeding feet rushing towards them as dark figures sprinted out of the brightness, men dressed head to foot in black who grabbed their arms and barked orders at them.

"Police! Hands above your heads! On your knees! On your fucking knees! Raise your fucking hands and get on your knees!"

The voices grew louder and fiercer – screaming at them until they submitted.

Draper peeped round, could see little but caught sight of Gavin Doyle, The Moose and Hugo Saunders lying flat on the floor each with a dark figure kneeling across their backs. Mr Cowie was still upright but being held in an arm lock. Then Draper felt a heavy foot on the back of his head as he too was flattened.

Once they were pinned down came a sound like the clicking of castanets as their hands were cuffed behind their backs. Wrists secured, they were lifted up into a sitting position facing into the light. Then came the sound of switches again as the lighting dimmed leaving them blinking as they tried to regain vision and focus. As they blinked, a large silhouette shuffled towards them speaking in a familiar brogue.

"Yeah, that's them alright. All of them: Mr Draper, Mr Saunders, Mr Doyle, Mr Moose and Mr Cowie."

Then a whisper: "Thank you, sergeant, and you're sure it's them?"

"Absolutely, there's no doubt about it, officer."

"Good. Thank you, sergeant."

Draper caught a quick glimpse of Sergeant McIlhenny as he wandered off into the shadows from whence he came.

31

Friday, 8pm
The Bull's Head, Yarmouth

"Your good health, Phil."

"Cheers, Mary."

"So, Saffie, what time's your father due to get here?"

"He wasn't specific. I think he said some time this evening. Though knowing Dad it won't be till after midnight."

"You're learning, dear."

"Mum!"

"Well, he's always been very generous with his time. He gives lots of it away – spends most of it with other people."

"Aren't you meeting up with him tomorrow, Mum?"

"Apparently. Eleven o'clock in here. We want to present a united front at the wedding."

"I'd love to see that! You two, together, having a drink."

"Saffron!"

"Och, you know you love him, really."

"Really?"

"Yes."

"I wouldn't bet on it. What do you think, Phil?"

"No comment! I think I might go and see how your gran's doing. She'll probably be wondering where we are by now."

"Coward! You'll get on famously with Saffie's dad, Phil."

"He's called Colin, Mum. And leave Phil out of this."

"Sorry, Philip."

"You're OK, Mary. We're good."

"OK, Saffie, I think we should order another drink, don't you? We'll need one if your dad's on his way."

32

Friday, 9pm

"Do you understand the continuing rights that I have read to you? With these rights in mind, is there anything you would like to say to me?" the custody sergeant asked, delivering the legal mantra in a dry monotone. "Mr Draper, do you have anything you want to tell me? Do you have anything to say?" he repeated growing sterner. "Have you any medical condition, physical or mental, you would like me to note? Would you like to see a doctor?"

Colin Draper shook his head. He didn't feel like talking much; didn't feel like listening much either. Was in shock. More worried about Saffie's wedding and what his mother was up to than his present predicament.

"I've read you your rights," the custody sergeant droned on through the legalese from behind the counter at the front of the police station. "I've explained your right to contact someone to inform them you're here, I've explained your entitlement to free legal advice and I've given you a copy of our Notice of Detention that lists *all* your rights whilst you're held here in custody. Is there anything you would like to ask?"

No response.

"Mr Draper, is there anything you don't understand? Do you need me to read you your rights in Welsh?"

Colin Draper slowly shook his head.

"No, I thought not. Now, would you like to sign the custody record to acknowledge receipt of your Notice of Detention?"

Again no response.

"Right then, take him down to a cell please, constable," the custody sergeant commanded as the National Crime Agency arresting officer – anonymous beneath a black riot uniform and body armour – handed Colin Draper over to the local police constable waiting to receive him.

As the National Crime Agency officer released Draper from an arm lock, the pressure on his forearms suddenly loosened. The tight hold had felt like it was cutting off the circulation to Draper's hands, the feeling in which was already compromised by the handcuffs he'd been clamped in behind his back.

Draper was bustled along a corridor, past swathes of *how to prevent* and *what to do* posters, down a couple of flights of steps and through a swing door into a longer, darker corridor; their footsteps resounding around the bare walls and floor. They entered a cell about the size of a disabled toilet, the only furniture a narrow concrete bed. There was a small square window with frosted glass above head height that let in a little light but offered no view. It was cold.

Draper slumped onto the bed.

"Hands!" the police officer barked.

Draper twisted round to present his hands as best he could. The policeman fiddled with the lock, removed the cuffs, turned and left.

Once on his own, Draper removed the Notice of Detention – a clump of information sheets stapled together that had been stuffed down his shirt – flung them across the floor, rolled onto his back and lay down along the small single bed, flexing his fingers and rubbing his wrists to restore some circulation. He shut his eyes and tried to process all that he'd been through since they were seized on the car deck and work out why they had been arrested. He presumed it must be for landing the drugs in Ireland. Why else? Why else would McIlhenny be there? However, he wondered what authority the Irish police might have in the UK, if any.

Apart from a long and bumpy ride in the rear of a van, not much had happened since they were apprehended. And that was the last he'd seen of the others. He imagined they'd all been brought to the same police station in a convoy, and that they too, like he, had had their possessions confiscated, been photographed, been swabbed for DNA, been dabbed for fingerprints and had their rights read. The police were obviously intent on keeping them separated.

The door of Draper's cell swung open and an officer entered.

"Here, take this," he said, passing Draper a mobile phone. "You're entitled to one call. Let someone know you're here."

"Where are we exactly?"

"Colwyn Bay. North Wales Police Headquarters."

"Right, right. Thank you."

"Make your call then pass me the phone back. I'm going to wait for it here in case you try anything daft."

Draper phoned the first number that came to mind.

"Hi, Mary, it's me. I appear to be in a bit of a bind …"

"Time of interview, 10pm Friday, 21st March 2014," the detective inspector said in routine fashion having pressed the red button on the cassette recorder. "And in the presence of Detective Inspector Keith Matthews and Inspector Geraint Price. Also present, Mr Draper's legal representative, duty solicitor, Ms Suzanne Stokes. Mr Draper, I have to caution you. You do not have to say anything but it may harm your defence if you do not mention when questioned something which you later rely on in court. Anything you do say may be given in evidence. Do you understand or do you need legal advice from Ms Stokes in private?"

Colin Draper, who was staring down and focusing on the interview room floor, shrugged.

"Right, Mr Draper, or shall I call you Colin?"

Colin Draper looked blank. Stayed mute.

"Would you like a lemon bonbon, Mr Draper?" DI

Matthews asked, thrusting a wrinkled paper bag of sweets in Colin Draper's direction. Draper shook his head.

"Shame, they're delicious. Inspector Price? Ms Stokes?" DI Matthews asked, offering the packet round and then stuffing the bag back into a pocket of his corduroy jacket when there was no response.

"OK, I think we can all presume that you know why you've been arrested?" DI Matthews continued, his annunciation compromised by a mouthful of bonbons.

"I have a vague idea," Draper replied, his eyes still fixed on the floor.

"Let me help you out with some detail then. You, Mr Colin Draper, are suspected of being responsible for the illegal importation of over a ton of a class A drug – uncut cocaine, to be specific – into the United Kingdom in contravention of the Customs and Excise Management Act 1979. If you are proven guilty in a court of law, this offence carries a maximum sentence of life imprisonment, an unlimited fine or both,'" DI Matthews said, then paused. "So, Colin, it looks like you've landed yourself in a spot of bother, doesn't it? Doesn't look like you'll be needing carpet slippers for a while."

Draper raised his head, turned and glanced at his solicitor who lifted an index finger to her lips in response.

"No comment."

"Mr Draper, the Border Force have found a little over a ton of uncut cocaine concealed inside your caravan."

"What! In the caravan?"

"Yes. In your caravan."

"Bloody hell!"

"You sound surprised, Colin."

"I ... I ... I didn't have a clue! Not a clue!"

"Well, I guess you would say that, wouldn't you? And I presume you know the street value of a ton of cocaine?"

Colin Draper shrugged again. Sat open-mouthed.

"Around two hundred million, Mr Draper. Pounds, that is.

That would pay for quite a few divorces and a good few weddings too, would it not?"

"But the caravan doesn't belong to me! It is not my caravan. It's got *nothing* to do with me! Absolutely nothing to do with me!" Colin Draper stammered gazing into DI Matthews' blue-grey eyes.

"Is there anything you'd like to tell us about the drugs, Mr Draper?"

"There's nothing to say. I don't know anything. They've got nothing to do with me. Nothing!"

"Look, Mr Draper, Colin. The drugs were found in your possession. You've been caught red-handed. However, it might help your case later if we can show that you cooperated with us now. Do you understand?"

"Mmm," Colin Draper mumbled.

"I'm sorry, Mr Draper. Did you say something?"

"YES, I UNDERSTAND!" Colin Draper shouted.

"Mr Draper, you know you don't have to say anything or answer any questions you are unsure of?" his solicitor whispered, leaning forward and placing her hand gently on Colin Draper's arm to placate him.

"It's OK. I've nothing to hide," he replied in a lowered voice. "I'm happy to tell them everything I know."

"Mr Draper!"

"No, it's OK, Ms ...? Ms Stokes?"

"But—"

"It's OK, I'm past caring at this point, Ms Stokes."

"Alright then, Mr Draper, let's not waste any more time. Where would you like to start?" DI Matthews asked.

"At the very beginning."

"In the words of Julie Andrews, Mr Draper, 'that's a very good place to start'," DI Matthews said in a manner which indicated that the quote was a regular part of his act.

Draper waited a few moments, gulped, looked up and began his story.

"From whenever we left London the trip seemed jinxed. Thanks to a puncture we nearly missed the ferry to Dublin. I wish we had. Then there was Mr Cowie's health scare, then the caravan got stolen and from then on things just got worse and worse. But the first time we really felt that our lives were in danger was after our second night in Donegal when I, along with Moose and the Reverend Saunders, woke up on a yacht out in the Atlantic. We'd been drugged and dumped there in the middle of the night and, obviously, this happened totally against our wills."

"What? Are you saying you were abducted?"

"Yes. We were abducted. And when we came round in the morning, adrift at sea, I found a note from our captors. It was addressed to me. It implied that our friend and travelling companion, Mr Doyle, was either being held as a hostage or would be a target should we not comply with their demands."

"Which were?"

"To sail the boat into the harbour at Downings and leave it there. It was only later on that we discovered it was laden with a large quantity of cocaine. We had no choice but to moor the craft, return to our lodgings and continue on with the rest of our holiday and leave Ballyhanlon as planned, or, as the note stated, we feared someone was going to harm Mr Doyle."

"Someone? Who?"

"A third party. We never knew. We still don't know."

"Where is this note? Did you keep it?"

"No."

"Mmm, convenient. Please go on."

"Whilst we came across the cocaine stored on the boat, none of us were aware that the cocaine had later been transferred to, and hidden inside, the caravan. We had no idea, none. Anything we did to facilitate the importation of the drugs into Ireland was done under duress – that is to say we thought our lives and the life of Mr Doyle, in particular, were in grave danger – but anything we did to facilitate the importation of the drugs into the UK was done without our knowledge."

Colin Draper took a deep breath and sat back in his chair.

"And that's everything I know."

"What, that's it? That's all you've got to say?"

"Yes."

"And you call that the whole story?"

Draper shrugged.

"I'd call that a well-rehearsed explanation, Mr Draper, but a little bit thin on detail. And what you have told us sounds more than a little far-fetched. Drugged? Dumped on a yacht? In the Atlantic?"

"It's the truth."

"Mmm. The truth, Mr Draper. It takes an honest type of person to tell the truth, wouldn't you agree?"

"Of course."

"But you are not an honest type, are you, Mr Draper?"

"I like to think so."

"But you have already admitted to the Irish police that you smuggled an old man onto the ferry and ashore in Dublin by hiding him in his own caravan. Would you say that was the act of an honest man, Mr Draper?"

"You're making that sound worse than it was."

"Sergeant McIlhenny told me he was quite shocked when he heard how you'd treated Mr Cowie. So when you say you are innocent of importing drugs into the UK, why should we believe you? It doesn't stack up, does it, Colin?"

"We didn't smuggle Mr Cowie into Ireland. We didn't do anything illegal. Mr Cowie isn't contraband. And when we realised we might have a problem getting him onto the ferry we all agreed that we couldn't and wouldn't leave him behind. We genuinely believed we were doing what was best for him."

"But what about the drugs? What about the two hundred million. That would come in handy, wouldn't it? Let's face it, we know you're a bit short of cash. You are, though, aren't you, Mr Draper?"

"No more than anybody else!"

"But your design business went under not so long ago, did it not? And you've recently been through a divorce."

"My client doesn't have to answer this line of questioning. His personal affairs are of no consequence."

"Really, Ms Stokes? We're trying to establish a motive here. It would seem that Mr Doyle's personal circumstances suggest that he might indeed have had a very strong motive," DI Matthews replied, leaning back in his chair and appearing to enjoy the badinage.

"It's OK, Ms Stokes, I don't mind."

"And it was a difficult divorce, was it not, Colin? And expensive? And it's left you a bit short. We know. We've checked. Your bank has confirmed you are in debt. You are running quite a sizeable overdraft too, we hear."

"It's an arranged overdraft facility and carefully financed. I buy and sell property. The overdraft's a large one, but it's paid off regularly."

"And your daughter's getting married on Sunday I believe? It's a pity you won't be there. And a wedding, Colin. That's a big expense, isn't it? I mean, how are you going to afford all of those costs on top of everything else? A share of that two hundred million would come in very handy any time now, wouldn't it? I mean, from my point of view, there's a pretty good motive right there for you to have been tempted into getting involved in a little bit of smuggling."

"But the wedding – I have it covered."

"I'm sure you do. I'm sure you do."

DI Matthews paused for a second, the only noise a bonbon being crunched.

"What about your so-called friends, Mr Draper? What about Mr Doyle, Mr Cowie, the Reverend Saunders and Mr Morris?"

"Mr Morris?"

"The one you call Moose?"

"Ah ... What about them?"

"How well do you get on with them? Good friends?"

"Very."

"That's not what I've heard."

"What do you mean?"

"I hear you spend a lot of your time arguing. '*They're always arguing*' is what I've heard. I've heard that a lot. Always arguing. It sounds to me you are more like colleagues than friends. More like a group of criminal associates on a job than a group of mates enjoying a golf tour."

"That's ridiculous, Detective Inspector. We're all good friends. And who's to judge anyway. We might appear to be bickering or slagging each other off, but that's what we do. It's our code. It's how we communicate. God save us if we were ever to be *nice* to one another ... you know, polite. In our circle you'd know there was something seriously wrong with your health if the others started being *nice* to you."

"Mmm, we'll see what your so-called friends have to say about that."

"Ask them. Please do."

"Yes, you can be quite sure I will, Colin," DI Matthews replied before pausing.

"Golf, Mr Draper."

"What about it?"

"How many rounds did you play on your golf tour? Did you play every day? Three or four times maybe?"

"Err ..."

"Just twice, I believe. Isn't that correct?"

"Yes."

"Some golf tour that then, Mr Draper?"

"Look, please believe me, I didn't have anything to do with the drugs. I knew they were on the boat because we stumbled across them when we were at sea, but I had no idea about the quantity or value. I knew there were drugs there, but couldn't do anything about it. We'd been abducted and I thought we were in danger. I thought one, or all of us, would get shot. I was frightened!"

DI Matthews paused again.

"I hear you came into contact with an Irish naval ship. I hear they towed you off a sandbank. That's correct, isn't it, Mr Draper?"

"Yes, but—"

"If you'd been abducted and weren't smuggling the drugs of your own accord, why didn't you ask them for help?"

"Because of our friend. Whoever drugged us and left us on the boat said in their note that he, Gavin Doyle, would be harmed if we sought help. They said that if we were to attempt to report anything regarding the trip to the authorities then our friend's safety would be subject to change – or words to that effect."

"Ah, the note again."

"Yes. And that was a clear specification."

"Right, right. So let's move on."

"OK."

"Semtex, Mr Draper."

"What?"

"You haven't talked to me about the guns and Semtex."

"What guns?"

"It seems that there wasn't that much cocaine in the caravan after all. Nothing like a ton."

"But you said—"

Colin Draper was on the point of protesting further when he felt a sharp kick on his shins. This he took to be Suzanne Stokes' method of applying a mute button. He took the hint.

"I was leading you on, Mr Draper. It appears that the boat you so masterfully navigated into harbour was also carrying automatic weapons and explosives bound for a dissident terrorist group."

Colin Draper looked up sharply, lurched forward then received another kick in the shins from Suzanne Stokes. He sat back in his chair and started to rock backwards and forwards in silence.

"I'm afraid that the importation of arms and explosives carries a mandatory life sentence under the Prevention of Terrorism Act 2005, Mr Draper. Mr Draper, Colin, it could be that you're in bigger trouble than we first thought. It might help your position, however, if you could give us the names and nationality of those you have been dealing with."

Colin Draper turned to his solicitor who shook her head as if to underline that he must, under all circumstances, say nothing.

"Mr Draper. Do you have nothing to say?"

Colin Draper looked down into his lap and bit his lip.

"Mr Draper?"

"No comment," Draper murmured.

"Moving on then. What about Mr Cowie?"

"What about him?"

"An odd man, don't you think?"

"Remarkable."

"What do you know about Mr Cowie?"

"Not much. He's Gavin's father-in-law. That's about it."

"And your friends, Mr Draper. They have a lot to say about you. A lot to say—"

"OK, I think my client might appreciate a comfort break at this point, officers," Suzanne Stokes interjected briskly whilst peering at her wristwatch.

"Are you kidding?" DI Matthews said cynically.

"No, I am not."

As Colin Draper was led back to his cell, his solicitor followed.

"So, what happens next, Ms Stokes?"

"They've arrested, cautioned and questioned you and now they are considering whether or not to charge you, either with the offence of the importation of a class A drug in contravention of the Customs and Excise Management Act or for the importation of arms under the Prevention of Terrorism Act or whether to charge you at all," Suzanne Stokes replied. "You'll be held overnight. Meanwhile they have twenty-four hours from the time of your arrest to decide whether to charge you with either of those offences and they'll probably want to question you again within that time frame too."

"Twenty-four hours? That takes us to when?"

"Up until nine o'clock tomorrow evening."

"Saturday night?"

"Yes."

"Shit! I've got to be in Yarmouth by tomorrow lunchtime. First thing on Sunday at the very latest."

"When's your daughter's wedding?"

"Six o'clock on Sunday evening," Colin Draper replied. "Ms Stokes, Suzanne, be straight with me, do you think there's even the slightest chance that I'll make it?"

"It all depends on whether they charge you or not, Colin, and then, if they do, whether they detain you until there's a magistrate's hearing. If the magistrates' court thinks there's a case to answer, they will refer you to the criminal court for trial. Then you will either be released on bail or held in prison on remand until your court date comes up."

"What if they charge me under the Prevention of Terrorism Act?"

"In my opinion, they won't. My bet is that they were only fishing with the guns and explosives story – throwing in a red herring to scare you, mixing up fact and fiction to see how you would react, what you might say – see what you may or may not know."

"But what if they do?"

"Then they can hold you for up to twenty-eight days."

"Shit!"

"I'm going to talk to DI Matthews now and see what I can

get out of him. Don't worry, Colin, if your story holds up then there's hope."

"I don't care what happens to me, Suzanne, I just want to get out of here and get to my daughter's wedding. I can't miss it – she'd never forgive me."

"I'll do my best. Let's see what tomorrow brings."

"Suzanne, I called my ex-wife and told her that I'm being held here. She thinks I've been busted for drink-driving. If I give you her number, would you please give her a call and get her up to speed on what's actually happened? And please ask her to reassure Saffie that I'll be there on Sunday."

"Of course."

"By hook or by crook, I'm going to be there, Suzanne. By hook or by bloody crook."

33

Friday, 10pm
The Bull's Head, Yarmouth

"Your father left me a rather strange message earlier."

"Oh?"

"Seems he's stuck somewhere in Wales."

"Wales!"

"Something about drink-driving, apparently."

"Is he OK?"

"I don't know, Saffie. His phone keeps going to voicemail. I'll try him again later. I'm sure he'll be fine."

"But Wales!"

"Yes, well, you know your father."

"How's he going to get to the wedding without a car?"

"There are trains."

"He'd better not be late!"

"Don't worry. He'll be fine."

"Better had be."

"Saffie?"

"What?"

"You didn't think to ask Harvey Alexander to the wedding, did you?"

"Harvey, the tennis coach? No."

"Not even to the evening do?"

"No. Why would I?""

"Oh, I was only being curious."

"Why, Mum? He's my tennis coach. I barely know him. What's it to you, anyway?"

"Oh, nothing. Just checking. Hang on, Saffie ... phone! Hello, yes, I'm she," Mary Draper said turning away and walking out of the bar with her mobile clamped to her ear. Within minutes she returned wearing a blank expression and ashen-faced.

"What is it, Mum?"

"Oh, nothing."

"Who were you talking to?"

"Oh, no one."

"Mum! Who was it?"

"Someone your father knows."

"Who, Mum?"

"His solicitor."

"Oh."

"No, not that one. Another one. This one's Welsh. Well, she sounds Welsh. Says he might not make the wedding service."

"What!"

"Says he's been unavoidably detained in North Wales."

"By whom?"

"The police. The North Wales Constabulary. It's not drink-driving. I'm afraid it's worse. Apparently he's been caught trying to import cocaine into the UK in a caravan."

"What?"

"At least we now know why he's spent so much time mucking about in boats all of these years, Saffie. Saffie, Saffie – don't cry! Please. Please. Oh, please don't cry."

"But, Mum!"

"Saffie, the solicitor says he's protesting his innocence. Who knows, he could be out tomorrow or, there again ..."

"How ... How could he, Mum?"

"You know your father, Saffie. Full of surprises."

"But ... What about my wedding?" Saffie asked, sobbing.

"Breathe deeply, darling, breathe deeply. There's plenty of time yet. Who knows? I'll call his solicitor in the morning and see what she has to say then. It's bound to be alright. Your father hasn't got the brains to be a master criminal."

34

Saturday, 8am

Colin Draper slept fitfully. There was little to disturb him, bar a persistent snorer at the far end of the landing, but thoughts of a long prison sentence had induced an insomnia that left him perspiring and short of breath. He couldn't help but dwell on the events of the past week, raking through the detail over and over in a search for new clues. The one occurrence that still had him foxed, and that he kept returning to, was Old Mr Cowie's near-death experience. There was something about catalepsy that he sensed they'd missed or he'd forgotten and hadn't been mentioned and was relevant. There was something he'd read on the subject and couldn't quite recall – a news story maybe or an entry online. He racked his brain to remember but couldn't and finally gave up.

The early morning dragged but eventually the cell door clanked open and a fresh-faced policeman entered with a tray and deposited a plate of toast and a cup of tea on the floor.

"Scoff that lot and I'll be back in ten. Apparently you've got a busy day ahead of you," the officer said, speaking with a melodious Welsh lilt. It was a relief to hear a friendlier voice.

Before long the constable arrived to escort Colin Draper from his solitary confinement.

"Where're we going?"

The officer didn't reply.

After a short walk Draper was ushered into an interview room. Suzanne Stokes arrived shortly after.

"Good morning, Mr Draper."

"Colin."

"Colin. I just want to get you up to speed."

"Did you speak to my ex-wife, Suzanne?"

"Yes. She was most concerned. She said she would do what she could to placate your daughter – Saffie, isn't it?"

"Yes, Saffie."

"OK. Here's how it is. I am expecting DI Matthews to either charge you or release you by nine o'clock tonight. However, they may apply to a magistrate for a restraining order to keep you here for another twenty-four hours."

"Is that likely?'

"At present I think it is. The offences you are accused of are very serious. They will probably consider that there is a risk of flight. That is to say, you could abscond whilst on police bail."

"Oh, shit!"

"Exactly. But we'll see."

"So, what do we do, Suzanne?"

"We wait."

"Wait?"

"Yes. Meanwhile they'll be running round checking out your version of events, trying to dig up more evidence and talking to witnesses. They'll also have a forensic team working overtime and be investigating any fresh leads."

"And in the meantime, I get to miss my daughter's wedding."

Following Colin Draper's consultation with his solicitor, the busy day predicted failed to materialise. The seconds crawled. There was plenty of time for analysis and theorising, however.

After a snack lunch the young police officer returned to escort Draper from his cell to a drab room on the floor above comprising a long table, half a dozen chairs and little else. It seemed to be some kind of meeting room.

"Sit here, please," the constable said, stepping back and standing to one side of the door with his arms folded.

Draper sat as requested and surveyed the room. There were windows, but the blinds were drawn. There was a green felt noticeboard covering the wall at one end of the room, but it was bare except for some drawing pins dotted about in a random pattern. The strip lighting overhead did nothing to soften the drab interior.

Growing restless, Draper began to examine his hands checking his fingernails and the quicks. They were chewed and raw. He closed his eyes for a second and tried to recall, yet again, what is was about catalepsy that was bugging him – something symptomatic maybe, he thought. Whatever it was he knew it was relevant. He sighed heavily, was on the point of giving up again when, moments later, it came to him in a flash. It wasn't a symptom of catalepsy he'd forgotten, but a cause. And with the remembering the scales began to fall from his eyes.

A minute or two later the door was opened and Gavin Doyle, Hugo Saunders, Old Mr Cowie and The Moose filed into the room chaperoned by four uniformed officers who directed them to sit around the table. The police officers left. At first the five of them were at a loss for words.

"Jesus, Colin, we're screwed. What have they said to you?"

"They've hinted I might be facing a life sentence, Hugo. Apparently I'm responsible for importing guns and Semtex into the country. If found guilty, I'm not only going to miss Saffie's wedding, but I am also going to miss the birth of her children, their christenings, their graduations, their weddings, the birth of their children and their children's children too."

"They're trying to scare us, Colin. They must know we're innocent."

"God knows, but then maybe some of us are more innocent than others, Hugo. Wouldn't that be the case, Gavin?"

"What? What the fuck are you on about, Colin?"

"You know damn rightly what I'm on about, Gavin!"

"I'd be careful what I was saying if I were you," Gavin huffed, getting to his feet and looking fierce. Old Mr Cowie tapped him on the arm and tugged at his sleeve to encourage him to sit down whilst pointing up to the black orb suspended from the ceiling.

"I think we'd better compose ourselves, gentlemen. I think we might have company. It wouldn't surprise me if our friends were watching and listening in," Old Mr Cowie cautioned.

"Well, unlike some, I have nothing to hide, Mr Cowie."

"What the hell do you mean?" Gavin Doyle asked abruptly.

"Catalepsy, Gavin. There was something about catalepsy that I couldn't quite recall. There was something about Mr Cowie's story that was bothering me. But then it came back to me ... and just now, as it happens."

"What, Colin? What do you mean?" Old Mr Cowie said, sounding affronted.

"I'd almost forgotten that, apart from the most obvious symptom of catalepsy i.e. the appearance of being dead and, apart from the possible causes, such as Parkinson's and epilepsy, there is another cause – one we missed and you failed to mention."

"What are you blabbering on about, Colin?" Gavin Doyle snarled.

"Cocaine addiction, Gavin. Catalepsy can afflict those in withdrawal from cocaine addiction. Check it out. No wonder when we found him at the beach car park, Mr Cowie assured us he'd be fine, because by then his caravan was jam-packed with the stuff. A ton of it, as it happens. No wonder we had such a struggle to get the caravan off that damn beach."

"That's ridiculous!"

"You like your cocaine, don't you, Mr Cowie? I bet you can't get enough of it, can you?"

"Is this true, Mr Cowie?" Hugo Saunders asked, his eyes widening in disbelief.

"How and where did you get addicted to cocaine, Mr Cowie?

It's not often you come across an octogenarian with a coke habit. Was it Gavin? Is this his work? Grief can drive you to do desperate things, Gavin. And there was poor Old Mr Cowie stuck in a holiday caravan in Lewisham with only his memories for company. I bet that led to an easy sell. You probably told him it was snuff the first time. '*Time for some of your magic snuff, Mr Cowie. You know you love it. Makes you feel years younger, doesn't it? And I know where we can get plenty more*'," Colin Draper said, staring at the old man.

Old Mr Cowie sat tight-lipped, peeping up at the CCTV camera.

"He's talking rubbish! He's making this up!"

"Am I, Gavin? I have to say I never figured you as an international crime boss. Where did you get the idea to use an eighty-something-year-old as a drug mule? No wonder we had to hide Old Mr Cowie on the ferry. We were slipping him into the country. No one was to know he was there. Then he was unwell – was that intentional? Couldn't have been. That's when Sergeant McIlhenny got involved, and you wouldn't have wanted that, would you? Or maybe that was part of the plan since you needed to get the caravan 'stolen' whilst the drugs were stashed on board."

"You're talking shite, Draper!"

"Shut up, Gavin! I want to hear what he's got to say," Hugo Saunders interjected.

"But, stone me, Gavin, involving the AA? That was a master stroke," Draper continued, warming to his theme. "I mean, getting them to transport the drugs back to Britain was a brilliant idea. Who's going to suspect the AA of importing drugs? Nurse an old caravan all the way to Donegal then ensure it's too knackered to drive home. Fantastic!"

"Don't listen to him. The divorce has finally scrambled his brains. It's all bullshit!" Gavin shouted.

"OK, Gavin. Let's look at this from another perspective: the boat. Whoever is, or was, behind the drug smuggling needed

Hugo, Moose and me to land the yacht at Downings. What better cover than a bunch of tourists out on a pleasure cruise? And that's kind of what gave you away. Who else knew I was qualified and had the experience to skipper a yacht, apart from Hugo and The Moose? And who was desperate for me to come on the tour in the first place? You, Gavin. It's obvious."

"Gavin was always very keen that we all go on the tour, Colin. Never seen him so enthusiastic for a sporting activity he normally despises," Hugo Saunders said frowning.

"Exactly. Golf and sailing. It's why he needed me to come."

"I'm sorry for my part in that, Colin."

"Please, Hugo, whatever you do, never invite me to go on a fucking golf tour again."

"Would someone shut him up!" Gavin shouted, jumping up and jerking towards Draper.

"No, Gavin!" The Moose growled, rising to his full height to block Gavin's path. "Sit down. I want to hear this too," he added before shoving Gavin back into his seat.

"Let's face it, Gavin," Draper continued, "you've always been the one with the entrepreneurial ideas. I mean, anyone who can come up with *Dogs Are Just For Christmas* is easily capable of duping their ageing father-in-law into becoming a drug mule. And I think we should all commend Gavin on his acting skills. Your dramatic performance in Dublin when we thought Mr Cowie was dead."

"I thought he was!"

"No, you didn't, Gavin! When I come to think about it, I bet it wasn't even catalepsy. I bet you made that up too. I imagine you slipped into his tea whatever it was you slipped into our drinks to knock us out on St Patrick's night. All the same, a great performance. As was your fake surprise when the caravan was pinched. Great acting. I remember you had tears in your eyes at the police station. When you turned away and started shaking we all presumed you were crying. Come on, admit it ... I bet you were laughing your head off. Then there was your dramatic performance when the caravan reappeared laden with your precious cargo, and, surprise, surprise, Old Mr Cowie, alive and well on board – another tour de force. I bet it was you who rang Sergeant McIlhenny to tip him off that the caravan was at Ballybrack in the first place. Oh, and, Mr Cowie, fancy you pretending to have slipped and banged your head when Sergeant McIlhenny arrived."

"I had!"

"And then there's your weird story about being kidnapped by gypsies. Fancy blaming the poor travelling community. And I bet it was you who loosened the wheel nuts on the caravan when you were lying low in Ballybrack. You know, enough to make sure the wheel fell off and banjaxed the caravan so we'd have to call the AA – just in case the weight of the coke didn't do the job first."

"You're making all of this up, Colin."

"Gavin, no one minds a bit of private enterprise, but did you really have to involve your friends as cover?"

"I really don't know what the fuck you're talking about!"

"All of which makes me wonder, Gavin, what criteria did you use to pick your drug baron? How did you find your drug cartel – Google? Yellow Pages? Did you put an ad in the *Bogotá Times*?"

"OK, Draper. I think you'd better shut up now. If we weren't stuck in a police station, I'd knock your fucking block off."

The Moose placed a hand on Gavin's shoulder to restrain him.

"And it's so bloody obvious now why you weren't dumped on the boat with us, Gavin. You had to take yourself hostage elsewhere. Very clever."

"Colin, I really don't think it's a good idea to discuss this now," Old Mr Cowie said, leaning back in his chair, sighing and gesturing towards the CCTV camera.

"What about the girl, Gavin? The dancer? Did she have anything to do with this?" Hugo asked.

"He won't say. But it's my guess she was always going to be useful in providing an alibi for him for when we were at sea. God knows what Karen would say."

"And what about the guns and Semtex?" Hugo Saunders added, raising his hands for emphasis.

"I don't think there were any, Hugo. They were a diversion to unsettle us and get us to talk."

"So, what are you going to do to get us out of this mess, Gavin?" Hugo Saunders asked in a schoolmasterly tone.

Silence followed as all eyes fell on Gavin Doyle. There was a long pause.

"I will say this once, and only once," he eventually said, articulating slowly and clearly: "I DO NOT KNOW WHAT THE FUCK YOU ARE TALKING ABOUT!"

Back in his cell Colin Draper paced up and down waiting for his solicitor to arrive. He was desperate to see Suzanne Stokes and let her know of his suspicions following the confrontation upstairs. Whilst waiting, he went over the events of the past week again, searching for any other clues that might prove his innocence – even combing through the comings and goings of The Moose and Hugo Saunders in case there was something they'd said or done that might implicate them as Gavin's accomplices. Growing impatient for Suzanne Stokes' to arrive and sensing the duty officers were ignoring him he created a ruckus, banging on the door and yelling out every few seconds.

It was over an hour before Suzanne Stokes finally arrived. Colin Draper immediately explained his theories about Gavin Doyle's involvement in the drug smuggling operation. She listened with interest.

"I'm sorry, Mr Draper, but no matter what new information you may have to offer them they are still going to hold you here for up to another twenty-four hours whilst they further investigate all key lines of enquiry. Which means—"

"I'm going to miss my daughter's wedding."

"We can't be sure of that, but since they haven't formally charged you yet it suggests to me that they're not confident that the Crown Prosecution Service will be interested in the case against you based on the evidence they've gathered so far."

"Which means?"

"They're not certain that a criminal prosecution would lead to your conviction at this point. That is, if the case against you was brought before a jury in a court of law, that they would necessarily find you guilty."

"But the police still haven't given up hope?"

"Actually, I am starting to suspect that, with you in particular, Colin, they're getting a little desperate. I think they believe that this should be an easy case to conclude but feel that there's something not quite right. I mean, why else would they have left you sitting in that room with the others earlier without charging you first?"

"Why wouldn't they?"

"Because in my experience that is a highly unusual way for the police to go about things. *Highly* unusual. That's not their normal procedure at all. But then a two-hundred-million-pound drug bust doesn't come their way every day. I imagine they're under a lot of pressure from the top brass to get an early conviction and I'd say they're worried about missing an open goal here. This is a case that will make international headlines and I think their chief constable will be very keen for those headlines to be positive. They'll try anything."

"Then surely my testimony about Gavin's involvement will help?"

"It will. From what you say, they'll have been listening in to your confrontation earlier. As a result they'll be double-checking what they heard right now. But, Colin, the reality is, if they haven't charged you by nine o'clock tomorrow night, they will have to release you anyway."

"That's all very well, Ms Stokes, but by then, it won't matter. I'm afraid it'll be too little, too late."

35

Sunday, 9am

Another restless night and another morning that dragged. Another tray of tea and toast later and the door of Colin Draper's cell was unlocked as his solicitor, DI Matthews and the fresh-faced constable entered.

"Could you come with us please, Mr Draper," DI Matthews mumbled.

They assembled in the interview room where DI Matthews ran through the standard police caution before starting his questioning.

"I've quite a few points to raise, Mr Draper, so please concentrate and think very carefully about your answers. What you say now could determine whether you will or won't be spending the next two decades in prison. Do you understand?"

Colin Draper nodded.

"*Do you understand?*" DI Matthews repeated forcefully. "A simple *yes* will suffice for the recording."

"Yes!" Draper replied in a sullen voice.

"What do you usually wear when you play golf, Mr Draper?"

"What?"

"What do you wear when you play golf?"

"Jeans and a polo shirt. A sweater if it's chilly. Waterproofs if it's raining. Why?"

"I didn't think jeans were allowed on a golf course?" DI Matthews continued.

"Eh? Excuse me, but what's this got to do with anything?"

"Please answer the question, Mr Draper."

"Golf clubs don't like blue denim jeans, but I wear black 501s. No one seems to mind or notice black jeans in my experience."

"Did you wear black denims on the Donegal trip?"

"Yes."

"How many pairs did you bring with you?"

"Two."

"Only the two pairs then."

"Yes."

"Same style and make?"

"Yes. Black Levis."

"Can you tell the two pairs apart?"

"Yes."

"How?"

"One pair has a rip across the seat now."

"How did that happen?"

"I got the arse caught on a nail."

"Recently? Where and when?"

"On the boat. Obviously, these ones, the ones I'm wearing, are my spare pair."

"When you say 'on the boat', which boat was that?"

"The *Contessa Rose*, the one we were forced to sail into the harbour at Downings in Donegal."

"And the torn pair, they are definitely the pair you were wearing on the *Contessa Rose*?"

"Yes. As I've just said, I tore them when I was on the boat. I tore them on a nail. Does it really matter?"

"Mr Draper, please believe me, it matters that you are positive about which pair you were wearing on the *Contessa Rose*."

Colin Draper shrugged. "I'm positive. The torn pair."

"And when did you change into the ones you've got on now?"

"When we got off the boat and returned to the Harbour Inn in Ballyhanlon."

"When?"

"When?"

"Yes. On what day and at what time? And please be as precise as you can."

"It was shortly after we found Gavin."

"How soon?"

"When we got off the boat we went straight to find him to make sure he was safe. We found him in his room at the Harbour Inn. It was between four and five on Wednesday."

"Sure?"

"Sure."

"Then what did you do?"

"I showered, got changed and went down to the bar."

"Sure?"

"Yes."

"Then what happened?"

"Not much. We stayed in the bar all evening and then went to bed. The next day we all got up and played golf. Shortly after that we were reunited with Old Mr Cowie when Sergeant McIlhenny took us to the spot where he'd found the caravan."

"Once you'd got back from the *Contessa Rose* and changed out of the torn pair of jeans – the pair you were wearing on the boat, you packed them away and didn't wear them again, right?"

"Yes."

"Why?"

"Because they were torn."

"And they – the torn pair – were definitely packed away and haven't been out of your bag since."

"That's correct."

"And no one could have had access to your bag or interfered with it?"

"No, it was locked in my room until we were leaving Ballyhanlon when I put it in the boot of Gavin's car."

"And you're sure of that?"

"Yes."

"And no one could have tampered with it?"

"No."

"Sure?'

"As I've just told you, it was locked in my room before we left the B & B and never out of my sight once we'd left it."

"Mr Draper, your mystery note, the note you say was written by your abductors, did anyone else see the note apart from you, your friend Moose and the Reverend Saunders?"

"No, I don't think so."

"You don't *think* so?"

"No. No, they didn't. I'm certain. Absolutely certain. No one else saw it."

"Could anyone else have handled it after you found it apart from you, your friend Moose and the Reverend Saunders?"

"No, not after we'd found it. No."

"Did you show it to or let Mr Cowie handle it or touch it in any way?"

"No, I couldn't have done."

"And why's that?"

"Because I wouldn't have had it with me by the time we went to pick up Mr Cowie and the caravan. You see, I was told to destroy it when we were at sea, you know, once I'd read it."

"And did you?"

"What?"

"Did you destroy the note?"

"Pretty sure, yes."

"Certain?"

"No, not certain. I can't remember actually doing it. There was a lot going on."

"Are you good at following instructions, Mr Draper?"

"I like to think so."

"Well, it appears you didn't follow the instructions very

carefully in this instance," DI Matthews said, holding up a small polythene bag with a folded piece of paper inside.

"Fuck! Is that it?"

"Yes, Mr Draper. It's your note. For the record I am now showing Mr Draper exhibit number CD06."

"Where was it?"

"You must have shoved it into the pocket of your jeans – the pair you say you were wearing on the yacht."

"How do you know?"

"We found it when we made a routine search of your belongings. It was still in the pocket of your torn jeans."

"Thank God! Is this good news then, detective inspector?"

"For you? Yes, it would appear so. It might be very good news indeed if you can confirm that no one apart from you and your two companions on the boat – Moose and the Reverend Saunders – saw or touched it."

"Yes! That would be the case! As I told you before, I got showered, changed and packed away my dirty clothes shortly after we got back to the Harbour Inn from the boat."

"And Mr Cowie definitely didn't see or touch the note?"

"No. He couldn't have done."

"Needless to say, forensics have analysed this piece of paper very carefully, Mr Draper.'

"Oh."

"So, can you explain why – apart from yours, your friend Moose's and the Reverend Saunders' – the note has Mr Cowie's fingerprints all over it?"

"I don't know. I can't say, unless ..."

"Yes, Colin. Unless it was Mr Cowie who typed it, printed it off, folded it and put it in the envelope by hand before it was left for you to find on the yacht."

"Mr Cowie?"

"Yes."

"Not Gavin?"

"No, his prints aren't on it. The paper has been analysed.

It's Tesco's own-brand paper. There's an open packet of the same paper stored in Mr Cowie's caravan, plus a laptop and printer. They all match up."

"Careless."

"Yes, very. And Mr Cowie's laptop makes for some very interesting reading."

"Fuck!"

"Mr Draper, the guns and Semtex. Worry not. We didn't find any. We threw that in to give you a fright and loosen your tongue."

"Oh, thanks very much."

"So, we can dismiss the charges under the Prevention of Terrorism Act."

"Thank God!"

"The charge of the importation of a class A drug. Let's come to that. Unfortunately ignorance is not a viable defence in law. You may have been coerced into smuggling the drugs ashore into Ireland but, by the letter of the law, you are still an accessory. So, do I think you are guilty of being an accessory? Yes I do. Do I think it could be proven before a jury in a court of law? No, I'm not so sure. Do I think we would get a conviction? Again, I'm not convinced. So, in light of that, we are going to release you on bail without formally charging you."

"Thank Christ!"

"But, I must caution you that you may well be required to return here to help us with our enquiries at a later date and to act as a witness in the prosecution of other parties at any subsequent trial should there be one. Do you understand?"

"Yes."

"Good."

"So, are you saying I'm—"

"Yes, you are free to go, Mr Draper."

"What about the others?"

"I can't divulge what will be happening to your friends

except to say that Mr Cowie is likely to be staying with us for quite a while longer."

"What about Gavin?"

"I'm afraid I can't comment."

Colin Draper signed for his belongings at the front desk and was directed through the main doors of the police station where he paused for a moment to talk to Suzanne Stokes.

"Thanks for your help, Suzanne."

"All part of the service, Colin. Anything else I can do?"

"If you don't mind, I'd be very grateful if you could call my ex-wife and let her know I'm on my way. I'm afraid my phone's dead."

As they concluded their conversation, Hugo Saunders and The Moose emerged through the front entrance behind them.

"Jesus! Am I glad to see you two!" Colin Draper said giving The Moose and Hugo Saunders a hug.

"It must have been the note that swung it, Colin."

"What about Old Mr Cowie?"

"What about the wedding, Colin?"

"I think I'm screwed, Hugo."

"What time's kick-off?"

"Six o'clock this evening."

"But it's only ten to eleven – you can still make it!"

"Yeah, if you've got a Ferrari handy."

"What about the Passat?"

"Where the hell is it?"

"Parked round the back of this place."

"How do you know?"

"I asked."

"Hang on, you're not suggesting we steal Gavin's car from a police station, are you?"

"You'd better not!"

"Fuck, Irish! How did you get out?"

"With no thanks to any of you. Especially you, Colin Draper."

"Don't they suspect that you're involved?"

"No, Colin, they do not. And yours – a great theory, but completely barking I'm afraid."

"Well ..."

"Well, I think you owe me an apology."

"Me! Why? There's a good chance I'm going to miss my daughter's wedding because of you, Gavin."

"Me? Old Mr Cowie maybe, but not me."

"Ah, Beverley. How is dear Beverley?"

"Look, he's shafted me just as much as he's shafted you. More probably."

"So, it wasn't your idea to go golfing in fucking Donegal then, Gavin?"

"Actually, it was his. He said he thought I needed to get away for a few days after Karen's passing."

"Remind me how long ago that was, Gavin."

"One year, four months and a day, Colin."

"And you're trying to tell me you knew nothing of what was going on?"

"No, nothing."

"Nothing about the drugs?"

"No, nothing. I mean, if I was involved with the smuggling why the fuck would I have suggested we let Sergeant McIlhenny know what had been going on?"

"When did you suggest that?"

"In the bar on Thursday night. Jesus, you and I had a discussion about it, Colin."

"And?"

"And I suppose you aren't aware that I was so desperate to find you on Tuesday that Bernadette and I set off the fucking hotel fire alarm? Why the hell would I want to draw attention to myself in that way? Why would I be looking for you if I knew you were on that bloody boat? Tell me, how did you feel when you woke up on the boat on Tuesday?"

"Terrible. Like I'd been knocked out."

"That's how I felt on Tuesday morning too. Whatever you'd

been given, I'd been given too. Didn't know where I was or with whom."

"Oh, I think you knew with whom, Gavin."

"Thank you, Hugo."

"What can I say, Gavin?"

"Nothing would be good, Colin."

"So, what about Old Mr Cowie?"

"As I say, he was the one that banged on about a golf tour. He was the one that was so keen for you to come too, Colin. Made out we'd be doing you a favour after your divorce."

"How did he know I like sailing?"

"Because sailing is something he likes to talk to me about. I'm sure that's why you came up in conversation. We talked about you a lot."

"Oh, thanks very much!"

"To be honest, I felt sorry for Old Mr Cowie too at that time. I wanted to take him away. Thought he deserved a break, especially after Karen died. Shit, poor Karen!"

"Oh, you're not going to cry again, are you?"

"Fuck off, Colin. I mean ... Jesus! Karen! She'd be heartbroken if she knew what her dad's been up to."

"He was using us as human shields, for God's sake, Gavin!"

"Now, I know that what he's done doesn't look good."

"Doesn't look good?"

"But he's not a bad man."

"Are you kidding?"

"He was probably bored."

"What!"

"Bored and lonely."

"Be honest, Gav, did you have *any* idea what he was up to?"

"None whatsoever."

"Really?"

"Really."

"And obviously I'm gutted. But still ... You have to admit, he had some nerve."

"Gavin!"

"I mean, two hundred million!"

"What do you think will happen to him now?"

"I don't know, Colin. I don't know and I don't really care any more."

"Well, you did say that he likes confined spaces. I'm sure he's going to enjoy plenty of that going forward.

"Unless—"

"Unless what, Gavin?"

"Hang on, lads, Colin's got a bride to give away. Are you going to drive us back down south or what, Gavin?" Hugo interjected.

"Do you think Colin deserves my help?"

"No, probably not."

"So, is there anything you'd like to say to me, Colin?"

"Err ... sorry, Gavin?"

"It's a start I suppose. So what now?"

"Sure, why don't we *all* go to the wedding, you too, Gavin."

"But I'm not invited, Colin."

"Listen, I'm the father of the bride, I'm footing the bill and if I say you're invited, you're fucking invited. End of. We're all going! We've travelled this far together, if I'm going to go to Saffie's bloody wedding, you're all coming too."

"Gavin?"

"What, Hugo?"

"If it wasn't you who spiked our drinks in the Harbour Inn, who did?"

"I don't know! It couldn't have been Old Mr Cowie but then maybe he wasn't working alone. I'm sure two hundred million can buy you plenty of backup especially somewhere where there could be dissidents lurking in the background.

"Right. That's enough flannel. We've a wedding to get to," Hugo said wandering off towards the rear of the police station whilst whistling the tune to "I'm Getting Married in the Morning".

36

Sunday, 3pm
Near Winchester, Hampshire

"Fuck it! Fuck your bloody car, Gavin!"

"It's not Gavin's fault, Colin. It's an old car and we've been doing eighty the whole way down. She's done pretty well up till now."

"Pretty well? Are you kidding, Hugo? What planet are you on? This is, without doubt, the most unreliable vehicle I've ever had the misfortune to travel in."

"She's done Gavin pretty well for the past ten years and two hundred thousand miles."

"Exactly. It's knackered. If *it* was a horse, it'd have been shot years ago and made into burgers."

Past Winchester – where Colin Draper managed to hire grey morning dress in Moss Bros. – and about a mile short of the M3, Draper, Gavin Doyle, Hugo Saunders and The Moose were standing, hands on hips, looking on as steam poured from under the bonnet of the Passat. They were still a two-hour drive from Yarmouth, and there were just under three hours left till the wedding car was due to collect Colin and Saffie for the short drive to the parish church.

Colin Draper watched as The Moose lifted the bonnet and stared at the radiator, trying to avoid the steam and boiling water spitting at him as he twisted the cap with his handkerchief.

"Judging from the overheating I'd say there's either a hole in the radiator or the head gasket's blown," The Moose mumbled.

"Oh, hooray for Jeremy fucking Clarkson here."

"Thank you, Colin."

"Right. Got to go," Colin Draper said, yanking off his shirt and unbuttoning his trousers.

"What?"

"Getting changed. I'm going to get my wedding clobber on, jog down towards the M3 and hitch a lift."

"Are you mad, Colin?"

"For going on a golf tour with you three? Yes. For buggering off now? No. Anyway, I'm not hanging around here for the rest of the bloody day, Hugo. Nothing and nobody is going to make me late for Saffie's wedding," Colin Draper shouted already stripped to his underpants, much to the entertainment of a passing tourist bus.

37

Sunday, 6.15pm

Ted Baker, organist at St Matthew's Parish Church, Yarmouth, loved weddings. Weddings called for a wider range of music over and above the modern hymns that the Reverend Kevin Wickford normally picked for Sunday service; Ted considered that the vicar's choices were better suited to a guitar and tambourine rather than a classic church organ.

Since many of the young couples that came to Ted for advice regarding their wedding music were happy to be guided by his expertise, these were the services where *his* taste often prevailed. As a result, weddings had become a platform for showcasing his talent and usually included the classic fanfares and marches he preferred.

Ted knew Saffie Draper well. She had been a familiar face at St Matthew's since she was a child, such was her mother's loyalty to the local church. It was a shame, he thought, that even though she was home from London most weekends, she was no longer a regular attender on Sundays. However, with the wedding to organise, Ted had seen more of her of late. He liked Saffie. She was a nice girl, polite and chatty.

Because of her family's long association with St Matthew's, and his affection for her, it was a pleasure for Ted to help select the music for her wedding. Both she and her fiancé Phil seemed grateful for, and were keen to accept, his counsel.

On the day, Ted was more nervous than usual. Most weddings involved fly-by-night couples unlikely to be seen in the church again until either a christening, a second wedding or a funeral, but Saffie was one of their own: a fourth-generation member of the congregation.

Up in the organ loft, a storey and a half above the choir stalls, Ted was flexing his fingers and running his eyes across the sheet music. As agreed, he was to play the Jeremiah Clarke "Trumpet Voluntary" for Saffie's entrance and procession; a performance piece to stir the soul. But the wait was growing interminable.

The small church was full; there was standing room only. The female guests, an eyeful in violet, peach and lilac – a cacophony of colour and cloth – and their men, either in grey morning dress or kilted in Stewart tartan, buzzed with gentle chatter – nervous, expectant and excited. Fascinator feathers frolicked as tittle-tattle reverberated around the pews.

Peering down, Ted caught the vicar's eye.

Father Wickford had meant to smile and nod back as a friendly gesture but forgot that this was *the* signal he'd agreed with Ted to let him know the bride had entered the church and to commence the opening bars of the "Trumpet Voluntary" so that the bridal party could process down the aisle for the wedding service to begin.

Ted launched into the first bars with energy and aplomb, confident of his touch. The congregation got to their feet gasping in expectation of the bride's appearance. Saffie must look ravishing, Ted thought peeking into the small mirror that had been taped to one side of the organ to allow him a view down the aisle to the church entrance and steps.

The bride was still standing at the doors, however, alone, arms crossed and shaking her head. Ted kept going; if needs be he could play the "Trumpet Voluntary" as if on a loop. He peeped across to Father Wickford who rolled his eyes. Ted played on.

Thankfully the organ was effective in drowning out the murmuring now filling the church. The guests had sensed something was wrong, which was confirmed when they turned round to see Saffie, all dressed up and ready to go, but rooted to the spot and looking anxious.

Father Wickford glanced at his watch for the twelfth time in under a minute. The hands had barely moved. Still, he couldn't resist checking to be sure, but he would try not to do so again – the congregation was growing restless enough without him orchestrating a panic from the front of the church.

Father Wickford berated himself. He now realised he should have spoken up and objected to the time that the bride and her mother had requested for the service. It was bad enough they had chosen a Sunday, the busiest day of his week. He'd only agreed because Saffie had said it was her birthday. But once the engagement had been announced and the wedding planning commenced, only he would have been aware of the dangers of organising the church service at a time so uncommonly late in the day. For no one but he would have been aware of the one-hundred-and-seventy-six-year-old marriage act that stipulates weddings must take place during the hours of daylight and that the archaic law might still apply. He simply forgot to mention to them that after sunset there can be no wedding.

Standing at the chancel steps and observing the shafts of sunlight beaming through the tall church windows, Father Wickford felt that, as long as they could get underway before half six, however, there was still hope they could rush through the essential elements of the wedding service and get the job done before dark.

If it weren't that the Drapers were personal friends, Father Wickford would probably have insisted on commencing the service without waiting another moment.

"We'll have to be starting very soon, Mary. There'll be nothing I can do if we leave it much longer. I have to perform the blessing before sundown," the vicar murmured sidling over to Mary Draper.

"What?"

"We have to do this before dark."

"Do we?"

"Absolutely!"

"Really?"

"Yes!"

"Can't we give Colin another ten minutes, Kevin? For Saffie? Ten minutes?"

"Mary, if we don't get going shortly, we'll have to postpone. It's the law!" Father Wickford pleaded, struggling to make himself heard above Ted Baker's virtuosity on the organ.

Mary Draper had had enough. She stamped her foot, left her front-row pew and stomped down to the church doors in a thinly disguised display of impatience and indignation.

"I see your father's late as usual, Saffie. Have you heard from him today?"

"No, Mum. Not yet. Have you?"

"His solicitor called me this morning to say that he's been released by the police and is on his way."

"Oh, thank God!"

"He obviously failed to make it to the house, though?"

"Obviously."

"Typical!"

"I waited and waited but it was getting so late and the wedding car had been outside for ages. Eventually I just gave up and came on ahead without him. But I'm sure he'll be here any minute, Mum."

"He'd need to be."

Saffie had been on the point of bursting into tears but she wouldn't cry now. Not now her mother was interfering. She'd had years of practise of biting her lip where her mother was concerned and wasn't going to be swayed by one of her belligerent interventions now.

"Don't worry he'll be here, Mum. He promised."

Mary Draper took a peep inside the church and was startled by the anxious faces staring back.

"Saffie, we can't wait for him any longer. Come on, *I'll* walk you down the aisle."

"Saffron, we need to start the service or it'll be too late. We can't start after dark, dear," Father Wickford urged as he joined them at the entrance. "The wedding would be null and void."

"He'll be here, Father Wickford. I know he will."

"Two minutes, Saffron. That's as long as we can give him."

"He'll be here, Father. He'll be here."

"Saffie, come on. *I'll* walk you down the aisle."

"Mother. If he's not here, I'm not getting married. It's as simple as that."

"But—"

"No buts. It's not bloody happening."

"Phil, you talk some sense into her," Mary Draper said to her future son-in-law as he wandered up to join them but who thought it wiser to say nothing, shrug and look a little clueless. He reached for Saffie's hand.

Ted Baker was still thrashing out the "Trumpet Voluntary" but had lost count of how many times he'd actually played it. Artistry was one thing, but by now he wished he were playing one of Father Wickford's simpler, more modern hymns on a guitar. Tiring fast, and just as he could feel cramp creeping into his fingers, a series of booming thunderclaps put the fear of God into him. The sudden explosions rattled the stained glass, caused some of the congregation to shriek and the youngest of the children to cry. Ted stopped playing immediately after the first bang, covered his ears and wondered if it might be necessary to evacuate the building.

The church was silent. The only sound the fruity roar of a four-stroke motorcycle approaching at speed then another ear-splitting explosion of what Ted now realised was a backfiring engine followed by the squeal of brakes and the crunching of rubber on gravel as the bike screeched to a halt. A moment later Ted saw the vicar's head reappear below him, smiling up at him and bobbing like a nodding dog in a car's rear window.

Ted smiled and gave a little wave before realising that this time he really was being given the starting signal, and so launched, yet again, into the opening bars of Jeremiah Clarke's "Trumpet Voluntary". It was hard for Ted to read the sheet music when there was so much commotion to distract him in the church below. He was relieved that, after so much practise and so many dummy runs, he more or less knew the piece by heart and could probably play it blindfolded.

As Ted peeked over the handrail he caught a glimpse of the mother of the bride bustling back down the aisle towards her seat in the front pew, her face a fiery red. The groom was scuttling along beside trying to placate her without getting in range of her handbag. The vicar, now holding station at the chancel steps, was offering benign smiles to one and all and attempting to elicit calm whilst wearing the exhausted expression of a broken man. Meanwhile, Ted watched Saffie in his mirror. She was still loitering at the church doors, her back to the congregation.

Every time Saffie turned to peer into the church towards the altar, her view was filled with a vision of her mother imploring her to step forward, but Saffie was not for moving, would not budge.

Ted was still staring at Saffie when he noticed her silhouette suddenly soften as she was approached by a man in morning-dress trousers, scuffed shoes and a dress shirt smeared with oil stains. They hugged. He was panting. Ted noticed that there were patches of sweat under the arms of his shirt, but through the oil and grime, however, he could make out the familiar figure of Colin Draper.

Ted was surprised to see Draper looking so dishevelled. Not like him, he thought. His cravat was hanging loose, his shirt was untucked and his waistcoat unbuttoned. He was carrying a grey morning-dress jacket in one hand and a matching top hat in the other.

"This is Roy, Saffie. He picked me up on the slip road to the M3 somewhere past Winchester!" Draper shouted over the rumbling motorcycle engine. "Cheers, Roy! You know, if you're ever in Greenwich ..." Draper added before passing back Roy's spare crash helmet and giving him a friendly slap on the back.

"Saffie, I'm sorry!"

"It's alright, Dad. Slow down and catch your breath."

"But I am ... I'm really sorry. Car broke down ... Hitched a ride on Roy's bike. Sorry I didn't make it to Granny's."

"That's OK, Dad. You're here now and you're going to walk me down the aisle, and that's all that matters," Saffie said, buttoning his wing collar and tying his cravat. "Now get your jacket and topper on and let's get the rest of your kit sorted out."

"And I'm sorry I'm not wearing a kilt."

"No one asked you to. And, anyway, I imagine a kilt would be a bit chilly on a motorbike, if not a little too revealing."

"*And* I'm filthy."

"You're fine, Dad. A chimney sweep is supposed to bring good luck to a wedding, but only if they kiss the bride," Saffie said leaning forward and offering him her cheek.

As Roy roared off with a wave, Colin Draper gave Saffie a peck on the cheek, threw on his jacket, donned his hat and gloves, retrieved his buttonhole from an inside pocket, balanced on either foot so as to buff the toe of each shoe on the back of his trousers and gave Saffie a wink.

"Ready, Dad?"

"Yes. Fine and dandy."

"Good."

"Oh, Saffie ..."

"What?"

"One thing ..."

"What, Dad?"

"You look stunning. So, so beautiful. I'm very, very proud."

"And so you should be," she replied, squeezing his hand.

"Oh, and one other thing ..."

"Dad?"

"Happy birthday!"

"Aw, thanks, Dad. You're a sweetie."

"Right! Shall we?"

"Dad!" Saffie hissed.

"What?"

"Your hat!"

"Oh, of course," Draper said with a sheepish grin before removing his topper before they entered the church.

The walk down the aisle was a short one but the significance was not lost on Colin Draper. His eyes were fixed on Saffie. He was elated to see her smiling so freely. Whenever he did glance away it was to take a peek at the wedding party waiting at the chancel steps ahead of them. The men stood stiff-backed; an immaculate tartan clan. Meanwhile, the mother of the bride had assumed a more serene disposition now that the formalities had commenced.

When they reached the steps, Colin Draper gave Saffie a smile, nodded at Phil, released Saffie's hand and slid into the pew behind her where his mother had saved him a space.

"Hello, Mum."

"Why were you so late, Colin?"

"I had a spot of bother, Mum."

"And why aren't you sitting with Mary?"

"Because we're divorced, Mum."

"Yes, I know that, Colin."

"Really?"

"Of course. Everyone knows that."

"So, why do you keep asking me how she is on the phone?"

"Because I like winding you up, Colin. And, all things considered, she's still my favourite niece."

"God, Mum. You are naughty."

38

Sunday, 8pm

"Why the hell did you let Saffie book this dump, Colin?" Mary hissed. "She could have had Osborne House, for Christ's sake."

Colin Draper paused before answering. The image of angry geese coming to mind.

"Many reasons," he replied, glugging from a champagne flute as he stood in the receiving line at the entrance to the local cricket club. By now the clubhouse was nearly full, the flow of guests past the bridal party in the lobby drying to a trickle and Colin Draper growing weary of having to explain his late arrival at the church to all and sundry. "Firstly, because she loves Yarmouth, Mary. Secondly, because it seems that this is about the only place that can accommodate our numbers and, thirdly, because Saffie could enjoy a party in a paper bag," he added. "Osborne House might have been fine for Queen Victoria, but not for our Saffie. With her it's not so much about *where* as about *how much fun*."

"She probably gets that hedonistic streak from you I expect, Colin."

"Oh, I do hope so."

"Well, this place reminds me of a school canteen."

"Did yours have a bar then, Mary? Mine certainly didn't."

"You know what I mean."

"So, where is he?"

"Who?"

"Harvey," Colin whispered, changing the subject.

"He's at a tennis camp in Barcelona. I'm sure there's plenty going on there to keep him busy."

"I bet there is, Mary. I bet there is."

"Shut up, Colin, here's Saffie and Phil."

"Mum! Dad! Thanks for setting aside the hostilities for my big day."

"Yeah, it's like the Christmas truce in the trenches but without the football," Colin Draper responded, trying to raise spirits but being met with an ominous silence.

"Are your father and I going to be sitting together, Saffie?"

"No, Mum. We thought we'd spare you that ordeal."

"So, who's going to tick off your dad when he starts licking his knife and blowing his nose on his napkin?"

"I'll keep an eye on him. Anyway, you're sitting either side of Granny. Not a traditional top table, but there you go. She'll keep you both in order."

"I suppose you're going to say a few words, Colin?"

"Naturally. And you, Mary?"

"Mum, you can if you want to."

"No, thank you, Saffron. I'm sure your father is dying to entertain our guests with his hilarious wit and repartee. I wouldn't want to upstage him."

"By the way, Saffie, did you see Moose, Hugo or Gavin slip in? I don't think they made it to the church," Draper said scanning the room.

"No. Don't worry, they're probably having a quick pint in The Bull."

Mary Draper rolled her eyes.

Despite his casual attitude, the choice of venue had seemed a bit odd to Colin Draper as well. When he had first visited the clubhouse with Saffie he too had noticed that the place bore a passing resemblance to a school dining hall. With its patchwork of navy and burgundy carpet tiles, the fluorescent strip lighting, the fading framed photos of cricket teams past, the shelves stacked with old trophies and shields, the serving hatch to the kitchen, the dartboard and jukebox, it was like they'd stepped through a time portal back into the nineteen seventies.

"Saffie's made a great job of tarting this place up, Mary."

"Yes, Colin. Give her her due, I suppose she's managed to make a silk purse out of a sow's ear."

"I like all the white."

"The white? That's her theme, Colin. I'm glad you noticed."

"Whose idea were the sprays of white carnations and shrouds of muslin? It's like a Bedouin tent in here."

"It's what Saffie does best, Colin. What do you expect from a set designer?"

"Fair enough."

Colin Draper made a conscious effort to control his drinking downing just the one glass of champagne – wanting to make a good job of his speech even if it was to be a short one.

After an interminable wait whilst the wedding photographer fussed over the bridal portraits, and as bored children started to run amok, the master of ceremonies rapped his gavel on the nearest tabletop and called upon the guests to take their seats. Saffie and Phil were applauded into the room and the meal commenced.

Draper looked around the tables. Still no sign of The Moose, Hugo Saunders or Gavin Doyle. He leaned back in his chair and gawped at Mary hoping to catch her attention, but she was too busy chatting to the matron of honour to notice.

Then it was time for Draper to speak, the words "please welcome the father of the bride" catching him off guard as the MC handed him the microphone.

Applause filled the room.

Draper swallowed hard then caught Mary's eye – who gave him an encouraging smile – and got to his feet to the sound of some raucous booing which he took to be Phil's friends' attempts at irony.

"What are we going to do about Maria?" *The Sound of Music*. Julie Andrews. Sister Maria. A loose cannon that no institution could contain. Need I say more?"

Someone yelled: "No!"

A cue for laughter.

"It takes little imagination," Draper continued, "for me to visualise Saffie skipping up a mountain pass or pirouetting across some rolling downs, arms aloft and singing, "The Hills are Alive with the Sound of Music". And now she has found her Georg Von Trapp with whom to share the Tyrol ..."

Draper rumbled on through the speech he'd learned parrot-fashion. It seemed only a matter of seconds before he was glancing at the last of his cue cards.

"... And so, without further ado, I would like to invite you all to stand and raise your glasses to toast the bride and groom ... *The bride and groom.*"

"The bride and groom!"

Draper was about to sit down and soak up the applause when he caught sight of The Moose sitting with Hugo Saunders on a table towards the rear of the room and Gavin Doyle on the next table over.

"You OK?" he mouthed. But they didn't see him.

"I hope that went OK," Draper whispered, as he sat back down next to Saffie.

"You did well, Dad. I'm really proud."

Draper grinned through the rest of the speeches, joined in the applause for Phil and then his best man and raised his glass and mumbled through the toast for the bridesmaids. He took little notice when the MC asked: "Is there anyone else who would like to say a few words about the bride and groom?" And didn't at first notice when his mother put her hand up.

It was only as she struggled to her feet that Draper realised what she was about to do. He touched her gently on the arm but she shrugged him off, stared out across the room and began to speak.

"One two ... one two," she croaked into the microphone in imitation of something she'd seen on television.

The MC pranced over, checked the microphone and gestured for her to continue.

"My name is Constance Draper. I am eighty-eight years old. For those of you who don't know, I am Saffie's granny. Phil's granny-in-law."

Enthusiastic applause filled the room.

Constance Draper waited patiently for quiet whilst the MC raised his hands to restore order and winked at Constance to encourage her to keep talking.

"Now, I am not going to lecture you or give you any tips but I just wanted to speak up as I am positive proof that marriages can be long and happy. Mine lasted over sixty years, " Constance said, then paused to allow the ensuing applause to subside.

"You see I was twenty-three when I married Saffie's grandfather, Ernest Draper. That was relatively late in those days. I was three years older than Ernie. We had to wait till he was twenty-one. So, you see, I've loved him for most of my life. Most of his. He died a few years ago. It's a pity really because I know he'd love to have been here with us today. You know, for Saffie and Phil. He loved family. Loved Saffie. I'm sure he'd have loved Phil. He'd have loved this wedding."

Constance paused again whilst waiting for a ripple of applause to subside.

"Well, that's it really. Only to say, look after one another. It can be a long life. Make it a happy one. There you are, thank you for listening. And here's to absent friends!"

There was a moment of complete silence before the room took Constance's cue, rose as one and repeated the toast *to absent friends* which was followed by more thunderous applause – a standing ovation.

Emotional, Colin sat down and buried his head in his hands. He felt his mother's gentle touch as she sat down beside him, and when the pressure eased, he rolled his head sideways to look at her.

"Thanks, Mum."

"What for?"

"Och, you know ..."

With the speeches over and the cake cut, the wedding guests moved out onto the veranda at the rear of the clubhouse whilst the floor was cleared for the dancing.

Colin Draper was busy exchanging idle chat when Hugo Saunders and Gavin Doyle sidled up. The Moose appeared to be deep in conversation with Colin's mother nearby.

"Did you get to the church on time, Colin?"

"Yes, but it was bloody close. You two alright?"

"Spot on."

"I see you're wearing your dog collar today, Hugo."

"Well, you know, social functions, tarts-and-vicars parties."

"All the same, here's to us," Colin Draper announced, raising his glass.

"One hell of a trip, eh? *Slàinte!*" Hugo Saunders said, clinking glasses with the other two.

"*Slàinte!* And one never to be repeated. And, I'd suggest, best not mentioned to anyone else either, Hugo. One to keep to ourselves perhaps."

"Could be out of our hands once the press get wind of it though, Colin. I wouldn't discount the possibility that there's a media storm headed our way."

"Say nothing."

"God, I wonder what Old Mr Cowie's doing?"

"About twenty years, I should think, Hugo. And if he does end up in prison, Gavin, I think things will have worked out rather well for him," Colin Draper said with a smirk.

"How come?"

"Think about it, free accommodation, free meals, free heating, free healthcare, free library, lots of activities, his own room and plenty of company and all paid for by the state.

Also, you won't have to sell his caravan or remortgage your house to pay for it, Gavin. It could set a trend for the elderly! Thousands of geriatrics up and down the country will be trying to get banged up in prison now."

"Maybe, but then again, maybe not in Old Mr Cowie's case."

"How come, Gavin?"

"He'll probably do a deal."

"What do you mean?"

"My bet is he'll turn the Queen's evidence. You know, in return for immunity from prosecution. He'll cut a deal. Shop the Mr Bigs in the operation and get onto the witness-protection scheme."

"Really? Old Mr Cowie, a supergrass?"

"Yes. If he's got any sense and is prepared to name names."

"So, he could do that? Do a deal?"

"To exempt himself from prosecution or get a suspended sentence? Yes, I believe so."

"Really?"

"It happens, Colin."

"That's crazy!"

"I don't have a clue where he'll end up, Colin, but wherever it is it won't be on my fucking drive."

"You have to admit the caravan scam was good though."

"He's no fool, Colin."

"And what if he'd got away with it? You know, got the caravan home to London and sold his coke on. Do you think he'd have given you a cut, Gavin?"

"We'll never know."

"Would you have taken it?"

"We'll never know that either, Colin."

"At least you've got your off-street parking back. Hold on, the music's started. Dance, Hugo? Gavin?"

"Why not?"

39

Monday, 9am

Colin Draper took no notice of the alarm clock for a good thirty seconds after the start of its mechanical rant. It was out of reach on the dressing table and he wasn't going to move. It was bound to stop sooner or later, he thought. But, God, it was persistent, and a painful reminder of the excess of the night before.

Draper blinked as he came to his senses, determined to remain face down with his head in the pillows without moving and wishing the ringing would go away. Then he got a dig in the ribs from what he presumed was an elbow.

The shock that he had company succeeded where the alarm clock had failed. He was awake and running through what he could remember of the night before.

Sex! Yes, he'd had sex! But before he could put a name and a face to the action, he heard a voice. It was shouting. It was urgent and persuasive.

"Do something about that fucking clock!"

Then Draper was aware of someone jumping out of the bed and dashing across the room with an athleticism that scared him.

"Man overboard!" he called out sarcastically.

The ringing seemed to diminish and appeared to be moving away from him, then ceased altogether. A short pause was followed by the sound of a clattering and a smashing of glass from the pavement below.

"That'll be that then," the voice said in triumph heading back his way.

That the voice was familiar was vaguely reassuring.

Draper felt the mattress undulate as the voice returned to reclaim its previous share of the bed. And as peace reigned, Colin Draper resumed his mental scroll through the previous night's events: the reception, the dancing, the drinking, the small talk. Whom had he spent time with? Whom had he hung around with? And who had hung around with him? There were the bridesmaids and a couple of Saffie's friends from college. He wouldn't – would he? No, definitely not. Then there were other family members and a host of family friends. No, nothing registering there either.

He remembered avoiding Mary for most of the evening and dreading that he'd have to have a brief conversation with her at some point – for Saffie – and also to confound those who like to wallow in the misery of other people's divorces.

That's right. Shit! Now he remembered as the night's events came back to him in a flood of fear, regret, embarrassment and laughter. Yes, he'd sidled over to Mary for a quick chat. And, yes, the conversation had been forced and perfunctory at first, lightweight and awkward. But then, after a brief pause, she'd said: "Colin, you wouldn't get me a wee top-up, would you?" waggling her glass in the way that had always annoyed him.

"What is it? Fizz?" he'd asked begrudgingly.

"It's the only thing that's going to get me through this fucking party."

They'd both laughed at that. A giggle at first but then really, genuinely, laughed. And they couldn't stop laughing – couldn't stop laughing at the absurdity of life, of divorce, of weddings and of petty social mores in general – the whole shebang. Then those in their immediate vicinity noticed them laughing and laughed with them too; a sense of unspoken understanding spreading through the room until all the guests were laughing at them, with them and for them.

"Here we go then," Colin Draper eventually said, trying to regain his composure through the occasional guffaw, "one glass of champagne for the lady coming right up."

A sarcastic cheer rose from those within earshot.

The chat was much freer when he returned from the bar. Draper remembered thinking how it was like being with someone new. Half-cut and flirting, he felt a burning in his loins. It should have made him wary, but his ability to resist temptation couldn't keep up with his inability to resist alcohol.

Amidst the flirty banter he remembered catching Saffie's attention. She'd been flying round the room all evening, dancing like a dervish in the midst of a sea of tartan. She winked at them both. Rightly or wrongly, Draper read this as tacit approval. Now he realised that Saffie was probably having far too much fun to give a damn about her parents' comings and goings.

Then he asked Mary to dance. Everyone smiled.

And before long, while the reception was still in full swing and they were still capable of walking unaided, they sneaked off to his hotel room. They hit the bed – opened the door and just collapsed across it, kissing and undressing. And he remembered her murmuring: "God, Colin! I've really missed this", and then her hands were reaching down inside his trousers. And he accepted her subtle invitation and rolled on top of her as she whispered encouragement.

But why he'd been travelling with his fucking alarm clock, he didn't know. Why he'd thought he'd need it on a golf trip he couldn't say. But that didn't matter now.

"Morning, Mary."

"Shit, Colin! What *were* we thinking of?"

"Not very much, obviously. I don't think *thinking* came into it. More to do with lust and animal instinct."

"Jesus, Colin. You just don't know when to shut up, do you?"

"That has been said."

"What do we do now?"

"I guess breakfast would be a good idea, Mary. I certainly need to do something about my bloody headache."

"Yeah. Me too. Are you OK?"

"I'll survive."

"What about us, Colin?"

"What about *us*?"

"Saffie can't find out!"

"Why?"

"Because we're her parents and we're fucking divorced, that's why."

"Don't remind me. It cost me three hundred grand and my house."

"Our house."

"And a yacht."

Colin Draper sat up and glanced at his ex-wife. She smiled back which rather surprised him. Then she leant over and gave him a peck on the lips which surprised him even more.

"God, Colin. Where did it go wrong?"

"Does it matter?"

"Were things *that* bad?

"Yes, obviously, or we wouldn't be living a hundred and forty miles apart. Actually, I've never said it before and I'm loathe to say it now, but I've never really seen you as good wife material, Mary."

"Fuck you! What are you on about?" she said looking sad and drawn.

"That doesn't mean to say I couldn't see you in that light now though," Draper said rubbing his side and laughing.

"Wife material? Wife material? What the fuck does that mean, Colin? How very Victorian. I was married to you for over twenty-five fucking years. If I wasn't *wife material*, why did you fucking marry me?"

"You know why. Because I was young and I fancied you—"

"And I was pregnant."

"And we weren't offered much choice."

"That's families for you."

"What I'm trying to say is, maybe things could be different now."

"How?"

"Well, I still fancy you, but maybe I have a better idea of how to be a good husband too."

"And what makes you think you could be a good husband?"

"Because I'm ready to be one."

"Well, maybe you're too bloody late, Colin."

"Am I? Are we?"

"Yes. *And* you're going to jail."

"No way am I going to jail. They're not going to charge me, I'm innocent and, anyway, there isn't any proof."

"I guess we'll see. And what about Saffie? What would she think?"

"She's a big girl. I'm sure she wouldn't care. I'm pretty sure it'd be a relief for her not to have to worry about us being on our own," Colin Draper said, lying back into the pillows.

"Really?"

"Yes. Really. And I hate being on my own, Mary. I miss you," Draper said in a calm, reassuring voice before blowing his cheeks out and sighing.

A long pause followed, only interrupted by his mobile phone ringing.

"Shit."

"Leave it, Colin."

"I can't, it's my mother," he replied whilst picking up his mobile. "Mum! Hello, sweetheart!"

"Colin, where am I?"

"You're at Saffie's wedding, dear. We're all in The Bull's Head, Yarmouth."

"Am I?"

"Yes, don't worry. I'm in the room next door, Mum. Do you fancy some breakfast?"

"That'd be nice, Colin."

"Right, I'll come and get you in ten minutes or so. I'm getting up now."

"You're not still in bed, are you?"

"Yes. It was a late night."

"How decadent."

"Indeed."

"How's Mary?"

"Do you know something, Mum, I think she's alright. She's fine. Just fine."

"You do talk some rubbish, Colin. Look, I'll see you in ten minutes. Come and get me. Both of you."

"Mum?"

"Yes, Colin."

"Oh, nothing."

40

Six months later
Caracas, Venezuela

Rafael Mendoza lit a cigarette, exhaled and then took a small sip of espresso. He was lounging at his favourite table, on the pavement outside his favourite cafe basking in the gentle heat of the early-morning sun. It pleased him that he could enjoy this simple indulgence directly across the street from the family business, Mendoza and Sons, fruit-and-vegetable wholesalers. He also relished the opportunity to interact with the passers-by, many of whom he would have known since childhood. The narrow backstreets of his neighbourhood were bustling with commuters making their way into the heart of the city. Up on the main road towards Caracas' commercial centre the street-food vendors were setting up their stalls, the air filling with the rich aromas of arepas, mandocas and pabellón criollo and other favourite fast foods.

Mendoza peered down at his watch, peeved that the couple due for a breakfast meeting were already ten minutes overdue. He did not like tardiness; didn't trust those who were late. But, as he looked up, he was relieved when he caught sight of them emerging from the crowd on the sidewalk. They were easily spotted; their movements slow and laboured amidst the frenetic tide of humanity. The man was old and hunched, the woman young and lean. She was supporting him by the arm and walking with great care lest she should cause him to lose his footing and fall.

"Ah, Mr Cowie!"

"Sorry to keep you waiting, Mr Mendoza. As you can see I'm not as nimble as I once was."

"You're here, Mr Cowie. Some would say that that is quite an achievement in itself considering your recent setbacks."

"Indeed, Mr Mendoza, indeed."

"Please take a seat," Rafael Mendoza said pulling out a couple of chairs for his guests and beckoning for them to join him at his table.

"So, Mr Cowie, how did you get here? I'd heard you'd had a bit of trouble with the authorities in your country," Mendoza continued whilst passing them both a menu.

"Yes, but a minor setback, I can assure you. Of course, I managed to satisfy them of my innocence."

"That simple, eh?"

"That simple."

"So, where do they think you are now – today – this week?"

"In hospital. For a procedure. Nothing too serious, mind. A hip replacement, or so they believe. Long enough for them to take their eyes of me while I take care of business over here of course."

"Good. And I hope your recuperation goes well!"

"Quite. Anyway, Mr Mendoza, though the major part of the last consignment failed to reach its destination, my assistant here managed to deliver enough of your fine produce to finance another run."

"As we say in Venezuela: *"Al mal tiempo, buena cara."*"

"Err ... Put a nice face to the bad times?"

"Something like that, Mr Cowie, something like that. So, have you arranged transport for the goods?"

"Yes."

"A yacht, I take it?"

"Yes, Mr Mendoza, a sixty-footer bought in auction as before."

"From here?"

"Yes."

"But be careful, Mr Cowie. You know how closely these transactions are monitored now."

"I know, but by the time we sail, I can assure you no one will recognise the yacht. Like many of us, it will have a false identity – a cloned registration."

"Crew?"

"My own this time. We live and learn, Mr Mendoza. They're going to accompany the merchandise the whole way over on this crossing. I'm handling the arrangements all the way from A to B."

"Good, good."

"And I presume you can supply the goods under the same terms as our previous arrangement, Mr Mendoza?"

"Ah, but first, Mr Cowie, excuse me, before we go any further, please ... Won't you introduce me to your friend, here?"

"Of course! Of course! I'm so sorry, I'm forgetting myself. Mr Mendoza, this is Bernadette, Bernadette McIvor. My right-hand woman. My personal assistant, you might say. She's family."

"Miss McIvor, I'm very pleased to make your acquaintance," Rafael Mendoza said springing to his feet, bowing and taking Bernadette's hand to give it a gentle shake.

"Likewise, I'm sure," she smiled.

"So, Mr Mendoza, will we try again? Another run?"

"Why not, Mr Cowie? Why not?"

"Good."

"And I expect you would like me to show you the merchandise, Mr Cowie?"

"Most certainly. I'd like that very much, thank you."

"Now?"

"Why not?"

"Miss McIvor, I am sorry. Please excuse us. We won't be a moment. Severiano here will take care of you while Mr Cowie and I attend to some business. *¡Oye, Severiano! Por favor,* *cuida a esta jovencita ... ¡Dale lo que quiera!"* Mendoza barked at the waiter hovering in the doorway of the cafe, whilst taking Mr Cowie's arm and helping him to his feet.

Bernadette loosened the top button of her crisp, white blouse, slunk down in her chair, lowered her sunglasses and started to browse through the breakfast menu.

Inside the wholesalers, Mr Cowie was led through a shabby front office to a warehouse at the rear comprising four aisles of shelves stacked to the rafters with produce. The sweaty musk reminded Mr Cowie of the humid atmosphere inside the Palm House at Kew Gardens.

Rafael Mendoza gesticulated for Mr Cowie to sit on one of the two chairs placed in an open space at the far end of the repository.

"It's very quiet in here. What time do your people start work, Mr Mendoza?"

"Like most civilised people, Mr Cowie, only after a good breakfast," Rafael Mendoza replied before starting to back away. "Mr Cowie, please excuse me for a moment, I need to fetch some paperwork for you," he added in a calm voice before turning to stroll through the door behind them.

Whilst waiting Mr Cowie sat patiently surveying the pallets of fruit and vegetables lining the walls, trying to calculate the viability of Rafael Mendoza's grocery business but knowing all along that it probably didn't matter whether it made much of a profit or not. After a while he began to wonder what the hell Mendoza was doing. He'd been gone for at least ten minutes and there was still no sign of him. Time was beginning to drag.

Mr Cowie suddenly felt his mobile vibrating in his pocket. He quickly retrieved it and made sure he pressed the home button to read the message before it made a sound.

What's going on? BM.

Sitting up and peering round to ensure Mendoza was out of sight, Mr Cowie tapped in a hasty message:

God knows. Weird! Sitting here like a lemon.

He pressed the send button then shoved his mobile back into his pocket, sighed and continued his quiet deliberations.

Deep in thought, Mr Cowie didn't notice the dark figure emerging from the shadows behind him. He didn't hear the figure creeping closer and was unaware of the gun being trained on his upper body and that its barrel was now only inches from the back of his head. He would have heard nothing and felt no pain as the single bullet punched a hole through the rear of his skull, the sound dampened by a silencer.

A second later Old Mr Cowie's head rolled to one side and his arms flopped from his lap as his torso slumped in the chair. The warehouse remained silent save for the steady trickle of blood from the exit wound in his forehead, dribbling onto the concrete floor and splashing slightly as it formed a dark red pool which began to ripple outwards into a shallow puddle beneath his seat.

"*Al mal tiempo, buena cara* ... Be positive even in the bad times, Mr Cowie. Be positive," Mendoza whispered over the corpse. He spat on the floor, nodded, then tucked the gun into the top of his trousers being sure to conceal it with his shirt tails and was on the point of returning to the street when he suddenly heard music. Elgar. "Nimrod". Just a few notes emanating from one of Mr Cowie's jacket pockets. Mr Cowie's mobile phone. Mendoza bent over the old man feeling for the device, patting him quickly, roughly, urgently till he found the vibrating lump. He immediately retrieved the phone, pressed the home button and lifted the device into the light for a better view of the incoming text message.

You OK? I'm bricking it now. BM.

Rafael Mendoza dropped the phone, sprinted across the warehouse, through the front office and back out onto the street heading for the street cafe. But the girl was gone.

Mendoza thumped the table sending crockery, cutlery and menus flying. There was no sign of her. He scanned the immediate vicinity then turned to the waiter hovering in the doorway.

"*¿A dónde fue ella, Severiano?*"

The waiter shrugged, spun round and walked back inside the cafe.

"*¡Mierda!*" Mendoza cursed, before jogging up and down the street whilst pogoing above the crowd every few yards in a desperate attempt to catch a glimpse of the young woman. But there was no sign. Nothing.

Bernadette was long gone. She had mingled into the crowd of early morning commuters walking at the same brisk pace so as not to attract attention, but then, when she turned onto the main thoroughfare at the top of the street, had started to trot – tottering along as fast as her heels would allow. She felt safer once she'd hailed a passing cab, got on board and was being driven away in the rush hour traffic heading for the airport.

She immediately reached for her mobile again, scrolled through the directory and dialled the chosen number.

"Hi, Gavin! It's Bernadette! Bernadette McIvor ... I seem to have got myself into a bit of a pickle. Could you please call me back? It's kind of urgent. I need your help. Yeah, please call, you know, just as soon as ..."